MY FATHER ALWAYS FINDS CORPSES

Books by Lee Hollis

Hayley Powell Mysteries
DEATH OF A KITCHEN DIVA
DEATH OF A COUNTRY
   FRIED REDNECK
DEATH OF A COUPON
   CLIPPER
DEATH OF A CHOCOHOLIC
DEATH OF A CHRISTMAS
   CATERER
DEATH OF A CUPCAKE
   QUEEN
DEATH OF A BACON
   HEIRESS
DEATH OF A PUMPKIN
   CARVER
DEATH OF A LOBSTER
   LOVER
DEATH OF A COOKBOOK
   AUTHOR
DEATH OF A WEDDING
   CAKE BAKER
DEATH OF A BLUEBERRY
   TART
DEATH OF A WICKED
   WITCH
DEATH OF AN ITALIAN CHEF
DEATH OF AN ICE CREAM
   SCOOPER
DEATH OF A CLAM DIGGER
DEATH OF A GINGERBREAD
   MAN

Collections
EGGNOG MURDER
(with Leslie Meier and Barbara
Ross)
YULE LOG MURDER
(with Leslie Meier and Barbara
Ross)
HAUNTED HOUSE MURDER
(with Leslie Meier and Barbara Ross)

CHRISTMAS CARD MURDER
(with Leslie Meier and Peggy
Ehrhart)
HALLOWEEN PARTY
   MURDER
(with Leslie Meier and Barbara
Ross)
IRISH COFFEE MURDER
(with Leslie Meier and Barbara
Ross)
CHRISTMAS MITTENS
   MURDER
(with Lynn Cahoon and Maddie
Day)
EASTER BASKET MURDER
(with Leslie Meier and Barbara
Ross)

Poppy Harmon Mysteries
POPPY HARMON
   INVESTIGATES
POPPY HARMON AND THE
   HUNG JURY
POPPY HARMON AND THE
   PILLOW TALK KILLER
POPPY HARMON AND THE
   BACKSTABBING BACHELOR
POPPY HARMON AND THE
   SHOOTING STAR

Maya and Sandra Mysteries
MURDER AT THE PTA
MURDER AT THE BAKE SALE
MURDER ON THE CLASS TRIP
MURDER AT THE SPELLING
   BEE

Stand-Alones
MY FATHER ALWAYS FINDS
   CORPSES

Published by Kensington Publishing Corp.

MY FATHER ALWAYS FINDS CORPSES

LEE HOLLIS

Kensington Publishing Corp.
kensingtonbooks.com

KENSINGTON BOOKS are published by

Kensington Publishing Corp.
900 Third Avenue
New York, NY 10022

All Kensington titles, imprints, and distributed lines are available at special quantity discounts for bulk purchases for sales promotion, premiums, fund-raising, educational, or institutional use.

Special book excerpts or customized printings can also be created to fit specific needs. For details, write or phone the office of the Kensington Special Sales Manager: Attn. Special Sales Department, Kensington Publishing Corp., 900 Third Avenue, New York, NY 10022. Phone: 1-800-221-2647.

KENSINGTON and the KENSINGTON COZIES teapot logo Reg. U.S. Pat. & TM Off.

Library of Congress Card Catalogue Number: 2025930440

ISBN: 978-1-4967-3892-9

First Kensington Hardcover Edition: June 2025

ISBN: 978-1-4967-3894-3 (ebook)

10 9 8 7 6 5 4 3 2 1

Printed in the United States of America

The authorized representative in the EU for product safety and compliance
is eucomply OU, Parnu mnt 139b-14, Apt 123
Tallinn, Berlin 11317, hello@eucompliancepartner.com

For Scott Beauchemin and Steve Kirklys

MY FATHER ALWAYS FiNDS CORPSES

CHAPTER 1

The heavily painted woman in her late sixties with teased-out blond hair and wearing a rainbow-colored caftan stood stoically in front of a defeated, hunched over man in a butler uniform in his late forties, his eyes downcast as she pointed an accusing finger at him.

"It was *you* all along, Reginald! How could I not see it before?"

"Because you don't *see* me at all! You're only concerned with your snooty, rich, well-connected social circle!" the man moaned. "But me? A lowly servant? I was nothing to you, so why would I ever come across your radar? But you're just playing guessing games. How could you possibly know that I was the one who killed Anthony Towers?"

"Frankly, I don't need to guess. It's the irrefutable proof I have uncovered that has done you in. That fingerprint we found on the night table lamp. We compared it to the one you left on the silver serving tray at my cocktail party yesterday. It was a perfect match."

"I'm a butler. It's literally my job to turn off the lights in Mr. Towers's bedroom!"

"The small cut on your left arm you explained away as a scratch from Mrs. Towers's Afghan cat, Millie. We found traces of your skin underneath the victim's fingernails from when he desperately tried fighting for his life as you strangled him in his own bed!"

"But what motive would I possibly have to do away with my employer, the man who signs my paychecks, who ensures my livelihood?"

The woman in the loud caftan locked eyes with the seemingly harmless butler. "You're right. Reginald Blackdown has no motive to kill Anthony Towers. But Scottie Campbell does."

The butler shivered.

"That's your real name, isn't it?" the woman continued. "From Modesto. Whose nine-year-old daughter was killed seven years ago in a hit-and-run accident when Anthony Towers was there to meet one of his mistresses and was driving drunk."

"H-How did you find out?" Reginald sputtered.

The woman confidently folded her arms. "Because Reginald claims to hail from Rhode Island and only recently relocated to the Coachella Valley, never having been west before, where he found a job working for Mr. Towers. But when I questioned Cecelia Marks, Mr. Towers's personal chef, she said she was serving a Cabernet with dinner from E&J Gallo Winery in San Francisco. You absentmindedly corrected her, saying the E&J Gallo Winery was from Modesto. How could you possibly know that?"

"I could have read it somewhere online as an amateur wine connoisseur!" Reginald protested.

"Perhaps. But you appeared to know a lot about a town you've apparently never visited. So, I sent my trusty sidekick, Hank, up north to do a little digging. Tell him what you found, Hank."

Hovering behind the woman was a tall, handsome young man in his early twenties with an impressive swimmer's build and who looked as if he had just stepped out of an Abercrombie & Fitch ad. He appeared nervous.

After a moment of silence, the woman swiveled around toward him. "Hank? Tell him what you found."

Like a deer caught in someone's headlights, the young man just stood there, frozen. "I . . . uh . . . Well . . ." Then he glanced behind him. "Line, please."

"Stop! Stop! Stop!" a man's voice bellowed. "Turn the lights up!"

Someone flicked a switch that bathed the expansive place with light, once an IMAX auditorium that had been converted into a theatrical playhouse.

Jarrod Jarvis rose to his feet from a seat in the third row and made his way to the aisle, marching downstage where his actors stood, all of whom looked at him apprehensively.

"Kent, we go on in front of an audience in two weeks. Please, you have to learn your dialogue. You can't just stand up there in a theatre packed with people and ask Ava backstage to tell you what to say."

"Sorry, Jarrod, but I'm wiped, dude. It was my girlfriend's birthday last night, and we may have stayed out partying a little too late at the Retro Room!"

His eyes were at half-mast.

Jarrod did not even want to guess what he might be on. "What part of 'we open in two weeks' are you not understanding, Kent?"

"Jarrod, does this caftan make me look fat?"

"No, Talia, you look beautiful," Jarrod insisted. He was used to stroking his leading lady's fragile ego. He had known a lot of insecure actresses over the years.

"I don't know. This thing is just so big and flowing and completely buries my figure," she pouted, raising her arms and whipping them around so the fabric almost looked like a round multicolored spinning top. "I mean, it's the end of the last scene in the play. I certainly don't want the audience expecting me to belt out a tune."

Jarrod stared at the actress, dumbfounded. "You lost me, Talia."

The man playing the butler chimed in. "She feels like it's time for the fat lady to sing."

"Ahhh," Jarrod sighed, dropping his head.

Kent snorted. "Oh, I get it. That's funny."

Talia sashayed to the edge of the stage and peered down at Jarrod. "I just don't see the harm in calling in the wardrobe people to review a few alternative choices."

"There are no wardrobe people, Talia. There is no wardrobe *person*. We have a rack of donated clothes in the wings. That's about it. This is local theatre. Not the set of a Scorsese movie."

Talia's eyes narrowed, her tone tense. "I don't mean to be difficult, Jarrod . . ."

Which meant she was about to become very difficult.

"But I am obviously the heroine of this piece. This is my big moment. The audience is watching me with rapt attention. I just think it would behoove the character to wear something a little more formfitting, something that flatters her figure and doesn't try to hide it."

"Talia told me she has a new personal trainer and has lost five pounds so far," the actor playing the butler said.

"Seven!" Talia corrected him.

Jarrod bowed his head, defeated. "Fine. Why don't you head backstage and see if you can find something you like better? Take five, everybody!"

The man playing the butler clapped his hands. "Goody! I have a lovely bottle of Glenfiddich 21 Year Gran Reserva and several shot glasses in my car. Anyone care to partake?"

Kent eagerly raised his hand.

"Ira, it's not even noon!" Jarrod protested.

"It's five o'clock somewhere in the world, as they say!" Ira said with a conspiratorial grin as he shuffled off stage behind Talia with Kent lumbering after him.

Jarrod rubbed his eyes with his right index finger and thumb and mumbled to himself, "It's like herding cats."

"Darling, don't despair! This production has *hit* written all over it!" a woman's voice projected from the back of the theatre.

"Yeah, well, obviously you haven't been watching any of today's rehearsal."

Jarrod did not even have to look to see who was speaking. He could recognize that singsong voice anywhere. "Good morning, Kitty."

Kitty Reynolds was in her early seventies, glamorous, a boozy delight, and most notably a former first lady of the United States. She swept down the aisle toward Jarrod with all the fanfare of a grand marshal at a gay pride parade. "Don't worry, sweetie, as one of my closest, dearest friends Broadway legend Bernadette Peters once told me, a bad dress rehearsal always portends to a great opening night!"

"We're still two weeks out from our actual dress rehearsal. I would welcome a lousy dress rehearsal. But right now, we are on track for a major catastrophe. I never should have let my ego get the best of me and agree to write and direct my own play!"

"Stop spiraling. This isn't the Lunt-Fontanne Theatre. It's the CV Rep in Cathedral City, California. You're putting too much pressure on yourself."

"Do you like the title?"

"*Evil Under the Palm Trees*?"

"Yes. Does it seem a little too on the nose? I mean I named the lead character Agatha after Agatha Christie, and the title is a spoof of one of her most popular books. It could come off as a little bit derivative."

"It's *perfect*," Kitty assured him.

"You really think so?"

"I know so. Because I have already spent money printing the

programs, and every single one of them, in big, bold black letters, says *Evil Under the Palm Trees*. So, suffice it to say we're not changing it."

Just Kitty's soothing presence was beginning to calm Jarrod down. He was going to get through this. At least that was what he kept telling himself. Ever since moving to Palm Springs from Hollywood after his husband, Charlie's, unexpected death, he had been trying to find himself, discover a purpose, some path forward in a life that he had not expected to have to take on.

Jarrod had always believed that he and Charlie would grow old together once their daughter, Olivia, was off to college and they were finally empty-nesters. In his mind, he pictured a seaside villa in Provincetown or a quiet little abode in a charming town in Mexico, or even some sprawling fabulous estate here in Palm Springs, a town teeming with aging gay men. But once you have a plan in mind, well, life has a habit of throwing you a curveball.

Jarrod's husband was a police detective, so there had always been a gnawing fear that one day the phone might ring and someone would bear the worst news possible.

An arrest gone awry.

Cut down in the line of duty.

There were so many times that Jarrod rested his head down on the pillow at night, fearing he might wake up to discover Charlie gone.

But it didn't happen that way.

Not even close.

It had all been so maddeningly ordinary. A weird spot on his back. A biopsy. The excruciating wait for the results. The gut-wrenching diagnosis. The months of treatment. And then, less than a year later, he was gone. Just like that. Jarrod was left alone with a thirteen-year-old daughter he and Charlie had been raising together.

But despite the devastating loss, Olivia, or Liv, as friends and family liked to call her, was now a thriving young woman, a graduate from the College of the Desert, after studying criminal justice in honor of her father.

That would be Charlie.

Not Jarrod.

Liv had shown zero interest in Jarrod's former profession, acting.

It was only recently that Liv had sat down to watch a few episodes of the 1980s television series *Go To Your Room!* Jarrod had been eleven years old when he was cast as the precocious youngest kid in the saccharine sweet Friday night sitcom that made him a household name.

That is, until the show was canceled.

Unlike many other former child stars, Jarrod never had to contend with greedy stage parents frittering away his fortune, or a well-publicized drug problem, or multiple arrests for assault or carrying an unregistered firearm. In fact, he lived a pretty normal serene life post-TV fame. Especially after he met his future husband when Charlie was still a beat cop.

Charlie had grounded him.

Made him feel safe.

Loved.

Whole.

So the shock of losing him had been a monumental struggle.

For both Jarrod and Liv.

Jarrod knew in his heart that by trying to shield Liv from all the pain he was going through, he had somehow managed to create a distance between them. He loved her deeply. She was his whole world. But he knew there was work to be done on their relationship.

It had been Kitty who encouraged him to stretch his creative muscles again. The two had met at a mutual friend's party several years ago and quickly became inseparable. Jarrod had always admired how Kitty had managed to effortlessly manage life in the spotlight when her dear late husband was serving as the nation's president. And Kitty always got a chuckle watching Jarrod come of age on *Go To Your Room!* She watched the reruns on TV Land with her own children for years. It was a match made in heaven. They bonded over the loss of their husbands and a love of the arts. And now Kitty was donating almost the entire budget of Jarrod's first directorial effort, an Agatha Christie–inspired comedy thriller that Kitty, much more than Jarrod, believed in and was determined to make a resounding success.

Kitty grabbed Jarrod's hands. "My dear, I'm so proud of you for taking the chance on this creative endeavor." She took a breath. "I know I pressured you to move forward, and I'm so glad we did. But listen to me, sweetie. I know best. You desperately need to take a break."

"I can't, Kitty. We're so far behind. And Kent isn't even off book yet. I'm not even sure he can read!"

"The best directors know when to stop to rest and recharge so they can return to a troubled project with vigor and a new sense of clarity."

"Where do you get this stuff?"

"Sondheim and I hung out in Newport one summer amidst a sea of bottomless mimosas. He had a lot of interesting things to say about his time in the theatre."

Jarrod glanced down. "Wow, you drop so many names, I'm going to need a Dustbuster to get them all off the floor."

Kitty crinkled her nose. "Don't avoid the subject. You need a night out where you're not consumed by this play. And I don't mean one of those drunken three-martini loud dinners with those lovely but incorrigible BFFs of yours."

"George and Leo."

"They can be bad influences."

"They saved my life after Charlie died. They're family."

"And I adore them. I just have something else in mind."

Jarrod eyed her suspiciously. "Like what?"

She furtively glanced behind her at a figure hovering in the shadows at the back of the theatre. Jarrod followed her gaze and could see the man but was unable to tell what he looked like.

"Well, you know Arthur . . ."

"Your primary Secret Service detail."

"Yes. Wonderful man. Very loyal. Well, he finally retired. We had a little party for him last week. I knew you wouldn't come because you were rehearsing, so I didn't bother inviting you. Anyway, his replacement started a few days ago. His name is Jim Stratton, and he is, well, how should I put this? As my granddaughter likes to say, he is a snack!"

"So he's good-looking."

"Oh, darling, Justin Trudeau is good-looking, and I told him so, but Jim, he's not just good-looking. He is in a league all by himself."

"Are you trying to play matchmaker with me and your new bodyguard?"

"Not bodyguard. Secret Service man. There is much more rigorous training involved. And yes. It's time you finally got back out there and started dating again."

"No, I'm not ready."

"It's been almost ten years!"

"And I'm not ready!"

Kitty took a step back, sizing him up. "You're what, fifty-five years old?"

"Fifty-eight."

"Oh, I didn't know you were *that* old."

"Is this your idea of a pep talk?"

"It's just that Jim's a little younger. Early to midforties is my guess."

"I'm not into younger guys."

"Well, you should be. Pretty soon, there are going to be slim pickings ahead of you because they will have all died!"

"Kitty, I appreciate you looking out for me, but—"

She put a finger to his lips and called to the back of the theatre. "Jim, how are we on time?"

Jim took a step forward, checking his watch. "It's ten thirty-seven. You have that luncheon at Spencer's at noon."

"Right. The meeting to discuss the McCallum Theatre renovations. We should leave soon."

Jim nodded.

As Jim stood in the light now, Jarrod could see him more clearly.

He had to admit to himself that Jim was indeed a stunning man.

Sculpted jawline.

Handsome face.

Beautiful brown eyes that matched his hair.

A killer body.

Definitely way too good to be true.

Kitty pivoted back to Jarrod. "Gorgeous, isn't he?"

"How do you even know he's gay?"

"Well, I make it a rule not to pry into the personal lives of anyone who works for me, or anyone who is assigned to protect me, but there have been a few little clues along the way and they seem to check all the boxes."

"For example?"

"One, he's never been married. Two, he works out at the gym a lot, and I mean *a lot*. Three, and this is the big one, he's a *huge* Taylor Swift fan!"

"That doesn't mean a thing!"

"Of course it does!" Kitty protested.

"Kitty, read my lips."

"No new taxes?"

Jarrod looked confused. "What?"

"That's what George H. W. Bush told the country. 'Read my lips. No new taxes.' And then what did he do? He raised taxes. I begged him not to make that promise. I told Barbara he was writing his own political obituary. But did either of them bother listening to me? No, they didn't. And then Clinton beat him in ninety-two."

Jarrod sighed and then tried to take another stab at it. "Read my lips. No matchmaking. Do you understand? I'm quite happy living my very simple, very quiet life with very little drama."

Kitty pursed her lips. "Fine. You do you."

"Thank you."

But Jarrod suspected from the knowing smile on her face that she was hardly ready to let this little mission of hers die a quiet death just yet.

CHAPTER 2

As Liv lay prone on her stomach in bed, hugging her queen-size goose down pillow, she could feel his finger trace the outline of the small butterfly tattoo on her spine. She had gotten it in high school during some rebellious, free-spirited moment, then instantly regretted it, knowing her father would no doubt hit the roof when he saw it. But she had been clever, never wearing open-backed clothing or always donning a light wrap over her swimsuit whenever Dad was around. In her father's outdated opinion, a tattoo was like graffiti on the body. As an old-school actor, he had taught her how important it was to treat the body as a temple by staying fit, especially not marring it with any kind of permanent ink. Sure, he had boasted a large neck tattoo in his twenties for a TV role as a gangbanger on one of the Law & Order shows—it's hard to know which one because there were so many back then—but once he had completed his part, it was easily scrubbed off with simple soap and water.

Liv still loved her tattoo, and not just because Ariana Grande had a small one just like it or because she was a huge Harry Styles fan and he had a giant one spread across his chest. She just thanked God she didn't get the name of her boyfriend at the time, Vlad, an exchange student from Russia, which she had seriously considered as an alternative. The romance busted up a few weeks later when she caught him kissing her frenemy Ava behind the bleachers in the gym in her junior year. At least she wouldn't have to endure the painful process of having it removed, like Pete Davidson and Demi Lovato.

A tiny butterfly she could handle.

"You hungry? I can make us some breakfast," he purred, rolling her over onto her back and gently kissing her belly button. "What do you got in your fridge?"

Liv suddenly sat up in bed, smiling, suspicious. "Why are you being so sweet? What are you up to?"

"Nothing!" he protested, raising himself up on his forearms and reaching over to steal another kiss, this time on her lips. "Can't a guy spoil his girlfriend every once in a while?"

Girlfriend.

Such a loaded word.

Liv was enjoying her time with Zel, but she would not exactly categorize them as a couple just yet.

They had only been dating a few months, hardly long enough to qualify as a full-blown relationship.

At least in her opinion.

All her friends believed otherwise.

He was cute.

That was not in dispute.

Not with his shaggy dirty-blond hair, piercing blue eyes, sweet smile, and lanky build.

Her heart skipped a bit when she first met him around a keg at an off-campus mixer after her graduation. They had both been students at the College of the Desert, although he was a year younger and now in his senior year and she was taking graduate classes, still trying to figure out her next move. Their paths had not crossed up to that point. He was in the film department. She was studying criminal justice. The chemistry was combustible. But she was not looking to date anyone. She had just broken up with the heir to a local air-conditioning and heating company who was studying economics with the hopes of one day taking over the family business. Although his parents owned a small company, their greedy show-off of a son acted as if they were the royal family of the Coachella Valley, and so his charms wore thin after some time and his true colors were revealed.

He was an obnoxious, narcissistic prick.

Boy, could she pick them.

Although Zel seemed different.

Artistic.

Sensitive.

Maybe she had not made such a colossal mistake this time.

Zel hopped out of bed and slipped into some boxer shorts before padding out of the bedroom.

Liv pulled the covers up over her breasts and stared into space, still wondering if there was a shoe out there ready to drop.

Zel returned a few minutes later, carrying a wooden tray with coffee and orange juice and some buttered toast. "There's like nothing in your fridge except some ketchup and a half-eaten grapefruit that looks like it's a month old."

"I rarely cook at home."

"I can see that. Sit tight. I'm going to run down to the store and buy us some proper food. How about a big, sloppy breakfast burrito?"

"Please don't. I have to shower and get to class," Liv said, stretching her arms and then tossing the covers aside and crawling out of bed.

Zel grinned and moved his eyebrows up and down like Groucho Marx. "Want some company?"

"No! You'll just make me late. Raincheck?"

"Okay," he said with a fake pout. "I gotta get down to my studio anyway. I hired this new assistant to help me out, and I'm still teaching him the ropes."

Liv stopped in her tracks and spun around. "You hired an assistant?"

"Yeah, can you believe that? There was money left over in the grant I got last year to start a whole new project." He paused, hesitating. "Which is what I want to talk to you about. But, hey, I know I'm keeping you, so we can discuss it later."

It was too late.

She was suddenly curious.

"What is it?"

"My last two films didn't exactly set the world on fire, and my professors, in all their expert wisdom, seem to think I keep too much of a distance between me and my subject. Today, you gotta be a part of the story, make it personal in order to be seen as an authentic voice, so I've been thinking about a subject that's much closer to me."

"Like what?"

"You."

Liv let out a surprised laugh. "*Me?*" Then she just shook her head. "Trust me, there's nothing interesting about my life." She turned on her heel and headed to the bathroom to brush her teeth. Zel followed her, hovering behind her as she squeezed some toothpaste onto her electric brush.

"That's where you're wrong!" Zel protested. "You have an incredible story to tell. Two gay fathers desperate to be parents. Finding a surrogate to make their dream come true. What happens after that?"

"Nothing! I know very little about her."

"Which is why I'd like to make a film about you reconnecting with her."

Liv mulled it over for about a millisecond. "No, I don't think so."

"Why not?" Zel whined.

"Because I'm not sure I'm ready to open up this can of worms. Dad rarely mentions the woman who gave birth to me, and maybe there is a reason for that."

"Which could win me an Oscar!"

Liv spoke with her mouth full of toothpaste. "*Really*, Zel?"

"Oh come on, you know I'm joking!"

Maybe.

But then again, maybe not.

Zel placed his hands on her shoulders. "Okay, I'm not going to push it. If you're not up for it, I respect that. It was just a crazy idea I had." He kissed her left shoulder. "I won't bring it up again."

She really did want to help him with his career.

But she just was not sure this was the right way to go about it. She was not anxious to go down a road that she would later regret.

Zel was halfway out the door when she stopped him.

"So, you really think this could be the one?"

Zel nodded vigorously. "Most definitely."

"And if it gets to be too much for me, we can immediately stop? No questions asked?"

He was starting to get excited. "Absolutely! You're the boss."

Liv sighed. "Fine. Do a little digging. I have no idea where she is. Last I heard from Papa Charlie when he was alive was that she had moved to Phoenix."

"Maybe your dad Jarrod knows where to find her."

"No. Let's not involve my father. At least not yet. I have a feeling he won't approve. Let's wait until you actually have something before we bring him into this."

"Roger that," Zel said, spinning her around and wrapping his arms around her waist. "I love you."

"No. Stop. It's only been three months. Take it back."

"I can't take it back. It's already out there," he teased.

"I can't have the 'I love you' thing hanging over our heads. You haven't even met my father yet."

"Okay, I take it back," he said with a wink. "For now."

He tried kissing her on the lips again, open-mouthed, but she pushed him back. "I haven't gargled yet. Now get out. I need to shower, and I still have to iron my clothes."

He bounced out of the bathroom, and as she stepped into the shower, she could hear him on his phone with his new assistant, eagerly describing their new project.

Liv ran the water and stepped under the showerhead. The warm water cascaded over her body. She closed her eyes and silently prayed that she had made the right decision.

CHAPTER 3

Jarrod sat at his long dining room table and stared out beyond the sliding glass door at the large kidney-shaped shimmering swimming pool with its cascading waterfall and symphony of lights, painting the water's surface with a mosaic of dancing reflections. The towering palm trees were silhouetted against the indigo sky, their fronds swaying gently in the breeze. It was as close to paradise as one could get. And yet, he felt especially alone tonight. Maybe because he was trying to uphold a long-held tradition, one he had started with his late husband, Charlie.

When they had lived together high up in the Hollywood Hills, they would have a date night every Friday at home.

Indian food take out.

A cheesy movie.

Snuggling in bed.

Making plans for their next exotic trip somewhere in the far reaches of the world, one that inevitably would never come to fruition due to Charlie's crushing work schedule as an LA homicide detective.

But although Jarrod had a passion for travel, he never got angry or restless with him because he knew that Charlie's work was vitally important.

So he never complained.

Not much anyway.

Jarrod had been an actor.

Complaining was part of his built-in skill set.

It had been almost ten years.

Time had mostly healed the giant hole in his heart.

But there were still moments.

Like whenever he craved Indian food.

Tonight, for instance.

He had returned home from play rehearsal and was famished, so he snatched up his phone and ordered food from Monsoon on GrubHub.

Paneer tikka.

Vegetable samosas.

Extra tamarind sauce.

Some papadam.

Instinctively he almost added an order of butter chicken. That was Charlie's favorite.

But he had caught himself.

Jarrod poked at the cheese cubes slathered with onions and peppers on his plate with his fork. He had already made short work of the samosas and papadam and most of the side of rice and only had a couple more bites to go. But then he allowed his mind to wander to thoughts of his life long ago.

The night they first met, Charlie, then a beat cop, was called to the scene of a raucous out-of-control party in Beachwood Canyon, which turned out to be just two people, Jarrod and his best friend Laurette, drunk on too many margaritas and howling so loud they had disturbed the neighbors.

The sight of the handsome uniformed officer standing in the doorway to Laurette's apartment had taken Jarrod's breath away. He was not sure Charlie was even gay when he chased after him once he left after giving them a stern warning, satisfied they would lower the noise level.

Jarrod had found himself out on the sidewalk next to Charlie's squad car, blathering on incoherently and nervously scribbling his number down on a napkin he had grabbed from Laurette's wet bar.

Charlie's poker face over his ridiculous and embarrassing attempt to ask him out only fueled Jarrod's insecurities when the hot cop finally hopped back into his squad car and sped away.

A week went by.

Crickets.

Jarrod even considered calling the police and reporting a prowler, hoping they might send that same strapping young officer he had hit on, but cooler heads prevailed.

Then he called.

Out of the blue.

On a Sunday morning.

His first day off in two weeks.

Jarrod had pretended not to recognize Charlie's voice when he answered the phone, but of course he knew right away who it was. Charlie suggested coffee. Simple enough. If either one of them decided they were not interested, then they would only have to endure about forty-five minutes to an hour of painful conversation.

But that turned out to not be the case.

Coffee led to a walk around West Hollywood, which led to dinner, which led to them heading back to Charlie's apartment on Fountain Avenue where they spent the rest of the night talking.

Yes, talking.

And only talking.

A rare occurrence when two gay men who are wildly attracted to each other finally get together with a bedroom nearby.

Then there was breakfast.

More talking.

And finally Jarrod driving home to Hollywood Hills. Totally and unreservedly in love.

It had been the perfect first date.

Charlie moved in six weeks later.

And they were never apart again until the day he died.

Jarrod stood up from the dining room table and carried his plate into the kitchen. He scraped the leftovers into a garbage bin underneath the sink.

He felt another presence in the room.

"What are you looking at?"

There was no answer.

He set the dirty plate and utensils down in the sink and turned around to confront a Maine coon cat with a sourpuss face, his majestic tail swishing back and forth in evident boredom. His golden eyes, usually sparkling with mischief, now held a glint of longing as if imploring for attention.

"You're not getting any, so stop staring."

Jarrod poured himself a glass of wine from the half-empty Cabernet bottle and padded into the living room with its vaulted high ceilings and mid-century decor. He plopped down on the couch to turn on the TV. He was planning on watching *Gladiator* with Russell Crowe, one of Charlie's all-time favorites. Charlie had always been more of a meat-and-potatoes action movie kind of guy, as opposed to Jarrod, who fell right into the gay stereotype of loving *The Devil Wears Prada* or *Mean Girls*. After an excruciatingly long rehearsal with his high-maintenance cast, Jarrod was in the mood to watch bloody sword fights and lots of heads cracking open.

The cat jumped up on the couch and nestled down in Jarrod's lap as he surfed through the streaming apps with his remote in one hand while stroking the back of his cat's neck with his other. "You're such a whore for attention, Barnaby."

Barnaby closed his eyes and purred loudly.

Jarrod tapped the remote, bringing up the movie but stopping short of pressing Play. He glanced down at the cat curled up in his lap. "Is watching this going to take me to a dark, messy place? What do you think?"

Jarrod reached under Barnaby's chin, rubbing gently, causing him to nod and purr even louder. "Yeah, you're probably right. We should watch something else. How about a camp classic like *Valley of the Dolls*? Charlie fell asleep during it long before Neely O'Hara's big emotional breakdown scene while I could recite every word of Patty Duke's fabulously awful dialogue!"

Jarrod now petted the top of Barnaby's head. "You could care less, couldn't you? I know, you liked Charlie better because he was the one who picked you out at the animal shelter. You literally crawled on top of the other kittens, crying at the top of your lungs for him to lift you up and get you the hell out of there. He couldn't resist you. But you should thank me. He wanted to name you Cartman, after his favorite *South Park* character. I insisted we call you Barnaby. After *Barnaby Jones*. Charlie had never even heard of *Barnaby Jones*. Buddy Ebsen as a senior citizen private eye? Come on, it was a TV classic. Lee Merriwether as his widowed daughter-in-law and loyal secretary? Great show. With lots of cool 1970s guest stars. I was one of them. Did you know that? It was my first acting credit. I was still a toddler at the time playing the abducted grandson of a wealthy bank president."

Jarrod chuckled. Over the years he had grown used to talking out loud to his cat. It made the house feel less empty.

"So, Kitty is trying to fix me up with a guy. He's very sexy but maybe a little too young for me. I don't know. Just the idea of dating. Ugh. What do you think?"

Barnaby was curled up in a ball, eyes closed and still purring.

Jarrod continued gently petting him. "I know what Charlie would say. He'd say it's time. You need to live your life. Don't keep pining over me. It's been ten years." He glanced over at a framed photo of Charlie in his police uniform from the late 1990s. "Wouldn't you?"

Barnaby shifted slightly, probably annoyed by Jarrod's incessant chattering, which was preventing him from drifting off to sleep.

Jarrod looked down and grinned.

"Okay, message received. I'll stop bothering you. But unlike everybody else in my life, I know *you* would love for me to stay home all the time and just hang with you all day and night."

That would be so easy.

Just committing to writing and directing this play had been a huge monumental decision, one he was already regretting.

His phone buzzed.

He glanced at the screen.

It was a text from Isis.

An old Hollywood friend he had not spoken to in years.

What a blast from the past.

He tried to remember the last time he had seen her—maybe it was Charlie's memorial.

But that was ten years ago.

What could she possibly want?

CHAPTER 4

Liv sat at her usual corner table at Starbucks, sipping her coffee, doomscrolling the latest headlines on her phone. The door chimed as it opened, and Liv looked up to see her father Jarrod striding toward her with purpose in his step.

"Dad, what are you doing here?"

"I need to talk to you," he said grimly, his eyes conveying a sense of urgency.

"How did you know I'd be here?"

"You're here every morning like clockwork. You're a creature of habit. Just like your Papa Charlie."

Liv checked her phone. "You'll have to walk with me. I'm late for a yoga class."

She downed the rest of her coffee and popped up to her feet, grabbing her yoga mat. Jarrod followed quickly behind her out the door and onto the street.

Outside, Liv slowed, falling in step beside him as they rushed down a bustling street full of tourists. "How's the play going?"

Jarrod frowned. "It's an unmitigated disaster. It's probably going to completely ruin my credibility both as an author and a director. I don't even know why I was foolish enough to say yes to this."

Liv scoffed lightly, a smirk playing on her lips. "Come on, Dad. You always say that, and then opening night sells out," she teased.

Jarrod shrugged with a sheepish grin. "Well, that's because I always hire an actor who looks like a porn star and have him pose shirtless for the poster advertising the play. Inevitably, all the gays will show up, no matter how bad the production is," he explained with a wink.

Liv rolled her eyes, shaking her head. "You're shameless," she remarked, though there was fondness in her tone.

"That's not why I wanted to talk to you. I recently heard from an old friend. Do you remember Isis?"

"Yes, I do. I overheard you and Papa Charlie talking about her. Wasn't she that fake clairvoyant who used to give you psychic readings?"

Liv, like Charlie, was a strict nonbeliever in any kind of otherworldly pursuits.

"Yes, but she isn't a fake. She actually has a real gift."

"Whatever, Dad. What kind of name is Isis anyway?"

"She was born in the seventies. Her parents named her after the *Shazam!/Isis Hour* from Saturday morning kids' TV. Isis was a goddess superhero who wore an amulet that gave her the power of animals and the elements."

"Sort of like a poor man's Wonder Woman?"

"The show was hugely popular. Her parents had no idea that one day Isis would be the name of a terrorist group that beheads people. It was very unfortunate for her. I haven't heard from her in years, but yesterday I received a text from her. She felt the need to get in touch with me because she had a vision in her mind, so I called her."

Liv sighed dismissively. "She gave you a psychic reading over the phone?"

"Yes, they can do that."

"So, are you going to win the lottery or something?"

"No, she didn't see me. She saw you."

"Me?"

"You were standing over a dead body."

Liv stopped in her tracks. *"What?"*

Jarrod nodded gravely. "It was definitely you. She recognized you from the Christmas card I sent out to everyone I know a few years ago. She believes the person you were standing over was murdered."

"Oh come on, Dad. What is this? Was she shuffling her tarot cards and turned over the death card or something silly like that?"

"No, the death card doesn't always mean literal death. But trust me, Liv. Isis is good. Real good. We have a long history. She's done this before. Years ago, when I was younger and living in the Hollywood Hills, she predicted the same thing with me. She predicted a dead body, and then I discovered the corpse of an old friend floating dead in his swimming pool, and it turned out to be a homicide."

"I have to be honest. I can't believe someone of your intelligence actually buys into this crap. It's so Hollywood, all this psychic and New Age-y stuff."

Liv started walking again.

She was just like her Papa Charlie.

"Look, Liv, I'm just a little worried—"

She raised a hand, cutting him off. "Okay, for the sake of argument, let's say she did see something. I'm planning to attend the opening night of your play. It's a murder mystery. There will be a dead body on stage."

"No, I told her about the play. That's not it. It's an actual dead body, and she senses real danger ahead."

Liv could not help but emit a derisive giggle.

"I know it sounds silly but—"

"You know, I really ought to call this woman and give her a piece of my mind for scaring you like this. You can be so impressionable."

She could see the hurt on her father's face and softened a bit. "So, she just called you out of the blue with this premonition? When was the last time you spoke to her?"

"I saw her at Charlie's memorial, but we didn't speak because I was too broken up to talk to anybody that day. And she called a few months before Charlie died. She predicted he would be leaving his job as a detective soon, which I found utterly ridiculous. Your father loved his work. He wasn't ever going to quit. But then, right after that, he got sick and died."

Liv could feel her cheeks burning with anger. "I can't believe you're putting any stock in this woman. It sounds to me like she's just trying to stir things up."

"She's never been wrong, Liv, at least not with me."

He started peppering her with questions about what was going on in her life. Trying to find any clue that might indicate there was some kind of trouble ahead, and she resented him for it. They hardly spoke as it was. Why try now? Just because some charlatan had come out of the woodwork with a cockamamie psychic prediction?

They had reached the yoga studio.

She leaned in to give him an awkward kiss on the cheek.

"I gotta go, Dad. We'll talk about this later, okay?"

Jarrod nodded, disappointed that she was not taking him seriously. Eyes downcast, he mumbled, "I'm sorry, Liv. I didn't mean to upset you."

"It's fine. I'll call you." She gave him a quick wave and bounded inside the studio for her class.

She knew she had just lied to him.

She had no intention of discussing this nonsense with him ever again.

A decision she would come to regret.

CHAPTER 5

Maude sat atop a barstool at Pete's Hideaway, nursing a cosmopolitan, legs crossed as her shimmering cocktail dress rode up her thigh, revealing perhaps a bit too much leg. Maude was loud, boisterous, wild, and fun and was snorting over a joke she had just made at her own expense while Liv could not help but chuckle along with Maude's infectious laugh.

Pete's Hideaway was a dingy, weathered, dark bar that featured local musical acts located just outside the main drag of Palm Springs. Maude had strong-armed Liv into accompanying her to hear her boyfriend, Clyde, a ginger-bearded, barrel-chested country western singer, whom she claimed was once a judge on a country music competition series on an obscure cable channel, though Liv had never heard of it.

Liv had agreed to come out tonight to support both Clyde and Maude almost a week ago, but during the time before the big show, the couple had split, amicably according to Maude, promising to remain the best of friends. What made it so awkward was that Clyde had written a love song specifically about his relationship with Maude, a heart-tugging, emotional ballad called "Together Til the End," which had come a lot sooner than either of them had expected.

Maude assumed Clyde would not perform the song as planned,

but Clyde's response was, "Why not? I'm not going to waste a perfectly good song just because we broke up."

Maude could hardly argue with his logic. And so, she decided to show up and hear his set despite the fact they were no longer an item.

Maude took a sip of her drink. "I can't stop thinking about what your father told you."

"Please try," Liv sighed.

"I totally believe in psychics. I had a reading once, and he told me I was going to marry a singer one day."

"You think he meant Clyde?"

Maude shrugged. "Maybe. But I'm still going to hold out for Harry Styles. Besides, Clyde and I are already kaput. There's no going back." She slammed her drink down. "What if it's me? What if *I'm* the dead body?"

"Maude, would you stop indulging my father's paranoia?" Liv scolded. "Let's talk about anything else."

Luckily Clyde came out and interrupted their conversation, performing a couple of classic covers, "Wichita Lineman" and "Smoky Mountain Rain," before segueing into his original songs. And when it finally came time to croon "Together Til the End," Clyde suddenly got very nervous and avoided eye contact with Maude, keeping his longing gaze trained on the very discombobulated and confused sixty-something bartender, Roy, who was probably wondering why the singer was singing a love song directly to him.

When Clyde finished, after forgetting some words and mangling a high note, he quickly announced that he was taking a break and scooted out back through the moth-eaten red curtain.

Liv and Maude lost it, erupting in laughter.

"If I knew being here was going to throw him off and mess up his set so badly, I would have stayed far away, but the big lug insisted!" Maude claimed. "I know he's back there beating himself up. Maybe I should go give him a pep talk."

"No, I know you! You two will just wind up back together for a few more weeks before you decide to break up all over again."

"I can't seem to quit him!"

"You've never been able to quit any of your boyfriends ever since junior high!"

Liv and Maude had met when Liv was twelve and she and Jarrod had first moved to Palm Springs after the death of her Papa Charlie. Maude was asked by the principal to show Liv around the school on her first day and they had been best friends ever since.

"Remember Jason Pappas? God, I had such a huge crush on him," Maude sighed. "He was so different from all the other boys in our class. He went through puberty early and had that sexy, hairy chest! I could barely breathe whenever he was around! We went out for about three weeks before he dumped me for Ainsley Goddard, the head cheerleader, who also developed early!"

"Of course I remember Jason. He was the first boy I ever knew who could grow a beard," Liv laughed.

Maude sipped her cosmo. "We're friends on Facebook. He still looks good. You know how most jocks peak during high school and then it's all downhill, with the lumpy dad bod and broken dreams? Not Jason. He's an entertainment lawyer in Los Angeles with a hot actress wife who's been on *General Hospital*!"

"I marvel at how you stay in touch with all your past boyfriends," Liv said.

"Of course. Why stay mad? I adore all my exes. Except Lenny, the king of the selfies! He never stopped. Everything we did had to be posted on social media! When he tried going viral by teaching his cat how to salsa, I knew our relationship was dancing on thin ice. When I ended it, it was six months of crying jags on Instagram and TikTok about how I had so ruth-lessly broken his heart, even though he was already dating someone else! Putz!"

"Believe me, I remember it all," Liv nodded. She had heard this story multiple times. It only took two cosmos before Maude usually started repeating stories.

"Well, I'm done with men!" Maude suddenly noticed Liv's skeptical look. "What?"

Liv caught herself and swiftly wiped the smirk off her face. "Nothing."

"You don't think I can stay single, do you?"

Liv wanted to be supportive.

She really did.

But the idea of Maude without a man in her life struck her as hilarious. She decided to strike a measured balance. "I love you no matter what, single or attached."

Maude eyed her suspiciously, then chose to let it go. "Okay, now that we're in boyfriend territory, what's going on with you and Michael Moore?"

Liv cocked an eyebrow. "Who?"

"The documentarian!"

"You mean Zel. Who is Michael Moore?"

"*Roger and Me, Bowling for Columbine, Capitalism: A Love Story*? He's super famous. You'd know who I'm talking about if you ever watched a little Netflix!"

"I get it. Zel makes documentaries." She paused. "He's fine."

Maude picked up on Liv's slight hesitation. "What? What's wrong?"

"Nothing! He's great, actually. Things are really good be-tween us," Liv protested.

Maude was picking up on something.

And as Maude was prone to do, she was not about to let it go, and Liv knew it.

"Liv . . ."

"He's working on a new film."

"What's the subject?"

"Me, I think."

Maude downed the rest of her cosmo and signaled the bartender to bring them two more as Liv quietly explained about Zel's plan to track down her surrogate mother.

"I don't like this. Not one bit!" Maude exclaimed. "Liv, I wasn't going to say this to you because it's none of my business, but I don't trust him!"

"You've made that abundantly clear from day one," Liv scoffed.

"No, I haven't! This is the first time I'm telling you."

It also only took two cosmos for Maude to forget something she had said many times before, believing she had held her opinion back, keeping it a secret until this very moment when actually she had not.

Liv was too exhausted to argue with her. "Okay, thanks for letting me know."

Maude grabbed Liv's hand. "I'm serious. I'm not comfortable with him dredging stuff up from your past. Who knows what he could find? It might be very traumatic for you."

Liv gently pulled away and said firmly, "Well, luckily this is my decision and not yours."

"Absolutely. No question. But as your best friend in the entire world, I reserve the right to offer you my humble opinion. And I think he's a loose cannon, mostly concerned with himself and his fledgling film career."

Liv looked stung by the no-holds-barred assessment.

"Come on, Liv, you *always* tell me what you really think of my boyfriends!"

Maude was right.

She did.

And so why was she so closed off to hearing what Maude thought of Zel? Perhaps she was afraid of hearing what she suspected might be true.

The bartender returned, placing two fresh cosmos in front of them.

Liv held up a hand. "I didn't order another one."

"I did," Maude said as she picked up her glass and slurped the rim. "We're going to need these if we're going to sit through Clyde's version of 'She Thinks My Tractor's Sexy.'"

Clyde returned to the stage as the bar patrons mustered up some scattered applause. When he reached for the microphone, there was some loud feedback, causing people to cover their ears. As Clyde reintroduced himself and encouraged everyone to tip the bartender and wait staff generously, Maude decided to turn to Liv and ask one more question before the show resumed.

"Have you told Jarrod yet?"

Liv stared straight ahead, not saying a word.

"I'll take that as a no. Why not?"

Liv threw her head back and sighed loudly. "Because there's nothing to tell. I'm not even sure Zel is going to follow through on any of this. He's constantly changing his mind on what film he should make next."

The intro to Johnny Cash's "Flushed from the Bathroom of Your Heart" blasted through the speakers as Clyde swayed from side to side, preparing to sing.

Maude leaned over and whispered in Liv's ear, "You need to let him know what Zel is up to because it affects him as well."

Liv, desperate to change the subject, turned and locked eyes with Maude. "I will. When the time is right."

And then Clyde drowned them both out with his high-pitched wailing.

CHAPTER 6

Jarrod dashed across the parking lot to InShape Fitness Center, his hand clutching his phone. He was very late for his group exercise class Forever Fit. He swept the barcode in the gym app in front of the reader. A red light flashed and he heard a beep, and the pretty young girl in spandex behind the reception desk welcomed him, chirping, "Have a great workout."

Jarrod rushed to the locker room to stuff his gym bag in a locker and grab his towel, and then he hurried past the treadmills and elliptical machines, half of which were not in use due to the lunch hour. He made a beeline to the exercise studio that was full of older people in their sixties, seventies, and eighties, all wearing T-shirts and shorts and sipping water from recyclable bottles and chatting each other up as if this was a social mixer at a retirement community.

Jarrod loved this class.

The oldest member was a ninety-two-year-old woman named Joan, who could do more push-ups than anybody half her age. Jarrod found her, and almost everyone else in the class, an inspiration to stay in shape.

He was still feeling bad about is ill-fated conversation with Liv. Springing Isis's prediction on her like that. He had not expected the blowback he had gotten from her. But she could be as stubborn as Charlie, and so it would be futile to try and mention it again.

Maybe she was right.

Maybe Isis was wrong and they had nothing to worry about. Maybe.

Grabbing some hand weights from the bin set up at the back equipment wall, Jarrod spotted his two best friends, George and Leo, surrounded by a group of flirtatious older ladies gossiping and giggling with their favorite local gay couple.

George was in his early seventies, a friend of Jarrod's for several decades ever since Jarrod made an appearance at the Hollywood Bowl, which George ran for five years, for a TV Theme Night that also featured a parade of stars from the fifties, sixties, seventies, eighties, and nineties who would come out on stage when their series' theme was played by the Hollywood Bowl orchestra.

One of the theme songs featured that night was from Jarrod's classic sitcom *Go To Your Room!* Jarrod had played the precocious youngest child in the family comedy, who even had his own catchphrase whenever he was about to be accused of wrongdoing. "Baby, don't even go there!" It was printed on T-shirts and on coffee mugs, and even to this day whenever a fan of the show approached Jarrod, they would ask him to strike his signature pose, left hand on hip, right finger wagging, and repeat that memorable line from their childhood.

Jarrod was always happy to oblige.

His fans were the ones who made him.

George had never seen the show when he met Jarrod at the Hollywood Bowl. He was already too old to enjoy the sitcom's simple-minded pleasures, but he and Jarrod hit it off after the concert with a bottle of champagne and became fast friends.

At the time, George had just met his much younger husband, Leo, a sexy Latin spitfire from Nicaragua. At the time Jarrod thought the age difference would doom their budding relationship, but now, almost twenty years later, they were still happily together, although they both pretended to be miserable in the marriage.

Jarrod took a swig from his bottle of water and set it down before joining George and Leo and their adoring entourage.

"I didn't think you were going to make it," George drawled. Sometimes he spoke with an affected Truman Capote–like Southern accent, even though he was born and raised in Chicago.

"Neither did I. I couldn't get Kitty off the phone."

"Please tell me she's planning another cocktail party. I love her parties. There are always so many interesting people there. And I deserve to rub elbows with all of them!" George declared.

"She is, but that's not what she was calling about. She's trying to fix me up with her new Secret Service guy."

Leo's ears perked up, and he excused himself from the gaggle of ladies fawning all over him. "Really? You're finally going on a date? Do you even remember how to go on a date?"

"No, but it doesn't matter because I told her no."

George feigned distress. "Darling, I know you loved Charlie deeply, we all loved Charlie—please, every straight woman and gay man and everything in between loved Charlie when they met him—but don't you think it's finally time you put yourself out there again?"

"You sound like Kitty," Jarrod groaned.

"I just don't want you spending endless nights locked away at home like some sad pathetic agoraphobic, rewatching old episodes of that insipid little sitcom you starred in over and over like Norma Desmond in *Sunset Boulevard* until you're either committed or dead."

"Jarrod's show wasn't insipid. I loved it!" Leo exclaimed.

"I rest my case," George said with a perfectly timed eyeroll. "My darling husband has no taste."

Leo was now in his midfifties but eternally youthful. He still had to keep up with his Energizer Bunny husband, who not only ran the Hollywood Bowl but was also a Vietnam veteran and Broadway dancer and now a city councilman in Palm Springs. Leo, smart as a whip, had expertly helped run his campaign. Jarrod was convinced it was Leo who had finally dragged him over the finish line, but Leo magnanimously allowed George to mop up all the credit.

"Stop fighting it, Jarrod," George said firmly. "We all know what Kitty wants, Kitty gets. Let her fix you up."

"All right, people! It's about that time!" David, the sixty-something Forever Fit instructor shouted as he tapped his phone to start the music that would blast out of the hanging speakers on the wall.

Everyone fanned out into four rows across the room. Jarrod, George, and Leo hung back in the last row. Ninety-two-year-old powerhouse Joan led the group of four in the front row, their combined ages adding up to about three hundred and fifty years. Cher started them out with "If I Could Turn Back Time," and David led the class in some simple warm-up choreography before they would begin to really sweat with box steps, double-timed running, and even the cha-cha.

Jarrod was in between George and Leo and just could not allow George to have the last word. "You do realize I'm in the middle of directing a play, which is taking up all my free time. Even if I wanted to go out with the guy, it's just not possible."

"When there's even a faint possibility of having sex, one always finds the time!" George announced. "Am I right, Fran?"

One of the women in her eighties standing in the row in front of George turned around and gave him an impish grin and wink. Then she glanced at Jarrod. "What are you waiting for? You're not getting any younger."

"I just don't understand why you won't even entertain the idea," George huffed.

"I know why," Leo offered. "He's scared. That's why he's been throwing himself into his writing and directing work at the theatre. It's a way to fill the void in his heart."

Several more women in front of them, eavesdropping, all spun around and nodded in agreement.

"Oh, Leo, that's so insightful," Fran said. "Where did you ever find such a smart, thoughtful, handsome husband, George?"

"A bathhouse in downtown LA," George deadpanned.

The women guffawed, a couple of them blushing.

"You need to be open to loving again, Jarrod," one of the women warned. "Take it from me. When my Harry died, I thought I would end up dying alone. But then I met Orson, and it's been a wild ride ever since. You never know what's ahead of you if you just keep an open mind and allow it to happen."

"Words to live by, Esther," Leo smiled.

The music, which had now segued to a Prince song, suddenly stopped.

Everyone in class froze.

David glared at the back row. "I'm sorry to interrupt your little coffee klatch back there, but we're here to work out!"

"Sorry, David," Fran mumbled.

"You need to try harder, Fran! Get your money's worth out of that new hip of yours!" David snapped. "Now everybody get your weights!"

He tapped his phone and the music continued.

George whispered to Jarrod, "What does Liv think about it?"

"I saw her yesterday, but I didn't mention it to her."

There was no way he was going to bring up the whole Isis drama because he knew they were both skeptics and would immediately side with Liv.

Leo scooted up to them, excited. "I heard Liv's seeing someone new. Well, who is he? What's he like?"

Jarrod shrugged. "I wouldn't know. I haven't met him yet."

George and Leo exchanged suspicious looks.

"Which is not unusual. Liv has to be really certain about a guy before she brings him home to meet me. Seriously, it's nothing to be concerned about. She'll introduce us when she's ready."

They did not believe him.

But they chose not to press it any further.

Jarrod did not believe what he was saying either.

As he returned to his place in line and began doing bicep curls along with everyone else, deep down he was concerned about not knowing anything about the new man in his daughter's life.

Charlie, the badass cop, the fierce protector, never would have stood for it.

He would have already done a background check.

Interrogated the guy.

Investigated his friends and family.

He would know everything about him before the poor guy even set foot on the welcome mat.

Jarrod wished he was more like Charlie.

Maybe then he and Liv might be a little closer.

CHAPTER 7

Liv pulled her car into a vacant spot in front of a one-story nondescript commercial building on Sunny Dunes Road two blocks west of Gene Autry Trail. It was not a scenic street by any stretch of the imagination, but it was home to an eclectic group of art galleries, graphic designers, and photographers alongside more traditional businesses like picture framing and home fixtures.

Maude, in the passenger seat, scrunched up her nose. "He couldn't find a place closer to downtown?"

Liv turned off the car and unstrapped her seatbelt. "That's so you, Maude. Always ready with a positive comment."

Maude ignored the sarcasm. "I'm just curious why he needs to rent studio space. I mean, can't he just work out of his apartment and save all that money?"

"Why don't you just ask him?" Liv sighed.

They both got out and walked toward a door that still had a "For Rent" sign taped to the glass. Liv knocked on the glass, and within moments Zel appeared, his face smudged with dirt and his shaggy blond hair astray. His shirt was open, and there was dust and grime spread all over his smooth chest. He unlocked the door and swung it open to greet them. "Come on in. We're just in the middle of cleaning the place."

Maude cocked an eyebrow. *"We?"*

Zel did not respond and just ushered them both inside. It was a large room with lots of wall space, a work table, and piles of cardboard boxes. There was a small bathroom with a grungy toilet and sink off to the side and a door leading to another room with some office space.

"Isn't it awesome?" Zel crowed.

Liv chose to be diplomatic. "I can see why you like it. It has so many possibilities."

Maude was more focused on a young man whose back was turned to them. He was in a ratty old T-shirt and khaki painter's shorts and was busy unpacking with the help of a box cutter. "Who's that?"

"That's my new assistant, Butch," Zel said, crossing the room to the young man. He turned around.

Liv was struck by his handsome face.

So was Maude, who audibly gasped.

Butch was in his early twenties with dark hair, penetrating blue eyes, and a laconic smile. Standing next to Zel, he was much taller and muscular with broad shoulders, in contrast to Zel's slim frame.

Zel clapped him on the back. "Butch, this is my girlfriend, Liv, and her friend Maude."

"Nice to meet you," Butch said.

Liv swore he winked at Maude when he spoke. She could see Maude's knees almost buckle. Then she looked at Zel. "You hired an assistant?"

"Yeah, I put an ad on Instawork, and Butch was the first person to respond within like fifteen minutes of me posting it. We met for coffee at Starbucks the other day and hit it off right away."

"I needed some part-time work to help pay for college," he explained, his eyes still focused on a slack-jawed Maude.

Liv glanced around the room. "There is so much space to

work with." She really wanted to ask how he could afford the place, let alone hire an assistant.

Zel started bouncing around the room. "I'm going to put my editing bay over here, and here I'm going to set up a little meeting space with a couch and some chairs and a coffee table. I'm going to buy a mini fridge for the kitchenette so I can serve cold drinks and have a coffeemaker on the counter over here. There's room for a desk and filing cabinet in the other room. Obviously it could use a paint job and the floors need to be buffed, but eventually it's going to look really professional."

Liv had to bite her tongue.

This place had to go for at least six to eight hundred dollars a month.

And how much was he paying his new assistant?

He could barely cover the cost of his apartment rent as it was.

Luckily she did not have to broach the uncomfortable topic of his finances because Maude was with her and had finally stopped staring at the sexy new assistant, Butch.

"How are you planning on paying for all this?" Maude blurted out.

Zel flinched slightly at the question but quickly covered and dismissed her with a wave of his hand. "I applied for a grant that will cover all of my expenses for the next six months while I work on my new project."

Maude pursed her lips, not convinced she was getting the whole story.

Zel's eyes widened with excitement. "Speaking of my new project, I have some good news."

Liv braced herself. "Oh?"

"I found her."

"Who?"

"Your birth mother."

Liv took a step back, suddenly flustered. "What? Already?"

Zel nodded. "Yep. It wasn't that hard, really. I just called the surrogate agency that your dads went to and had to fill out some online forms and got a name, and then Butch helped me track down an address."

"They just gave you her name?" Liv asked incredulously.

"I said I was Jarrod Jarvis."

"You posed as my father?"

"I didn't think you would mind. We agreed together to do this, didn't we?"

Liv knew there had to have been much more involved than just saying her father's name over the phone to get ahold of this extremely confidential information.

Zel failed to notice her distress, or he was willfully ignoring it. She couldn't tell which.

"So, she's been living in Desert Hot Springs for the last two years. Apparently she moves around a lot. I'm curious to know why. Her name is Candy Lithwick. Does that ring a bell?"

Liv nodded. "Yes. I always remembered my dads mentioning someone named Candy whenever I'd ask questions about my birth. I just never had any burning desire to seek her out."

"Until now," Zel beamed. "Okay, I haven't reached out to her yet, but when I do, I'm going to ask her to speak about her experience on camera, and maybe we can do a sit-down interview with the two of you."

"Zel . . ." Liv whispered.

"What, baby?"

"I-I'm not sure I'm ready for all this."

Zel deflated. "Why? What's wrong?" His eyes darted toward Maude, suspecting she might be the cause of Liv's misgivings.

"Things just seem to be moving so fast. I'm not even one hundred percent sure yet that I actually want to go through with this."

"But I thought we decided this would be a great project for me, for us?"

"I know, it's just—"

"I'll be with you, holding your hand the whole way. You're not doing this alone."

Maude could not take it anymore. "Why do you keep pushing her? Can't you see she's changed her mind? She doesn't want to do this! Stop badgering her!"

Maude's sharp words finally penetrated Zel's overzealous demeanor, and he quickly backed off. "You're right. I'm sorry, baby, I didn't mean to pressure you. If you're not ready, I respect that. I'll just find another subject to work on. And when you're ready, if you're ever ready, then we can talk."

"I'm sorry," Liv whispered, frowning.

Zel enveloped her in a hug, gently stroking the back of her hair. "No, baby, I'm sorry. I know how overbearing I can be when I'm excited about something. This is my fault."

She could see the disappointment written all over his face and felt herself wavering again. "Look, you just caught me by surprise. I know how important this is to you, so I'm not officially saying no yet. Just let me think about it some more."

Maude released a heavy sigh.

"So, if you're cool with it, would it be okay for me to continue working on it before you make a final decision? Just in case you decide to go for it?"

Liv nodded. "Okay."

"Liv . . ." Maude said through gritted teeth.

"No, Maudie, it's fine."

"I know I get so excited sometimes that I forget boundaries. I can't help it. I'm an only child," Zel said with a wink.

So was she, for that matter.

Then he kissed her lightly on the forehead. "Thank you, baby."

She brushed his lips with her own.

Then he kissed her back more passionately, causing her to swoon and almost forget there were two other people in the room.

She had to admit, despite his flaws, he was a great kisser.

Maude cleared her throat and snorted. "Why don't you two get a room? Or use the one back there since you're probably paying a fortune for it."

They both turned their heads to see Maude and Butch, closer together now, ardently checking each other out.

"Why don't you?" Zel joked.

And from the expressions on their faces, it appeared to Liv that they might do just that.

CHAPTER 8

With practiced strokes, Jarrod swam his twentieth and final lap. He glided through the water, turning his head to the side for a gulp of breath as he strained to reach the other end of the pool. His goal for the day was to have done thirty laps, but he felt a cramp in his leg and decided to call it quits at twenty.

When his fingers touched the tile of the pool's shallow end, he pushed back, his feet touching the bottom, and stood up, the cool water clinging to his skin like a revitalizing embrace. He exhaled and opened his eyes, catching a glimpse of a man standing at the pool's edge.

For an instant, Jarrod's heart skipped a beat.

Charlie?

Was that Charlie?

Maybe his ghost?

A bittersweet ache surged within him.

What was happening?

Was he going completely mad?

But then there was the dawn of recognition.

No, of course it was not Charlie.

This man was much younger.

Just the spitting image of Jarrod's dear departed husband.

It was Charlie's brother Brody.

"Nice form, Michael Phelps," Brody joked as he reached for the plush terrycloth robe draped over one of the lounge chairs and handed it to Jarrod as he climbed out of the pool.

"Brody, what are you doing here? Why didn't you call?"

"I hadn't planned on just dropping in unannounced. But I found myself passing through the Coachella Valley on my way to LA, and the next thing I knew, I was using Google Maps to swing by and say hi."

Jarrod gave his brother-in-law a wet hug and then turned around as Brody helped him slip on the robe. Jarrod tied it at the waist. "I thought you were in Tucson."

"I was. But it was time to get out of Dodge. I needed a change."

"Weren't you dating someone?"

"Yeah, Cinda. Didn't work out. Her family hated me. Except her little brother, who is a huge wrestling fan."

Brody was a former pro wrestler hired by the WWE when he was just twenty-three years old. He was cast as a villain, playing Blackheart, a vicious, no-holds-barred menace who cheated his way to the top with lots of eye gouging, hair pulling, and surprise wedgies. His character never came close to winning a title, and after a knee injury, Brody was let go when his contract expired.

Jarrod hated violence, but he and Charlie never missed watching Brody's matches on TV. He had an undeniable screen presence, and women (not to mention a lot of Jarrod's gay friends) drooled over Brody's chiseled physique. Now in his late thirties, he was not as buff as he had been in his prime, but he was still a force to be reckoned with, even with his slight paunch.

"I'm sorry I never got the chance to meet Cinda."

"Don't be. She was a cold fish. We never should have been together."

This statement had a familiar ring.

It was something Brody always said after breaking up with a girlfriend. But he never showed much interest in examining why he chose women he should never be involved with, and Jarrod had no intention of pushing it.

Brody had always been kind of a lost soul and a bit of a mess, and Charlie was always bailing his little brother out of trouble for years. They loved each other deeply and always had each other's back. But mostly it was Charlie rushing to the rescue, and not the other way around.

Since Charlie's passing, Brody had been wandering the country aimlessly, gutted by the loss, trying to find a path forward, but so far in Jarrod's estimation, not succeeding.

Brody often found himself on the opposite side of the law, quite unlike his straight-laced, by-the-book detective brother. Jarrod had spent a lot of money bailing Brody out of jail for several minor infractions like bar brawling or public nuisance charges, sometimes paying off loan sharks or setting him up in a new locale where nobody knew him so he could start fresh with some seed money. He did not have to, but this was Charlie's baby brother, and Jarrod understood the emotional pain Brody was going through on a visceral level because he was experiencing the same thing. Jarrod could not help himself. He had somehow become Brody's de facto guardian angel, or as George liked to put it, "His fairy godmother!"

Jarrod sat down at a patio table and poured himself a glass of orange juice. "Would you like some?"

"Got anything stronger?"

"I can make you a mimosa."

Brody wrinkled his nose.

"Not strong enough?"

"How about vodka? That goes good with orange juice."

"I'm a gay man living in Palm Springs. Of course I have vodka. But it's not even ten o'clock in the morning."

Jarrod was uncomfortable with Brody's drinking because he used alcohol to mask what was going on inside him until he could no longer hold it in and there was some kind of outburst.

Which the alcohol just exacerbated.

But he also did not want to argue with him.

It was probably best to just acquiesce and give the guy what he wanted to drink.

Besides, Jarrod had once been to a champagne brunch with George and Leo and was sipping his mimosa on the patio when he noticed several old men at the bar next door, guzzling down shots of whiskey. Jarrod lifted his flute, and without any sense of irony, remarked, "How sad those poor guys feel the need to drink so early in the day." Then he took a generous sip of his fifth mimosa. George and Leo had not let him live down that comment even to this day.

Alcohol was alcohol.

No matter what the proof.

Brody followed Jarrod inside to the wet bar in the living room, where Jarrod mixed him a screwdriver. He handed Brody the cocktail glass. "So tell me. What's in LA?"

Brody shrugged as he took a swig. "I hear there's this young manager, used to be an agent at CAA, who has opened up his own shop and is signing new talent. He specializes in pro wrestlers. I've been working on a new character and thought he might be interested in meeting with me."

Jarrod's stomach churned.

He knew whenever Brody found himself in desperate circumstances, he would try to revive his career in wrestling as some solution to his current problems. It never worked out, and then, left with little choice, he would go find himself a minimum wage gig for a while in order to try and get by until the next big opportunity.

"What about your knee?"

"It's mush. I know. But there's a doctor in Tucson who hooked me up with some new pain meds, so I hardly feel it at all. I honestly think I'm ready to get back in the ring. I can't wait too long. I'm closing in on forty."

None of this sounded good to Jarrod.

But he did not want to come off as an overbearing mother.

"So, when's the meeting with this manager?"

"I don't have one yet. A buddy of mine got me his number, and I've called a few times and left messages, but so far I haven't heard back. My buddy says I should be patient, he's a busy guy, but I thought maybe I'd try a more aggressive approach and just show up at his office and try to charm the receptionist into letting me see him."

Not good.

Not good at all.

Jarrod was already envisioning getting a call from Brody after he was arrested for trespassing when he refused to leave the premises until he got a meeting with this potential new manager a.k.a. savior.

"I think your buddy might be right. In my experience, aggressive behavior can be off-putting. When Tim Burton was casting *Batman Returns*, Sean Young showed up at the studio dressed as Catwoman and demanded to see him, and he hid under his desk until security finally escorted her out. She came off as insane and was never seriously considered for the part."

"I have no idea who Sean Young is."

"You're so young."

"But I get your point."

"Do you have a place to stay in LA?"

"I have an ex-girlfriend, one of the few still speaking to me, who says I can crash on her couch. She's living with a new boyfriend, so it's not like she wants to rekindle anything."

"How does the boyfriend feel about you staying with them?"

"Not great."

"That sounds awkward and awful."

"Well, I don't have any money for a motel, so it's just going to have to do in a pinch."

Jarrod bit his tongue.

Don't do it.

Don't do it, he told himself again.

But then, of course, like so many times before, he found himself racing to the rescue.

"No one's staying in the casita at the moment. Why don't you crash here? That way, you have a place to stay, and you can hang out with me, just until you get a meeting with this manager on the books."

"Are you serious? That is so generous of you."

Jarrod wanted to put a time limit on it.

Three weeks.

A month, tops.

But he refrained.

Brody was family.

He could never envision himself kicking family to the curb.

"Thank you, Jarrod. And I want you to know, I'm not going to be some lazy-ass freeloader. I'll do my share of work around here. I'll clean your house."

"I have a housekeeper."

"I'll do some gardening."

"I have a gardener."

"I'll skim the pool. Wait, let me guess, you have a pool guy."

Jarrod nodded.

"I'll find a way to make myself useful. I promise."

Jarrod laughed. "Just think of your time here as a mini vacation to clear your head and get some rest."

And hopefully get your act together, Jarrod thought but refrained from saying it out loud.

Suddenly a high-pitched voice pierced the air.

"Uncle Brody!"

Jarrod whipped his head around to see his daughter Liv flying out the open sliding glass door from the house and into the backyard, arms outstretched and running toward her uncle.

Jarrod was perplexed. "How did she—?"

Brody gave him a wink. "I may have texted her and given her the heads-up that I was in town today."

As Liv flung her arms around Brody, he lifted her up off the ground by the waist, just as he had done so many times before when she was growing up.

Liv adored her uncle.

And she had an incalculable positive effect on him. Whenever Liv was around, it was as if all his internal trauma and turmoil had never even existed. Liv was now smothering his face with kisses as he set her back down on the ground.

"How long can you stay?" Liv asked.

"Your dad graciously invited me to hang out here, so I guess I'm going to be in town for a little while."

"That's wonderful!" Liv gushed, hugging him again.

Jarrod watched his daughter with mixed emotions. On the one hand, he loved the fact that she was so closely connected with her Uncle Brody, a reminder of her father Charlie. But on the other hand, her enthusiasm shone a light on the distance between her and Jarrod. It had been weeks since Liv had stopped by the house, and then it was for a birthday party for Leo, whom she also worshipped.

She kept her visits to a minimum, Thanksgiving and Christmas and a few other special occasions. He knew they had grown apart in the years since Charlie died, and Jarrod was acutely aware that the estrangement was mostly his fault. He had been so destroyed, so crushed by Charlie's death, it took him a long while to emerge from his grief, which might have been at the expense of paying more attention to his only child.

But despite the fact he could now pinpoint the cause, he still had no idea how to fix it.

Or if it was even possible.

But seeing her euphoric reaction to Brody riding back into town like a conquering hero returning from battle just made him feel more isolated from her than ever.

CHAPTER 9

Liv was blindsided when she arrived at Zel's studio. She had raced over the moment she received an ominous text from Zel instructing her to come to the studio just as soon as possible, that it was an emergency.

Fearing some kind of accident or injury, Liv's mind began filling with worst-case scenarios as she sped across town.

But when she burst through the door, she found Zel calmly setting up his camera and some lights. There were two empty chairs and a woman with dirty-blond hair teased out, her back to Liv, chatting with Zel's assistant, Butch.

Zel lit up at the sight of her. "Hey, babe."

"What's going on? What's the emergency?"

Zel winked at her and then walked over and lightly took the blond woman by the arm and gently steered her around to face Liv while signaling Butch to capture the moment with his phone camera.

Liv did not recognize the woman, who was in her late forties, early fifties.

But then she had a sinking feeling who it might be.

Zel turned to make sure Butch was getting it all on video before he finally spoke. "Liv, I'd like you to meet Candy . . . your birth mother."

"*Surrogate* mother," Candy corrected him in a raspy, nervous voice.

Liv nearly doubled over, gut-punched, struggling to maintain her cool. "H-Hello."

"I was finally able to get in contact with her, and after chatting with her, and getting to know her a little bit, I felt it would be great if you two finally met and maybe did a little sit-down joint interview for the documentary," Zel explained.

"A *what*?" Liv gasped, in shock.

Candy suddenly picked up on Liv's reticence. "Did he not tell you I was coming here today?"

Liv shook her head. "No, no, he did not."

Zel's smile tightened. "Excuse us just a moment, Candy; we'll be right with you." He then scooted over and gently guided Liv out of the studio and into a small office space he had set up for himself, whispering, "Babe, I know I sort of just sprung this on you, but I felt it was important to capture your raw reaction to meeting Candy for the first time, and believe me, you were absolutely perfect!"

He touched her arm and Liv stiffened.

"This is so not cool, Zel. This was an ambush, plain and simple. You should have given me some warning."

"I know, I know, I went back and forth about giving you a heads-up, but I decided it would be best for the film to see the actual reunion before you sit down together and answer questions in a more formal setting."

"What's best for the *film*? What about what's best for me? You can't just manipulate my emotions on a whim. I am not the least bit emotionally prepared for this. We had an agreement. I was going to decide if I wanted to move forward."

"And you said I could keep working on it until you made your final decision," he said quietly.

Liv rolled her eyes.

That was pushing it.

Zel threw up his hands. "You're right. I'm sorry. I overstepped again. Boundaries, remember? I just wanted everything to be real and unrehearsed. I was afraid if I gave you time to prepare, the reunion might come off as preplanned or scripted and less authentic. But I see now I lost sight of being sensitive to your needs. Liv, forgive me. We can call the whole thing off. I can send Candy home right now."

Liv waffled.

She was curious to talk to this woman.

But she was still deeply angry with Zel for how he had arranged it.

She took a deep breath. "No, we're both here now. Let's just do this."

Zel perked up, relieved. Then he dashed back into the studio to give Candy an indication on how they were going to proceed, what kind of questions he was going to ask.

Butch ambled over to Liv, who had wandered back into the studio, still shell-shocked. "Hey, um, do you have a second?"

Liv snapped out of her stunned state, finally noticing him. "Uh, sure. What is it?"

"So, your friend, Maude, um, is she single?"

"Yes, she is."

He nodded, relieved. "Awesome. She's so rizz. I was thinking maybe I'd ask her out, unless you think she wouldn't be into it."

"I'm sure she would love to go out with you, Butch."

Butch lit up. "Seriously?"

"Seriously."

"Butch, can you help me out over here?" Zel barked.

Butch turned and nodded before whipping back around to face Liv. "How can I get a hold of her?"

Liv handed him her phone. "Give me your number, and I'll have her text you."

Butch excitedly tapped his number into Liv's phone.

"Butch!" Zel bellowed.

"Coming!"

He bounded away to assist Zel in attaching a small mic to the inside of Candy's blouse.

Steeling herself, Liv marched over and sat down in the chair opposite Candy.

Zel could sense her unease as he clipped the small microphone to Liv's lapel and snaked the wire down inside her jacket to keep it hidden from view.

He whispered in her ear. "You look beautiful."

She did not respond.

She was still mad at him.

Once satisfied with both their appearances, Zel stepped behind the camera, setting up his shot, as Butch fussed with the lights.

Soon they were ready to begin.

"Okay, rolling. Checking sound?" Zel turned to Butch.

Butch was now monitoring the audio recording equipment. "Speed."

"And . . . action," Zel said softly before speaking in a clear, crisp, authoritative voice. "Thank you both for being here. Candy, Liv, this is a profound moment. How does it feel finally meeting each other, now that Liv is an adult?"

Candy glanced at Liv, not sure who should speak first. But Liv was still in the midst of processing and obviously wanted Candy to go first. "It's surreal, actually. I've thought about this day for years."

Liv nodded, tension lining her shoulders. "Yeah, it's, um, strange."

That's all she could think of to say.

Zel poked his head to the right of the camera so they could both see him. "Candy, you carried Liv for nine months, brought her into this world. What made you decide to become a surrogate?"

Her smile wavered slightly. "Um, well, I wasn't ready to have children of my own yet. I was very young, but I wanted to help others to experience the joys of parenthood. It felt like the right thing to do."

"And the money?" Zel asked.

"I'm not going to lie. I was broke. I was hoping to go to school and study to be a nurse. So, yes, the money helped."

She nervously glanced back at Liv, who was stone-faced.

"Liv, how does it feel meeting the woman who carried you?"

Liv swallowed hard, her voice small. "It's a lot to take in. I've always known I was a surrogate child, but meeting Candy, I don't know, it's different."

"Candy, did you feel an attachment to Liv during the pregnancy?"

Candy paused, emotions flickering across her face. "Of course. It's hard not to. Carrying a life inside you for nine months . . . you can't help but feel connected. It's lovely to see what a poised, beautiful young woman she turned out to be."

"Thank you," Liv whispered.

"What about you, Liv? Do you feel any connection to Candy?"

"I guess. I mean, it's weird, right? She's not my mom. I have my parents who raised me, my dads, they're my family."

"Candy, did you ever wonder what happened to the child you carried after she was born?"

Liv wanted to put a stop to this right now.

She had been through enough.

But before she could, Candy spoke quietly. "I did. But I understood that once the baby was born, my role was over. Jarrod and Charlie were wonderful and open to me staying in touch, but I didn't want to intrude on their lives."

"Liv, knowing Candy wonders about you, how does that make you feel?"

Liv paused, conflicted. "I don't know. It's a lot to process. I didn't expect this—"

Zel did not wait for her to find the rest of her words. He quickly turned to Candy. "If Liv wanted to form a relationship with you, would you be open to it?"

"Of course. I've always had a special place in my heart for the child I carried, even after I went on to get married and have kids of my own."

"Talk about your children. What are they like?"

"I have two, a boy and a girl. They're grown up now and mostly on their own." She appeared very guarded and not eager to share many details, which struck Liv as odd.

"And Liv? What about you?"

She glared at Zel. "I don't know. It's a lot to take in. I probably need time."

"Of course," Candy agreed, not wanting to pressure her.

"I'm sure this has been an emotional meeting for both of you. Thank you for sharing this moment with us."

"Is that it? Are we done?" Candy asked.

"For now. Hopefully you will both be open to continuing this conversation," Zel said as he turned off his camera.

After a few pleasantries, Candy thanked Zel for bringing her and Liv together and quickly left, sensing there was an argument brewing between the two of them.

Butch also found an excuse to fly the coop, claiming he needed to go buy a new battery pack for one of the body microphones.

Zel braced himself as Liv finally erupted, lashing out at him.

How badly he had handled all of this.

How unfair it was for him to keep her in the dark.

She understood why he had made the decision, but it gave her no voice, no say in her own story, and it was hurtful and unfair and demonstrated a complete lack of empathy.

And then she stormed out of the studio.

Zel chased after her like a chastised puppy dog who had just gotten swatted on the nose with a newspaper. He begged her to forgive him, promising to keep her in the loop on everything from this point forward.

If she did not kill the project right now.

But Liv just wanted to end the whole discussion.

She needed time to think.

Without Zel around.

As she got in her car, Liv gave him one last stark warning. "If you ever pull something like this again, we're through. Do you understand me? Done. Finito."

And then she pressed a button and rolled up the driver's side window, nearly crushing his fingers before he yanked them free, and peeled away.

She fumed all the way back to her apartment because she knew that despite his groveling apologies and assurances, he was obviously thrilled with the painfully uncomfortable footage he had shot this afternoon.

He was on his way to making a great film.

CHAPTER 10

The midday sun cast a warm glow over the elegant estate as Jarrod pulled up in his car, a small smile playing on his lips. He had eagerly accepted Kitty's invitation for a game of tennis, relishing the thought of spending the afternoon with his dear friend.

Bounding up the stone steps to the grand entrance, racket in hand, Jarrod was greeted by Kitty herself, her radiant smile slightly marred by a hint of discomfort.

"Jarrod, darling, I'm so sorry, but my damn knee is acting up again," Kitty explained, a touch of regret in her voice. "I should've called you earlier to cancel."

Jarrod, masking his disappointment, brushed it off. "No worries, we can play another time. You should get that checked out."

"I have. The doctor says I'm going to eventually need a replacement, so I'm putting all that unpleasantness off for as long as possible."

Jarrod tapped the strings of his racket with the palm of his hand, joking, "You're just using that as an excuse because you're afraid I'm going to wipe the court with you again."

"In your dreams, Andre Agassi," Kitty howled. "Since you're already here, I thought we could have a light lunch by the pool, if that's all right with you? Renata has made her world-famous empanadas."

"Count me in! I love Renata's empanadas!"

Jarrod followed Kitty inside through the opulent home with its high ceilings and walls filled with historical photos of her husband's presidency, including Kitty rubbing elbows with world leaders, royalty, and celebrities.

They emerged out onto the sun-soaked patio. Jarrod stopped short at the sight of a man sitting at the table near the pool, his back to them, reading a book.

Jarrod instantly recognized him.

It was Jim Stratton, Kitty's new Secret Service man, casually dressed in a burgundy Lacoste pullover shirt and khaki shorts that showed off his thick, muscled legs. His face was buried in his book.

A sense of dread suddenly swept through Jarrod.

Was Kitty's knee really acting up?

Or was this all part of a ploy to get him and Jim together?

He could not be sure, but from the hint of mischief dancing in Kitty's eyes, he would bet this had all been orchestrated as a part of her obsessive matchmaking mission.

"I invited Jim to join us. I hope you don't mind," Kitty blurted out so fast that Jarrod did not even have time to object.

Jarrod's place at the table was set up next to Jim, very close together in fact, while Kitty took a seat across from them so she could observe their interaction like Jane Goodall studying a couple of curious primates.

"Jarrod, I didn't get the chance to formally introduce you to my new Secret Service agent, Jim Stratton, when we dropped by the theatre the other day. Jim, this is my best, best friend, Jarrod Jarvis."

Jim stood up from the table and shook his hand. "Nice to meet you, Jarrod. Kitty's told me a lot about you."

"I just bet she has," Jarrod said with a wry smile. "I hear you're a big Taylor Swift fan."

Jim's face flushed with embarrassment as he turned to Kitty. "You told him that about me?"

"It's nothing to be ashamed of, Jim. Taylor Swift is the closest thing this country has to royalty. I almost had to take out a mortgage on this house to get my hands on some concert tickets for my grandchildren!"

They all sat down at the table. Kitty's cook, Renata, had already brought out a plate of her empanadas along with some salsa and guacamole and bowls of Mexican rice and refried beans. There was also a pitcher of margaritas in the middle of the table, which Kitty reached for to pour into three margarita glasses lined with salt and wedges of lime.

Jim raised his hand in protest. "None for me, Kitty."

"Oh, Jim, please! One tiny cocktail is not going to kill you."

"I'm on duty. I could get fired."

"Who's going to tell? Not me! You need to have more fun. Jarrod is loads of fun. He could definitely teach you to relax more. Now, Renata makes the perfect margarita. If you don't take a sip, she'll be horribly insulted."

Jarrod guessed that Renata did not care one way or the other if Jim drank her margarita.

This was all about Kitty trying to loosen him up.

Jim sighed and raised his margarita glass. He knew he was not going to win this one. "To Renata."

"To Renata!" Jarrod and Kitty said in unison before they all clinked glasses and took a sip.

There was an awkward silence.

Jarrod reached over and picked up the book Jim had been reading. "*Giovanni's Room* by James Baldwin."

"Yeah, my ex recommended it. He used to think I didn't know enough about gay history, so he was always giving me his favorite books to read."

"I never read it. What's it about?" Kitty prodded.

"It's set in the 1950s, and it's about an American man in Paris who grapples with his feelings for a bartender named Giovanni, and it delves into the complexities of desire, self-acceptance, and the struggles to fit into societal norms during that time period. I gotta admit, so far, it's pretty good."

Kitty spun around to Jarrod. "Jarrod, what are you currently reading?"

"Nothing. I'm too busy directing my play these days."

"So, what was the last book you read?" Kitty pressed.

Kitty was making this conversation more forced and uncomfortable by the minute.

Jarrod bit into an empanada and took his time chewing to buy himself more time to think. "It was called *Less*. I don't remember the author's name, but it won the Pulitzer Prize, I think."

Kitty scrunched up her face. "What does the title mean? Less than what?"

"Less was the last name of the main character. He was a struggling novelist who embarks on a whimsical world tour to escape the heartbreak of turning fifty." Jarrod glanced over at Jim, who stared at him blankly. "It might not speak to you since you've got a long way to go before you hit fifty."

"Not *that* long!" Kitty interjected.

She clearly did not want their age difference to be an issue.

Jarrod could see Jim's unease over Kitty so obviously pushing Jarrod onto him, and he decided to change the subject. "How long were you with your ex, Jim?"

"Ten years. He was older than me. I was in my early thirties when we met, and he was in his midforties. He broke up with me when he met someone else, someone younger than me, in his twenties at the time, but then . . ." He paused. "I probably shouldn't go into all that."

Kitty was now wildly curious. "No, please do! Tell us!"

Jim sighed.

She was the boss.

He did not have much of a choice.

"But then he had a stroke and the new guy bolted, so I came back to take care of him and nurse him back to health. But unfortunately he never fully recovered and passed away about two years ago."

Jarrod and Kitty sat motionless.

Neither had expected to hear this.

They both self-consciously took another sip of their margaritas.

"So, he traded you in for a newer model, but then when he got sick, you came back. That's very generous of you, Jim," Kitty marveled.

Jim shrugged. "He didn't have anyone else in his life. He had two grown kids from a marriage when he was young, but they wanted nothing to do with him because he was gay. I couldn't let him go through something like that all alone."

Kitty, more intrigued now than ever, pressed Jim for more details about his past. His life as a beat cop, then homicide detective, before he was recruited for the Secret Service. Still relatively new to the position, he had been assigned a lower-profile task, looking after a widowed former first lady in Palm Springs. The risk of armed terrorists climbing the walls of her Rancho Mirage estate to kidnap her was admittedly remote.

But as Kitty continued peppering him with more questions, which he politely answered, it struck Jarrod that Kitty was doing all the work, not him. Jim addressed Kitty through most of the lunch, acknowledging Jarrod a few times, but the man was technically still on the job. He had pushed the margarita away, refusing to imbibe any more after the initial toast.

He was a professional.

Handsome.

Smart.

Hell, he was reading James Baldwin.

And blushing at the mention of his passion for Taylor Swift made him all the more adorable.

When pressed by Kitty, Jarrod shared a little about his past life as an actor in Hollywood, even though Jim had never heard of his show *Go To Your Room!* or any of his other major acting credits for that matter, with the exception of a voice-over he did for a Cartoon Network superhero show that Jim used to watch as a kid. He also mentioned Charlie but did not go into too much detail, except to say he had also sadly passed away.

But Jim did not follow up, asking if he was seeing anyone at the moment. And for Jarrod's part, he failed to ask Jim the same question. So it was up to Kitty, who managed to get both men to admit they were both currently single.

But the fact was, despite Kitty's herculean and blatant attempts to find common ground between them, they just did not seem to have much chemistry.

Perhaps it was because Kitty was pushing too hard.

Or maybe they were just too different.

Despite her efforts to keep the lunch going, Jim finally got a call from the field office and excused himself, leaving Jarrod and Kitty at the table.

"Well, I found that incredibly productive," Kitty concluded.

"How so?" Jarrod scoffed.

"You came into this not even certain he was gay, and now we know he reads James Baldwin and became the caretaker to an ex-lover who had been cruelly dumped by his twinky boyfriend! How heroic is that?"

"You can stop right there, Kitty."

"What? Don't you think he's perfect?"

"Yes. For someone else. I'm not interested in dating anyone right now, as I've explained to you multiple times. So, I beg you, please do not, repeat, do not interfere with my personal life."

"What life? You have no life! I'm just trying to help get you one, dear," she huffed, finishing her margarita. "If I can get a nationwide mental health campaign going in the first six months of my husband's presidency, I can find you a boyfriend!"

This was not the first time Jarrod had heard that challenge from Kitty.

It was time to play hardball.

"Don't you think that perhaps the reason you're trying so hard to play matchmaker for me is because you're basically projecting? You miss your own husband so desperately, the man you adored during fifty years of marriage, that seeing me find someone fulfills that need in you?"

"I have no idea what you're talking about!" Kitty spit out defensively. "And when did you start tossing out all this psychology mumbo jumbo?"

Jarrod grinned.

Kitty always got defensive when faced with a hard truth.

She gingerly rubbed her left knee. "You know, my knee is feeling better. How about we play a set before you leave?"

Jarrod cocked an eyebrow. "I thought it was your right knee that was giving you trouble."

"Don't be sassy. I did not fake pain in my knee just to arrange a date between you and Jim. I'm not that Machiavellian," Kitty protested, hauling herself up to her feet and marching into the house to find her tennis racket.

Jarrod could not help but grin because he knew Kitty's strong denial simply meant that she had done exactly that.

She had learned many lessons from her years in the White House.

Focus on serving the common good.

Collaborate and build coalitions.

And most importantly, when backed into a corner, deny, deny, deny.

CHAPTER 11

Liv had not expected to see her father at home. Usually he had rehearsals on Sunday afternoons, and knowing what a perfectionist he could be, and with opening night just a couple of weeks away, she knew he could be very strict about doing as many last-minute run-throughs with the cast as possible. But when she breezed up the stone walkway to his house, he had startled her by appearing at the front door to greet her.

"What are you doing here?"

"I live here," Jarrod deadpanned.

"I mean, I thought you'd be at the theatre."

"Ira has strep throat and Talia claims to have a migraine, but I know that's just an excuse so she can attend her niece's wedding in LA today, and Kent's just being a pill as usual, so I canceled rehearsal today. What are you doing here?"

"I'm picking up Uncle Brody. We're going to hike the Murray Canyon Trail."

"Oh . . ." Jarrod squeaked, a look of disappointment flashing across his face. "He's out back, doing crunches, trying to resuscitate those rock-hard abs per usual. I'll go get him."

Jarrod turned to leave before Liv stopped him. "You're welcome to join us . . . Now that you're free."

Her father turned back and studied her expression, trying to gauge whether she really wanted him to join them or if she was just being polite, having been caught making plans that did not include him.

"No, I've got work to do. I'm still rewriting the script."

"At this late stage?"

"I keep thinking I can improve it, make it better. Believe me, I'll be at this until the curtain goes up, and even then I'll probably keep hammering at it, changing things that don't work throughout the entire run. Your Papa Charlie always said I couldn't be bothered watering the hedges once a week, but I would work tirelessly through the night in order to nail the perfect line of dialogue."

A wave of nostalgia washed over her at the mention of her other father, Charlie. She noticed Jarrod looking down at his shoes, getting misty-eyed.

"He would be proud of you," she said sincerely.

His eyes rose to meet hers.

She knew he needed to hear that.

It frustrated her that she and Jarrod had grown apart over the years. Whenever she tried to pin down a specific reason, she could not because it had been a gradual process, a slow sleep walk, and now she just had no idea how to get close to him again.

Brody bounded in from out back, shirtless, sweat dripping down his face, which he wiped off with a towel, his broad chest and arm muscles glistening. "Hey, Princess, just let me change and then we can head out. I got some clean clothes in the laundry."

"Sure, Uncle Brody."

He sprinted up the stairs.

She turned her attention back to Jarrod. "Hey, Dad, do you still keep in touch with my surrogate mother?"

"Candy?" Jarrod asked, surprised. "No. I mean, not really. Why do you ask?"

She wavered, not sure if she should reveal their recent reunion just yet. "No reason. I've just been thinking about her lately, like what kind of woman she was?"

"Your dad and I didn't know what to expect when the agency paired us with her. But she turned out to be a nice girl, with a good heart, who seemed genuinely interested in helping us bring you into the world. For that, we'll always be grateful."

"Why didn't you stay in touch?"

Jarrod thought about it for a moment. "I'm not really sure. Charlie and I were very clear with her that we were open to her remaining a part of your life after you were born, and she did pop around occasionally for a while. She would bring you toys. But then when you were still just a toddler, maybe three years old, she just kind of dropped out of our lives. We never saw her again. We heard through the grapevine that she had met a guy and was pregnant, so we figured she probably wanted that to be her focus, starting her own family."

"You never considered trying to reach out to her as the years went by?"

"Honestly, no. We felt that pulling away was her choice so we wanted to respect her boundaries. I'm curious. Why the sudden interest in Candy again? Are you thinking of trying to find her?"

"No!" Liv barked at the top of her lungs.

Jarrod was taken aback.

He knew her habit of talking loud and fast when she was not being entirely truthful, but to his credit, he chose not to call her on it.

Liv felt terrible.

She wanted to tell him everything.

How she had just seen her, thanks to Zel.

And about her conflicted emotions during their reunion.

And Zel's notorious role in planning the whole surprise.

But she demurred.

She was not prepared to show all her cards just yet.

Not until she learned more.

Because she worried Candy was hiding something.

She had been so careful during their interview, so guarded, as if she was fiercely determined to paper over key aspects of her life.

Which just made Liv all the more curious to find out what those aspects might be.

Brody clambered down the staircase in a fresh aqua-blue tank top, shorts, and hiking boots. "Okay, I'm ready. Is Steven Spielberg joining us?"

"No, he's working at the studio," Liv laughed.

"What's his name again? Zeke?" Brody asked.

"Zel. Short for Zelmer."

"I can see why he shortened it," Brody cracked before scuttling into the kitchen.

"Am I ever going to meet this new guy in your life?" Jarrod sighed. "How long have you two been together already?"

"Just a few months. It's still kind of new."

She did not want to admit to him that she was still figuring out whether she even wanted to stay with him after the stunt he pulled ambushing her with Candy.

She knew that Jarrod could tell there was more to the story, that her hesitation was not because she had just met him and was still getting to know him herself or that it was just a casual thing that might not last, but again, her father chose to remain mum and not make her feel uncomfortable.

Brody returned with two bottled waters. "Gotta keep hydrated. We're in the desert. Ready to go?"

Liv nodded. She spun around and gave her father a quick peck on the cheek. "I'll bring him by soon. I promise."

"I'm going to hold you to that."

And then she followed Brody out the door.

She was consumed with guilt. Although she did not feel as close to her father as she wanted, she still hated lying to him, or at least blatantly omitting the truth.

And she knew, in the end, the truth always had a way of coming out.

CHAPTER 12

When Liv let herself through the gate to the common area of her apartment building near downtown Palm Springs, her heart started racing and she felt a gnawing sensation in the pit of her stomach. She had always had an innate sixth sense, an invisible radar attuned to the slightest hint of danger. The common area was quiet, the kidney-shaped swimming pool still and glistening from the moonlight. Her eyes darted around in search of a presence, but there did not seem to be anyone wandering around.

And then she saw him.

He was lying on one of the chaise lounges, arms folded, his face hidden by the hood of a dark sweatshirt. He had really big feet, and she could not tell if he was asleep or staring at her. Her whole body shivered even though it was still over seventy degrees on this warm autumn night. She reached into her bag and fumbled for her keys, keeping one eye on the prone body, fearing it might suddenly rise and rush at her.

She rummaged frantically, her fingers touching her mints, her sunglasses, her package of tissues, lipstick, trying to find her keys. She glanced down in her bag, finally spotting them jammed into a corner nestled behind her wallet. She quickly scooped them up, shuffling through them for her apartment key, and then jammed it into the keyhole, glancing back at the man lying on the chaise lounge.

He was no longer there.

In the few seconds she had taken her eyes off him, he had vanished. But she felt no wave of relief, only more anxiety and apprehension.

Before she could yank the key to the right and unlock the door and slip inside to the safety of her home, she felt a hot breath on the back of her neck, causing the hairs to stand up. She crinkled up her nose from a foul smell, a combination of cigarettes and whiskey. She withdrew the key from the lock, slipping it between her thumb and index finger, ready to use the metal as a weapon, something to scratch a face or even gouge an eye, if necessary.

She stood absolutely still.

Then she heard his voice. "Good evening."

It was a deep, scratchy, raspy growl, a voice damaged from constant smoking. Although he added a slight lilt, hoping to make himself sound less threatening, it failed to help.

Liv slowly turned around to face the man, still clutching the key between her fingers.

He took a step back, realizing he might be too much in her personal space and was making her uncomfortable.

He was tall, lanky, and imposing.

She raised her hand with the key ready to strike. "Who are you? How did you get in here?"

"One of your neighbors was kind enough to let me in. Really sweet girl with red hair and the cutest freckles."

Maggie in 2A.

Always so trusting.

Never heeding Liv's stern warnings to be more careful, not to just always assume everyone had good intentions.

"She's not supposed to do that."

"Well, I told her I was your brother."

A jolt of fear shot through Liv. She tightened her grip on the key, moving back away from him, her shoulders touching the door, ready to lunge forward at him if she had to defend herself. "What do you want?"

He reached up and pulled the hoodie down, finally revealing himself. His face did nothing to reassure her. He seemed to have a permanent scowl, his thin lips pursed tightly together, and gray empty eyes from what she could see from the light above her doorway. His head was shaved like a skinhead. His hands were plunged deep in the pockets of his sweatshirt, and she was afraid he might pull out some kind of weapon to use on her.

He stared at her for a few seconds before responding, as if he somehow expected her to recognize him. "I'm Dale."

"Dale?"

"Candy's son. She didn't mention me?"

He stepped further into the light.

She could see the clear physical resemblance between them and relaxed a little but still remained on guard. Candy did say she had two children but never mentioned their names.

"I'm sorry to just show up like this, but when Mom told me I had a half sister, I don't know, I just felt like I really wanted to meet you."

"How did you find me?"

Dale chuckled. "You can find anybody on the Internet. I'm pretty good at that kind of stuff. Do you mind if I come in for a few minutes?"

Liv still had a gnawing sense of dread. "No. It would be better if we talked out here."

Dale shrugged. "Sure. I get it. I don't blame you. I'm basically a stranger. Mom never really told us about you either, so you can understand why I'd be so curious to meet you after you got in touch with her."

She wanted to explain that it had been Zel who had reached

out to Candy, not her, and she was not ready for any of this, quite frankly. But she also did not want to immediately send him on his way and possibly risk upsetting him because there was no telling what kind of person he was or how he might react.

She could tell he was younger than her, maybe only nineteen or twenty, despite his hardened features.

"Dale, I would really like to talk, maybe sit down with you and . . . What's your sister's name?"

"Jewel."

"Sit down with you and Jewel over coffee sometime and get to know each other, but it's been a very long day, and I don't mean to be rude, but I'd really just like to go inside and go to bed."

"Of course. We can do this another time. I'm so sorry I startled you. Mom taught me better manners than this. I'll leave you alone. Have a good evening."

He turned to leave, and she felt a wave of relief wash over her.

But then he stopped just a few feet away and spun back around again. "Can I get your number to text you?" He tapped his phone and then handed it to her. "Just type it, and I'll save you in my contacts."

She reluctantly took the phone and started tapping numbers. She thought about purposely giving him one wrong digit, saving herself from his texts, but she chose not to and ended up giving him the correct number. She certainly did not have any kind of sense that he was lying to her. It seemed perfectly logical that Candy would tell her other children about her, that it would undoubtedly pique their curiosity. But this Dale guy gave her the willies. There was something off about him. Something she could not quite trust. She handed his phone back to him.

"Thanks. I'll be in touch." He attempted a smile, which was crooked and insincere.

He did a half turn, then frustratingly stopped again, refusing to let her go inside. "Hey, Mom mentioned that your dad was a big-time actor in movies and TV."

Liv nodded. "Yes, he was a very popular child star in the 1980s and was a working actor for many years, but he's pretty much retired these days."

"That is so cool. He must have a lot of Hollywood connections."

"Well, like I said, he's really no longer in the business. After my dad Charlie died, he moved here to Palm Springs and left all that behind."

"Wait. You had two dads? I thought your mother couldn't have kids or something, which is why they needed my mom. She didn't tell me . . ."

Probably for a reason.

"It was nice meeting you, Dale, and I look forward—"

"Do you think I can meet him?"

"Who? My dad? Um, yeah, sure, eventually when we—"

He cut her off again. "When?"

"I don't know. Text me and maybe at some point—"

He widened that crooked, awkward smile. "I have an idea I'd like to talk to him about. Maybe he can introduce me to the right people and could help me get it off the ground."

"Dale, I think it might be a bit premature for me to—"

He did not seem to care what she thought. "You'd be doing me a huge favor. I mean, family helps family, am I right? I'm there for you, you're there for me." He winked at her. It did not strike her as a friendly gesture. To her, it seemed to suggest that he was acknowledging that there was no way she was ever going to get rid of him, now that they had met and he knew where she lived. "Anyway, no pressure. Think about it. I'll be in touch."

He slowly backed away, still forcing that smile, before spin-

MY FATHER ALWAYS FINDS CORPSES / 79

ning back around and laconically shuffling across the common area toward the side gate, whistling a country tune.

Liv hurriedly opened the door and scooted inside, slamming it shut and locking it behind her with the bolt and the chain before throwing her back against it.

She had a sinking feeling that she had just opened Pandora's box, releasing all the troubles and woes that would plague her life, and that it would be impossible to ever stuff them back inside again.

She braced herself for what was about to come.

CHAPTER 13

When Liv showed up at Zel's studio later that evening, she found him working at his computer, editing the footage from the interview between Liv and her surrogate mother, Candy. Butch sat at his side, observing, taking everything in. There was a pizza box on the scuffed wooden coffee table and empty blue-and-gray cans of Red Bull scattered on the floor to keep their energy level up as they probably planned on working through the night.

Liv had to clear her throat in order to get them to notice her at first since the door to the studio had been unlocked and she had just let herself in, but when he caught sight of her, Zel jumped to his feet and ambled over to give his girlfriend a tight squeeze.

"Hey, baby, I didn't expect to see you tonight. I'm teaching Butch the basics of editing so he can keep working when I'm out doing interviews."

His eyes wide and his fingers jittery, probably from the heavy jolt of caffeine from multiple Red Bulls, Butch raised his hand to greet her. "Hi, Liv."

"Good evening, Butch," she replied politely before turning back to Zel, who nuzzled her neck. "Zel, we need to talk."

She felt him stiffen, but he propped up his happy face, not wanting her to spoil the mood, although she could tell he knew what was coming.

But Liv was determined to press on. "I had a visitor at my apartment tonight."

Zel cocked an eyebrow, curious.

"Dale, Candy's son."

Zel lit up. "Do you think he might be willing to be interviewed?"

"I don't know, Zel. He told me he wants to be in the film business, so maybe, but that's not what I want to talk to you about."

"You should watch my cut of the interview with Candy. It's so good. We really captured the awkwardness and uniqueness of the situation. I want to build from that as you two get to know each other so when I interview you again, we'll be able to see how far you two have come, how you're both more open—"

Liv held up a hand in front of his face. "Zel, stop! Enough!"

Zel reared his head back, wounded. "What? What did I do?"

"Nothing. It's just that this Dale guy really spooked me. He was kind of creepy."

Zel shifted into protective boyfriend mode. "Did he hurt you in any way?"

"No, no he just surprised me, and I got a weird vibe from him. I didn't feel comfortable around him . . ."

"Then I will make sure you never have to be in the same room with him if we use him in the film."

"Zel, I think we should put the brakes on this whole project. At least for now."

He froze.

This was the last thing he wanted to hear.

He called back to Butch, who was chewing on a slice of pizza, his glasses glowing softly, emitting an ethereal hue from the computer screen. "Butch, do you mind stepping out so we can talk privately?"

Butch stuffed the rest of the pizza slice in his mouth and stood up, grabbing his phone. "Sure, I'll just . . ." He looked around, not sure where to go. Then he reached into his shirt pocket and extracted a pair of earbuds, popping them in both ears. "Be in the next room listening to some Olivia Rodrigo." He scurried out.

Zel gripped Liv by the shoulders, making direct eye contact. "Baby, I understand how difficult this must be for you, dredging up the past like this, but you gotta trust me, this doc is gold. I also got a line on a couple of film festivals whose awards officially qualify you for the Academy Awards if we place in competition. That would be a game-changer for us."

He was not hearing her.

Despite her concerns, it was still full steam ahead.

"You won't regret seeing this through, I promise you." He tried to kiss her, but she turned her head away.

He knew he had not convinced her.

Suddenly there was a knock at the door.

Zel checked the time on his phone. "Who could be dropping by this late?"

Liv's stomach tightened. "It might be him. Dale. Candy's son. He may have followed me here. I don't want to see him again."

They both stood there, not sure what to do.

There was another, more forceful knock.

Whoever was at the door was not going to go away.

Zel finally registered concern. He led Liv away from the door and placed her off to the side, out of view. Then, steeling himself, he walked over and opened it.

It was not Dale.

A young couple huddled just outside the door. She was short, barely five feet, wide and top heavy, with frizzy dull brown hair and too much makeup on an otherwise attractive face. Next to her, practically crowding her out, was a six-foot-tall linebacker with a bent nose no doubt broken in a brawl, muscles aching to burst out of a tight Arizona Wildcats sweatshirt. Both wore matching frowns.

Zel kept his hands on the door, ready to slam it in their faces if he got a bad feeling. "Can I help you?"

The girl spoke first. "Yeah, I got this address off my mother's calendar. She was here the other day. Candy Lithwick?"

Liv quietly exhaled from her hiding place.

Oh no.

Another one.

"Yes, I know Candy," Zel answered evenly, not willing to divulge too much at this point.

"I'm her daughter, Jewel."

Zel offered his hand. "Nice to meet you, Jewel. I'm Zel."

She did not shake it. "Are you the guy who came out of nowhere filling her head with all sorts of crazy thoughts, forcing her to embarrass herself for some bull TV interview?"

Zel sighed. "Nobody forced her. She was happy to do it." His eyes flicked to the bruiser accompanying her, who no doubt could crush Zel's head with his massive bare hands as easily as squeezing a lemon.

Jewel noticed Zel quaking with fear. She smiled cryptically. "This is my boyfriend Gunnar. Big, isn't he?"

Zel nodded, speechless.

"Here's the thing, Zeke."

"Zel."

"I don't care. What I do care about is you worming your way into my mother's life and telling her all kinds of things she wants to hear just so you can exploit her."

"That is not my intention. I just invited her to participate in a documentary—"

Gunnar slammed a giant paw down on Zel's shoulder, causing him to wince in pain. "She's not done talking."

Zel nodded.

Message received.

"I'm just curious. Ma says this woman she gave birth to is a really nice, pretty girl, very sweet, and that tends to make me very nervous."

Zel looked confused. "Why?"

"Because nice, pretty girls always get the most attention at the expense of the rest of us who aren't so pretty and nice. Gunnar and I are planning on getting married and starting a family someday soon, and we want to do it in the house where I grew up out in Desert Hot Springs."

"I'm not following you."

Gunnar crunched Zel's shoulder harder, this time causing him to welp. "Try harder."

Liv was not about to allow the brute to break any of her boyfriend's bones, no matter how much he deserved it for bringing all of them down upon her. She stepped out and joined Zel at the door, surprising Jewel and Gunnar. "I'm Liv."

Jewel snickered. "Well, if it isn't Little Orphan Annie." She looked Liv up and down. "Ma was right. You're so classy and poised. Like a Kardashian."

Liv ignored the comparison. "I don't know what you think I want from all this, but I'm not an orphan. I have a family. And I have zero interest in coming after anything you feel you might be entitled to."

Jewel leveled a skeptical gaze at her. "Gunnar's done a lot of work on Ma's house, fixing the plumbing, putting on a new roof. We've invested way too much to just lose it all now. And Ma's not doing too well with her diabetes and chronic heart issues. She might not be around a whole lot longer, so we just want to make sure we're not going to run into any problems from you down the road."

Liv could not believe this was her half sister.

Whatever fantasies she might have harbored about eventually forging a relationship with Candy's children dissipated in a flash. "Like I said, I don't want or need—"

Gunnar suddenly pointed a thick finger across the room. "Hey, that dude's recording us!"

Liv and Zel spun around to see Butch, having returned from the other room, holding his camera up, the red recording light blinking. Before any of them could react, Gunnar lunged forward at a surprised Butch, who dropped his phone and scrambled out of the room again. Gunnar stared down at the phone that was face up on the floor, right light still blinking, and then stomped on it several times with his size-thirteen boot, smashing and cracking it.

Nobody else moved.

When he was done, he marched back over to join Jewel, a smug look on his face.

Jewel shook her head in disgust and then poked Zel's chest with her finger. "You may have conned my mother into thinking she could be some glamorous movie star, but I'm not buying any of your bullshit. So, leave me out of it! Do you hear me?"

Zel slowly nodded.

She then turned to Liv. "As for you, if I get even a whiff that Ma might be revising her will, and believe me, I will because her lawyer is Gunnar's uncle, then I will be back here, and next time I won't be so warm and friendly."

Liv had heard enough threats from Jewel. She marched toward them with grim determination, forcing them back out the door far enough so she could slam the door shut on their threatening faces. "Goodbye, Jewel. Thanks for stopping by."

Liv and Zel stood absolutely still, listening.

Butch poked his head back in the room to see if the coast was clear but did not say a word.

They all heard Jewel and Gunnar talking outside the door but could not make out what they were saying. Finally, they heard a truck roar to life and speed away. Zel dashed over, pulled back the curtain slightly, and peered out before heaving a huge sigh of relief. "They're gone."

Butch bent down and snatched up his phone to examine it. "It's pretty trashed, but maybe I can still save what I recorded."

Liv walked over and wrestled the phone out of his hand. "No, Butch! We're done."

Zel remained quiet.

"Enough is enough." She hurried over to Zel's desk and began to rifle through a stack of papers. "Where is the waiver I signed allowing you to use me in your documentary?" Papers were flying everywhere. "Where is it, Zel?"

Resigned, he skulked over to the desk and unlocked a drawer, pulling out a folder. Liv plucked it out of his hand and ripped it up, tossing the remnants into a trash can. "I want no part of this project anymore, do you hear me?"

She could tell Zel's mind was racing, trying to come up with one more reason they should continue.

But he knew it was hopeless.

Candy's kids had effectively killed his award-winning documentary.

Defeated, his shoulders sank and he gazed down at the floor, nodding slightly. "Okay."

Then, fearing he was about to lose her as his girlfriend, he redoubled his efforts to reassure her, rushing over and grabbing her by the hands. "Liv, I'm sorry. I feel awful causing you any kind of pain. I thought I was doing what was best for you, but I can see now I was wrong. The whole project was misguided, and maybe I just couldn't see past my own ambition."

Okay, this was a start.

"My relationship with you is way more important than a documentary, I promise you!"

She let him kiss her.

He was saying all the right things.

She just was not sure she should believe him.

CHAPTER 14

Jarrod raised a skeptical eyebrow. "I beg your pardon?"

Kent pouted and shrugged. "I've been in two other plays, and both times I slept with the director, and you haven't made one move on me this whole time. Did I do something wrong?"

"Kent, you're not even gay. You have a girlfriend."

He shrugged again. "So? One of those directors was a woman. I'm very fluid when it comes to who I go to bed with."

"No! This is not happening. We are not going to have an affair."

Kent pouted. "Why not?"

"One, you're too young for me. Two, it is totally unprofessional. Three, if Ira ever found out you banged me and not him, he'd quit the play, and opening night is just around the corner and we simply can't afford to lose him now."

"Do you want me to sleep with Ira?"

"No! That's *not* what I'm saying! I don't want you to sleep with anyone! Just learn your lines. That's all I ask."

Kent sighed, resigned. "Okay, whatever."

What was it with this generation?

"Now where's Talia? We need to rehearse the opening scene."

Ava, the stage manager, appeared from the wings. "She just called. She's home drinking hot tea with lemon, trying to preserve her voice."

Ah yes.

Talia was suffering from a sore throat.

Jarrod had heard from a couple of her previous directors that whenever she felt she was not receiving enough attention from her director, she suddenly would come down with some malady, in this case, a sore throat and possible laryngitis. She would sit out rehearsals for a few days, keeping everyone on pins and needles, praying for a speedy recovery. She would always miraculously reappear at the eleventh hour, full of vim and vigor, ready to slay the critics on opening night.

Jarrod had decided to indulge her. Of all his major cast members, Talia was the most prepared, the most ready to go on. Ira was still overacting too much, shouting his lines to the rafters. And then there was Kent, sweet, dumb Kent, who now was slumped in a seat in the first row of the theatre, pouting over Jarrod's rejection, texting on his phone, probably trying to line up a new sexual conquest after rehearsal.

Jarrod noticed Ava smiling and waving at someone in the back of the theatre. He turned around to see Liv hovering by the entrance, quietly waving back to Ava, not wanting to disturb her father.

"Ava, let everybody take five. We'll pick up with the opening scene when we're back and you can stand in for Talia."

"Sure thing, boss."

Ava disappeared back into the wings as Jarrod waved Liv down the aisle to join him.

When she reached him, Liv went in for a quick hug. "How's it going?"

Jarrod rubbed his eyes with his thumb and forefinger. "We'll get there. I hope." Then he exhaled a long breath and smiled. "I'm happy you dropped by. What's up?"

He knew she would never just show up at a rehearsal for no reason. Liv always seemed to have something on her mind whenever she came to see him. He wished just once she would come by the house to hang out and talk, catch up on each other's lives, with no problem to solve or prickly situation that had to be dealt with.

"There's something I need to talk to you about."

And there it was.

She looked pained, nervous.

Jarrod studied her troubled expression. "Is it serious?"

"Maybe. I've done something without telling you first, and now it's gotten a bit complicated, and I'm not sure how to handle it anymore."

Jarrod braced himself. "Okay."

She paused, collecting her thoughts, and then everything just poured out. How Zel had reached out to her surrogate mother, Candy, for a film project and how Candy's two rather unsavory adult children had begun popping up, making demands, one wanting to meet Jarrod, the other making threats, fearing Liv was trying to horn her way into Candy's life in order to get possession of her house. It was crazy, and scary, and she should have told Jarrod much sooner because then maybe he might have helped talk her out of it.

"You're probably so mad at me right now!"

As Liv prattled on, near tears, Jarrod reached out and squeezed her hand. "Liv, Liv, I'm not angry. I'm not. It's your choice, and your choice alone, whether or not you want to have some kind of relationship with Candy."

She sniffed back tears. "But I think I made a huge mistake. Those kids, they were so . . . aggressive. I never should have let Zel start searching for her."

"Zel?"

"The guy I'm seeing."

Jarrod could see the guilt written all over her face. The elephant in the room was that Jarrod had yet to meet him.

And he had suspected all along this had been Zel's idea.

"Liv, if you've changed your mind, just keep your distance

from Candy and her family from this point forward. Leave it to her to contact you, and hopefully her kids will realize you're not a threat and I'm not a meal ticket, and maybe they'll just go away quietly and this will all be over."

Liv appeared unconvinced.

"So, it was Zel who got the ball rolling on all this?"

Liv nodded. "He was so excited about finding her and interviewing her, and I just didn't have the heart to say no. I didn't expect it to turn into such a big mess."

"He seems like a very passionate, ambitious young filmmaker," Jarrod said, trying to be tactful.

Liv frowned. "Dad, I'm sorry I haven't introduced you. I guess I was waiting to be sure if I wanted to be with him for the long term, and right now . . . I don't know, he was so sweet and charming and caring when we first met, but lately I've been seeing a whole new side of him, and I'm not sure I want to stay with him."

Jarrod could see how conflicted she was and felt sorry for her, but there was also a part of him that was happy that she was finally talking to him about something that was going on in her life and that she needed his advice.

Finally, finally, they were having a real father-daughter moment.

"Might I suggest something?"

Now it was Liv's turn to brace herself. "What?"

"Let me meet him and I'll make my own assessment. I will give you my full, unvarnished opinion."

Liv scoffed. "I don't doubt that."

"But no matter what I think of him, I will respect and support whatever decision you make. I'll even invite Brody to join us so he can give you a second opinion."

"Promise me you won't play the overprotective dad too much, okay? It can be so embarrassing."

"I will be on my best behavior. Now go on. Text him. See if he's free tomorrow night."

Liv hesitated, but then began typing out a text on her phone.

Within seconds, Zel wrote back, confirming he was available and telling her how much he was looking forward to finally meeting her father.

There was no going back now.

CHAPTER 15

Sorry, babe. Can't make it. Working late. Will call you tomorrow.

Liv stared at the text on her phone, her cheeks burning. She had just helped her father set the table. Uncle Brody was outside prepping the grill for the steaks. Jarrod was in the kitchen, tossing a salad. There was a cobbler bubbling in the oven. The wine was open. Everything was ready, and now Zel was going to be a no-show.

Jarrod could see her from the kitchen and instantly noticed her grimacing. "What happened?"

"He's not coming."

Jarrod set his salad tongs down on the counter. "What? Why not?"

Liv shrugged, frustrated. "He says he's working late. He's always working late. I'm surprised he even remembered to text me. Usually he just loses track of time, and I never hear from him until the next day when he calls to beg for my forgiveness." Liv marched into the kitchen, joining her father. She picked up the serving plate with four seasoned raw slabs of filet mignon. "I'm going to take these out to Uncle Brody. No need to wait anymore."

Jarrod put a hand on Liv's shoulder. "I'm sorry."

"What have I been doing? How long am I going to put up with this? I should've seen the signs much sooner."

She could tell her father had a lot to say, but he chose to stay silent, allowing her to continue to vent.

"There were so many red flags. I never should have allowed him to pressure me into dragging poor Candy into this film project of his. It's been one big headache from the start. I should've put a stop to it sooner, and now it's become a whole awful complicated mess."

Brody strolled in from the backyard through the sliding glass door. He was wearing a tight T-shirt and some ragged shorts and a black apron that said "This is a Manly Apron, For a Manly Man, Doing Manly Things, While Cooking Manly Food." He had always been a cut-up. "What'd I miss? You two look so serious."

"Zel canceled," Jarrod replied quietly.

"Loser," Brody growled.

Jarrod folded his arms. "So, what are you going to do?"

"I'm going to stay and enjoy a delicious dinner with my dad and my favorite uncle and I'm going to have a double portion of the peach cobbler with a ton of ice cream and really eat my feelings, and then I'm going to go home and work on my break-up speech, the gist of it being about how his behavior makes me feel like I'm not a serious priority in his life except as a muse for his work, and I plan to deliver it tomorrow morning at his studio, and then when I have completely washed my hands of him, I'm going to treat myself to a spa weekend in Santa Fe, far away from him and Candy's creepy kids."

"Why don't I tag along with you when you dump him? If he gets out of line, I can pound his puny head into the ground," Brody offered, his muscled chest puffed out.

Liv gave him a wry smile. "He won't get out of line. I fully expect him to grovel and plead and beg me to reconsider, at least until his documentary gets into Sundance. After that, he probably won't even care." She handed the plate of steaks to Brody. "Here, I'm starving."

"Coming right up, your highness," he said with a wink before dashing back outside, where the orange flames from the grill were now dancing in the wind.

"Promise me you'll call and let me know when it's over and done with," Jarrod said.

Liv nodded.

She was not going to allow this to spoil their evening. When the three of them finally sat down at the dining room table with their perfectly cooked steaks, twice baked potatoes, and salad, Liv made sure to steer the conversation in any direction that was away from Zel. She did not want to give that man any more of her energy. She was embarrassed enough and wanted to put this all behind her.

After coming through on her promise to eat a huge helping of cobbler, she offered to clean up, but Jarrod insisted that she focus on the task ahead and that he could clear the table and load the dishwasher on his own. She could barely stand up from the table she was so stuffed, and after enjoying one more glass of wine with Brody in the living room, she headed home, her head spinning with ideas on how to end things with Zel.

When she arrived back at her apartment building, she very cautiously entered the front gate after parking her car, half expecting Dale or Jewel to spring out of hiding and pounce on her, but fortunately there did not seem to be anyone lurking around in the bushes.

She let herself into her apartment, and within minutes she was lying in bed, going over what she was going to say to Zel the next morning, before she finally drifted off to sleep.

She woke early. It was not even six a.m. yet. But she jumped out of bed and took a quick shower, blow-drying her hair and throwing on a short-sleeve canary-yellow blouse and some blue jeans and slipping into some sandals.

After fortifying herself with two cups of strong coffee, she was finally ready. She had a rough idea of what she was going to say, and she was already feeling a rejuvenating freedom when she got in her car and took the ten-minute drive over to Zel's studio.

Parking out front, she walked up to the door and found it slightly ajar. She pushed it open some more and poked her head inside. "Zel?"

There was no answer.

She knew he usually crashed here instead of going home to his own place whenever he got lost in his work. In fact, he had not spent one night at her apartment since signing the lease on this new work space.

She stepped inside the studio.

Suddenly she felt a sense of dread in the pit of her stomach.

Something was not right.

It was so eerily quiet.

And that's when she saw him.

Lying facedown on the floor, his head twisted to the side, a small pool of blood next to it. The back of his head had been bashed in with some kind of blunt object.

"Zel!"

She hurried across the room and around to the other side of his body where she could finally see his face. His mouth was wide open in shock, and his glassy eyes stared up at her in total disbelief, as if he could not believe this had happened to him.

She knew right away he was dead.

And that someone had murdered him in cold blood.

Perhaps Isis the fake psychic was not so fake after all.

CHAPTER 16

Jarrod dropped everything after receiving the frantic call from Liv. He could barely make out what she was saying because she was screaming and hysterical. He quickly turned off the stove where he was scrambling eggs in a big frying pan, shut off the oven that was baking his veggie tots, and switched off the coffee maker before dashing out the door to his car. He had thought about waking Brody and have him accompany him, but there was no time.

Liv desperately needed him.

He jumped in his car and raced over to the studio, his mind reeling from what Liv had just told him.

Screeching up in front of the building and nearly rear-ending Liv's car, he hurried inside, where he found his daughter on the floor, balled up in a corner, eyes closed, crying. She could not even bring herself to look at the body sprawled out on the floor on the other side of the room.

Jarrod bent down and enveloped Liv in a hug. "It's okay. I'm here, sweetheart. I'm here."

Liv buried her face in his chest, arms slung around her father's neck, sobbing. She tried catching her breath a few times but could not and kept heaving.

Jarrod gently patted her on the back with his hand. "Did you already call the police?"

He could feel her shaking her head. Sniffing, finally able to speak, she whispered, "I-I was in a panic . . . I wasn't thinking . . . I just thought to call you . . ."

Jarrod slowly helped her to her feet and reached for his phone in his front pocket. "We need to call them right now so it doesn't come back to haunt us later."

Liv, wiping away tears, gave him a curious look.

Jarrod had watched enough crime dramas on television, having appeared as a guest star many times throughout his childhood and early adulthood, to know the longer you waited to bring the police to a crime scene, the more suspicion might dog you during the official investigation. He typed 9-1-1 into his phone and reported the incident. The dispatcher informed him that officers were on the way and to stay on the line.

That's when he heard a thump outside the door.

Liv heard it too, and they both froze.

And then they could hear voices speaking softly to each other and the front door creaking open.

Jarrod instinctively grabbed Liv by the arm and pulled her off to the side. They crouched down behind Zel's editing bay. Jarrod's heart was in his throat, fearing the killers—there were two voices—had come back to the scene of the crime. Liv hugged herself, keeping her head down, trying not to sniff or make any kind of sound.

The voices grew louder.

It sounded like a man and woman talking.

Giggling.

And then as they entered the studio, there were piercing screams from both of them as they discovered Zel's corpse lying on the floor in front of them.

"Oh my god!" the woman cried. "Zel!"

Liv, recognizing the voice, suddenly shot to her feet.

It was Maude and Butch, both horrified, their faces pale, their bodies shaking. The sight of Liv suddenly appearing caused Butch to yelp in surprise again.

Jarrod slowly rose to join her.

Maude covered her mouth with her hands as she glanced back down at the body. "What on earth happened here?"

"I-I don't know," Liv stammered. "I came over this morning and found him like this. I-I couldn't believe it. The police are on their way."

Jarrod could not stop himself.

He inched over closer to Zel's body to get a better look, mindful not to contaminate the crime scene. He noticed some dirt scattered about on the floor, spread out as if the killer or killers had tracked mud or clay into the studio, the soles of their shoes caked with dirt. He bent down to inspect the distinct texture of the composition of the soil.

Liv grabbed Maude's hands and forced her to avert her eyes from the body and look straight at her. "Were you and Butch here earlier?"

"No, we were, um, we were at my place," Maude answered shakily.

Butch appeared to be in a trancelike state as he watched Jarrod circle the body, examining the scene for more clues as if he was unable to comprehend what had happened here.

"All night?" Liv asked.

Maude nodded. "We had a date, and we wound up back at my apartment where he, uh, spent the night."

As Jarrod rejoined them, Butch managed to collect himself and put an arm around Maude's waist. "We were up talking half the night and then woke up late, so Maude offered to give me a ride to work since I don't have a car right now."

Sirens wailed in the distance.

Within minutes, the studio was swarming with police. Officers cordoned off the crime scene and questioned those present. Everyone carefully recounted their stories, and before long, Detective Lamar Jordan of the Riverside County Homicide Division was barreling through the door. He was a tall Black man in his midforties, gruff on the surface, but his brown eyes betrayed a detectable kindness, which suggested to Jarrod that the stereotypical seen-it-all, brusque exterior he no doubt adopted from TV detective shows was mostly just an act.

Liv watched in awe as her father confidently marched up and introduced himself to Detective Jordan, explaining how his daughter had discovered the body and then called him, how he had been careful not to touch the corpse but how he did notice a possible clue, pointing out a large shoe print on the dusty floor along with the strange unidentified dirt and clay particles, most likely left behind by the killer since Zel was presently barefoot.

Detective Jordan stared at Jarrod blankly.

There was a long, uncomfortable pause.

Then Jordan cleared his throat, scowling at Jarrod, vaguely recognizing him but not quite able to pinpoint from where, and said dismissively, "I'm going to need you all to step outside."

Jarrod took a deep breath and was about to speak again, but Jordan did not give him the chance. "I'll have one of my officers come get you when I'm ready to talk to you."

Signaling a baby-faced rookie cop in his early twenties, Jordan watched long enough to see the officer escort Jarrod, Liv, Maude, and Butch out of the studio before turning around and continuing his work.

Left standing on the sidewalk outside under the watchful eye of the nervous-looking rookie cop, Liv and Maude comforted each other while Butch remained in a perpetual daze. Meanwhile, Jarrod seethed with anger over the fact that he had not been taken seriously by Detective Jordan.

Actors are always ridiculed whenever they try to do anything outside the realm of show business. They're constantly told by news commentators to curb any political speech, to mute any strong opinion they might have, and just perform like the trained monkeys they're perceived to be. But actors are citizens too, and like everyone else, they have the right to speak their own mind. And Jarrod had been doing that his whole career and was not about to be muzzled now.

Actors also detest being ignored.

And that's what Detective Jordan was doing.

Ignoring him.

He had once had a small role playing a public defender in a television movie on Lifetime depicting the aftermath of a fatal shooting during a carjacking. A young married couple were on their way home from a Lamaze class when a robber appeared out of nowhere, forced his way into their car, and shot them both, stealing the wife's wedding ring and some loose cash. The police targeted a small-time hood with a record and arrested him with the flimsiest of evidence, never questioning the husband's story. Jarrod's character came in to take the case of the small-time hood, believing he was innocent. As it turned out, the husband had lied and staged the whole murder, making up the carjacking. The police had gotten it completely wrong because they were too anxious to believe the upstanding citizen and railroad the more obvious suspect in order to quickly wrap up the case.

That story had always stuck with Jarrod.

Sometimes the police can have blinders on. They miss key evidence in order to create a desired narrative. And given his daughter's relationship with the victim, he wanted to make damn sure they got it right this time with his help.

Even if they did not want it.

CHAPTER 17

Detective Jordan looked peevish as he stood behind a podium that had been set up outside the Palm Springs Police Department. He hovered over a cluster of microphones from the local news stations that had been hastily placed in front of him. It was evident he wanted to be anywhere else but talking to a bunch of reporters shouting questions at him about the latest homicide in his hometown. Jordan's hostility toward the press was not a secret, especially when he did not have much information to share with them, but the local politicians expected him to give the community an update, and so, begrudgingly, here he was, just trying to get through it.

A reporter from the local NBC affiliate raised her hand and shouted, "Do you have any suspects at this point, Detective Jordan?"

"Not at this point, no. But we are considering the possibility that this murder might be connected to a rash of break-ins that have occurred recently throughout the Coachella Valley," he said before pointing to another reporter from the Desert Valley Sun newspaper. "Yes. You."

"If that's your theory, why wasn't anything taken from the location where the victim was found?"

"We don't know yet what, if anything, was taken. This is an

active investigation. We're still interviewing people who knew the victim and would have knowledge about what was stored there. There is also the possibility that Mr. Cameron surprised the thieves, and in a panic, they struck him with a blunt object to incapacitate him and immediately fled the scene, but this is all conjecture at the moment. We still have a lot of work to do."

"I don't buy any of this," Liv groaned, staring doubtfully at the television set. "It makes no sense."

Jarrod took a sip of his red wine as he sat on one end of a white leather couch in George and Leo's condo. "I'm with Liv. I don't think this was a random robbery. A wrong place, wrong time kind of thing."

George and Leo, who were sitting in matching white leather chairs, both with glasses of white wine, nodded in agreement. Leo glanced lustfully at the television screen. "I don't even pretend to know what might have happened, but what I do know is that Detective Jordan is outrageously hot!"

"He needs to smile more," George huffed, gulping down his wine.

George and Leo had declared Thursday evenings as "Thirsty Thursday" when Jarrod would come over and they would relax with a couple bottles of wine and recap their various weeks. Liv had decided to join them tonight because they all wanted to watch Detective Jordan's press conference together to see what progress had been made on the case.

Which appeared to be very little.

At least on the surface.

The police had a tendency to keep the specifics of their case heavily under wraps.

Liv angled her right hip in George and Leo's direction. "I believe Zel's murder had something to do with the film project he was working on."

Jarrod's eyes widened. "Are we talking about Candy's kids?"

Liv shrugged. "You didn't meet them, Dad. They both gave off a really bad vibe. And Jewel's boyfriend, he was so big and nasty, like a Bond villain's henchman, what was that guy's name, Chompers?"

"Jaws," George corrected her.

"Well, whatever his name is, I certainly think he's capable of violence," Liv insisted.

Jarrod set his wine down on the glass coffee table. "But why? What would be their motive? You said yourself, the son was focused on making a Hollywood connection with me and the daughter was threatened by you establishing a relationship with Candy. None of that had anything to do with Zel."

Liv paced back and forth. "They could have showed up at Zel's studio to threaten me again, and things just got out of hand. I don't know. I just can't shake the feeling that this is somehow all connected, and that it's my fault."

"*Your* fault?" George gasped. "That's absurd."

Jarrod stood up and crossed to his daughter, resting a hand on her shoulder. "George is right, honey. Zel was the one who coerced you into starting this whole surrogacy project in the first place. Not you. So stop blaming yourself. Besides, we don't know who else Zel may have had problems with in his life, or if Detective Jordan is actually correct and this was just a robbery gone awry, and Zel didn't even know the person who killed him."

"It wasn't random," Liv declared.

"How do you know?" Leo asked.

Liv glanced at Detective Jordan still holding his press conference, a pained expression on his face as he answered more protracted questions from the gaggle of reporters. "I feel it in my bones. Someone deliberately murdered Zel. And I'm afraid the police are going to rush to arrest somebody so they can close the case just to make the city feel safe again."

"Why don't you have your dad look into it?" George joked.

Liv spun around. "What are you talking about?"

"When he was an actor in Hollywood, he used to be an amateur sleuth on the side. He would poke his nose in all kinds of cases that he shouldn't have," George smiled.

"George, please. That was a long time ago. Let's not relive all that," Jarrod begged.

Of course George ignored him. "Your Papa Charlie hated it. He was the cop in the family. Not Jarrod. But did that stop him? No. He was a regular Nancy Boy Drew."

Liv, gobsmacked, stared at her father. "Why am I just learning about this now?"

"Because it was silly and dangerous and I got myself into a few scrapes playing detective. And George is right, Charlie was *not* amused. He was worried I was going to get myself killed, and he turned out to be almost right on more than one occasion. In fact, it was a real strain on our relationship, so I eventually stopped."

"How often did you get involved in homicide cases?" Liv asked, still in a state of shock.

"I don't even remember . . ." Jarrod fibbed.

George shot a hand in the air. "I do. There was Willard Ray Hornsby, the guy you got caught kissing at the gay rodeo by a paparazzi, who outed you to the whole country, which nearly cost you your career. He was found dead floating in his swimming pool on the same night you were throwing him a birthday party. It turned out to be a murder, and your father solved the case. And then there was the guy who keeled over from poisoned champagne at your manager Laurette's wedding to that Latin lothario who turned out to be gay. You solved that one too. Who am I forgetting?"

Leo piped in. "The actress in London, Claire somebody, when you were doing that Agatha Christie–type play in the West End. The police suspected you were somehow involved, so you had to investigate on your own to clear your name. Trust us, Liv, your father was always finding corpses!"

Liv gaped at her father, shaking her head in disbelief. "I really need to google you more."

"Like I said, it was ages ago. Those days are long in the past," Jarrod insisted, waving them off.

"I would say your father doesn't like to brag, but we all know that's not true!" George chuckled.

Liv pulled her blazer tight around her waist. "Well, maybe I get this burning need to play detective from you, but I can't let this go. I need to know what happened and I don't trust Detective what's-his-name to do the job." She bussed her father's cheek, then walked over and did the same to George and Leo. "Good night, boys. Thanks for the snacks and wine. I'll call you tomorrow, Dad."

"Good night, honey," Jarrod said.

And then she marched out the door, a woman on a mission.

The three men sat silently for a moment.

Finally, Leo spoke. "I'm just going to say it. She's exactly like you."

"I better have a talk with her tomorrow. I don't relish the idea of her willingly putting herself in danger by investigating a murder."

George snorted. "Now you know how Charlie felt."

Leo hauled himself to his feet and refilled Jarrod's wineglass. "Look, she's not going to let this go. She's like a dog with a bone, just like you. She needs to know that she's not even tangentially responsible for Zel's murder."

"Tangentially? My baby's a walking thesaurus," George quipped.

"You're just jealous that you didn't come up with such a fancy word," Leo said as he crossed to the kitchen to uncork another bottle of white wine for his husband.

"You know, this reminds me of when I was dancing with Twyla," George said.

Leo cocked an eyebrow. "Who?"

"Twyla Tharp. Famous choreographer. Way before your time," Jarrod explained.

George plowed on, ignoring them. "Twyla was choreographing a unique piece, exploring the father-daughter dynamic through dance. Their movements mirrored emotions, a dance of protection, guidance, and trust."

"Move it along, sweetheart, my eyes are starting to glaze over," Leo cracked.

George gave him a withering look. "In the Tharp piece, you could feel the tension and release, the way they moved in sync yet with their own unique styles. Similarly, the father and daughter harmonized their skills. His experience complemented her fresh perspective. It was like witnessing a pas de deux. Two individuals moving as one, exchanging roles seamlessly, leading and following in perfect rhythm."

Leo grinned. "I knew my husband could be pretentious and insufferable, but he's really outdone himself this time. It must be all the wine."

Jarrod leaned forward. "What are you trying to say, George, in your typical long-winded treatise?"

Leo popped the cork out of the wine bottle. "Wait. I've got it. I think he's saying you should help Liv look into this case because it might bond the two of you, which is something you've been wanting for a long time! Did I get it right?"

George proudly tapped his nose in the affirmative. "I'm so proud of you, baby."

Jarrod plopped back down on the couch, contemplating.

They were right.

He and Liv had grown apart.

Perhaps this could be a way to finally bring them back together.

It just might be worth a shot.

CHAPTER 18

Liv had not had much time to tidy her apartment before her father showed up at her door the following morning. Her cupboards and refrigerator were bare, so she had run out to the market down the street to buy some cinnamon rolls, K-pods for her Keurig coffeemaker, and a quart of milk. She scrounged around her tiny pantry for some artificial sweetener packets, not remembering how Jarrod took his coffee.

Jarrod arrived promptly at nine o'clock, having called earlier to announce he wanted to come by and talk to her about Zel. What she had not expected when her father sat down at her kitchen table and took a bite of the pastry she had bought for him was his suggestion that they team up to look into Zel's murder.

She balked at first. She had planned on launching her own quiet inquiry, talking to people who knew Zel, not playing father-daughter detective team with her dad. But now that she was aware of her father's penchant for crime solving years ago when he lived in Hollywood, she was slowly warming up to the idea, and it was not due to the hot pumpkin spice coffee she was drinking.

As Jarrod began peppering her with questions about Zel, those people close to him, she slowly began to realize just how little she actually knew about her boyfriend's life in the short time they were together.

She had to think hard. "I know both of his parents have passed, and he has one sibling, an older brother."

"Where is he?"

"He lives in Sweden, I think, with his wife. No wait, Switzerland, not Sweden. In a small village outside Zurich."

"Do they get along?"

Liv nodded. "I believe so. I mean, Zel didn't really talk about him much. They rarely had any contact except maybe once every two years when he came to the States for a visit. Zel never traveled to Europe to see him. He doesn't even have a passport." Liv could read her father's mind. "I know. How could a documentary filmmaker not have a passport? I was bugging him all the time to get one, just in case an international story fell into his lap that he could make a film about."

"Do you know if someone has contacted the brother yet to let him know about Zel?"

Liv shrugged. "There must be a number on his phone we can call, but I have no idea what his passcode is."

"What about friends?"

Liv racked her brain. "Zel never really socialized with anyone outside of my circle of friends, including Maude, of course. He was much too focused on his work. I asked about some of his classmates at the College of the Desert, where we first met, who he used to hang around with when he was a student, but he never seemed interested in seeing any of them. I'm sorry I can't be more helpful, Dad. I'm just so embarrassed. You would think I would be able to tell you more."

Jarrod reached out and touched her hand. "I had this wonderful acting teacher who once who told me, 'It's always in the details. They make the picture complete. Memories have a tendency to come back to you when you're not trying too hard.'"

"But where do I start? Who would want to hurt him?"

"What about his new assistant? How much do we know about that guy?"

"Maude likes him a lot. He seems to be a nice guy, but I honestly don't know. Plus, he pretty much has an airtight alibi. He stayed over at her place the night of the murder. They were together the whole time."

"And you said you never saw Zel interacting with any former classmates from college?"

"That's right." A thought suddenly struck her. "Wait a sec. I remember hearing him on the phone with one of his film professors once, not too long ago, asking for his advice on a project. Zel called him his mentor."

"Do you remember his name?"

"No. But it sounded Russian."

"How many Russian film professors could there be teaching courses at the College of the Desert?"

Liv leapt to her feet and scrambled into her bedroom. She returned carrying her laptop, set it down on the kitchen table, flipped it open, and fired it up. It took her less than thirty seconds to access the college's website and find the professor's name. "Professor Illya Lipovsky."

"You can't get more Russian than that."

Liv scanned down his profile page. "It says he has office hours today from ten to twelve."

Jarrod downed the rest of his coffee and stood up. "I'll drive."

The College of the Desert was a twenty-minute trip, which Jarrod made in less than fifteen. Spread across a sprawling area, the campus combined desert landscapes with contemporary architecture and facilities, an oasis amid the arid terrain, with manicured lawns, palm trees swaying gently in the desert breeze, and vibrant bursts of greenery contrasting against the sandy hues of the surroundings.

Jarrod parked his car in the student lot, and he and Liv

made their way across the campus to the faculty building where they found Professor Illya Lipovsky hunched over his desk, smoking a vape pen, and grading papers. He had the classic look of a college professor: messy hair, scraggly beard, glasses. The only thing missing was a tweed jacket. He was wearing a Tommy Hilfiger dress shirt with the sleeves rolled up and khaki pants. Liv knocked gently on the door, which was ajar. He did not acknowledge them at first. He just continued reading a printout on his desk. Finally, when he reached the end, after scribbling a few notes down with a red pen, he deigned to look up from his papers. "Yes?"

"Professor Lipovsky, I'm Jarrod Jarvis." Jarrod paused, half expecting him to recognize him from his film and TV work. He was a film professor, after all, with a vast knowledge of Hollywood history, one might presume, but, alas, Lipovsky just stared at him blankly.

Trying to recover, Jarrod turned to Liv. "This is my daughter, Liv."

Liv could see he vaguely recognized her, probably from when she was a student on campus studying criminal justice.

"I am . . . I mean was Zel Cameron's girlfriend."

Lipovsky finally showed a hint of humanity, hauling himself up from his desk and welcoming them into his cramped office. "I was so sorry to hear about Zel. What a tragedy. I fully expected him to have a long, successful career as a filmmaker documenting our times. I hope they catch the ghoul who took his life."

"That's actually why we're here," Liv said. "I know Zel thought very highly of you, and we were hoping you might help us find whomever might have had a motive to kill him."

Lipovsky reared back, surprised. "I thought the police said it was a random burglary, that the killer was not someone he knew."

"That's the working theory, but we don't want to leave any stone unturned. What can you tell us about Zel?"

"I have nothing but praise for Zel's raw talent as a film-maker, but as for his character . . ."

Jarrod and Liv exchanged pensive looks.

"What about his character?" Jarrod asked.

"Zel had a knack for borrowing other people's ideas. Too liberally, if you ask me."

Jarrod raised an eyebrow. "Borrowing ideas?"

Lipovsky smiled ruefully. "Let's call it what it was. He'd out-right steal concepts, scripts, even camera shots from his peers' projects. It didn't earn him any friends here on campus, that's for sure."

"So, he wasn't liked by his fellow students?" Jarrod asked.

Lipovsky laughed. "That's an understatement. He'd strut around campus with an air of entitlement. Like the world owed him. His fellow classmates despised him. They'd pour their creativity into their work, only for Zel to swoop in and snatch it up when they weren't looking and claim it as his own."

"Why wasn't he expelled?"

"Because he was crafty. No one could outright prove he didn't have the idea first. There was really nothing the disciplinary com-mittee could do, so he continued to get away with it, causing more resentment and animosity."

"Professor Lipovsky, could you make us a list of the stu-dents who had a beef with Zel? That would be a huge help."

"I don't have to. I can just email you my class roster from Zel's time in the program. He was despised by *everybody*. Each and every one of them wanted to kill him."

After a few taps on his keyboard, Lipovsky's printer roared to life and spit out two pages, which he handed to Jarrod, who quickly perused the list.

Liv peered over her father's shoulder as he skimmed the pages. There had to be about thirty names. This was going to be a long process going through each and every one of them as a possible suspect.

They thanked the professor and left the faculty building, crossing the campus back toward the student parking lot where they had left Jarrod's car.

Jarrod noticed Liv being unusually quiet. "Anything the matter?"

She stopped, visibly shaken. "I'm just a little spooked by hearing such an unflattering portrait of Zel. It just shows my incredible lack of judgment. How could I be so in the dark about his true character?"

Jarrod hugged her. "Honey, you can't beat yourself up. Listen, back when I was an actor, I dated lots of men in Hollywood who turned out to be world-class schmucks before I met Charlie. Users, abusers, grade-A losers. It takes kissing a lot of frogs to finally get to your prince. And believe me, your dad was a prince among men."

Liv noticed Jarrod's eyes welling up at the mention of Charlie, but she could see him visibly trying to hold back the tears so he would not cry in front of her.

It was sweet and touching, but it could not stop her from worrying about how easily she had fallen for someone with such a questionable character.

And it was only driving her to learn more about just who Zel Cameron was.

CHAPTER 19

The Dusty Mug Pub, located just outside downtown Desert Hot Springs, had seen better days, but the parking lot was still packed with pickup trucks and motorcycles belonging to their very loyal clientele.

Jarrod had read a few reviews online about the establishment, mostly warning strangers off the seedy bar because there were routinely drunken brawls from the quick-tempered customers, and there was even a shooting last year, though luckily no one had been killed.

Liv had tracked Jewel's social media accounts and quickly came upon a pattern of her hanging out here with her boyfriend, Gunnar, pretty much every Friday night, where she downed multiple gin and tonics until she mustered up enough liquid courage to sing a few staples for the bar's weekly karaoke night.

Jarrod and Liv had decided to take a chance and drive out to talk to both Jewel and Dale about Zel's murder and see if they might have any useful information. Both father and daughter found it odd that Liv's half siblings had come crashing into her life with, if not menacing, at least suspicious intent just before Zel wound up dead.

When Brody happened to overhear them making plans to

drive out to Desert Hot Springs, he had insisted on accompanying them. He was big and ripped and intimidating in his own right, and so they welcomed his protection. Brody was thrilled to tag along as muscle because he had been feeling guilty about taking advantage of Jarrod's hospitality and felt that this might be a way to say thank you for providing him with a temporary roof over his head until he got his act together.

The three of them piled into Brody's beat-up truck since Brody had deemed Jarrod's Mercedes too showy and ostentatious for such a dive bar as the Dusty Mug Pub and would probably draw too much attention to themselves. Jarrod, relieved, had quickly agreed, and twenty minutes later, they were pulling into the gravel parking lot.

As the three of them strolled inside, Jarrod instantly spotted Jewel and Gunnar sitting in a corner booth, arguing. Gunnar looked blotto, and the proof was the five empty Corona bottles all around him as he was busy guzzling a sixth. Jewel was already on her third gin and tonic, judging by the empty glass count in front of her.

Jarrod turned to the bartender. "I'll have a martini, extra dry, with three blue cheese olives." He turned to Liv. "What will you have, honey?"

Liv struggled not to laugh.

Brody cleared his throat and tapped the bar with his hand. "We'll take three Coronas."

The bemused bartender nodded and ambled away, returning with three bottles and setting them down in front of them. "Lime?"

"We're good, buddy, thanks," Brody said, sliding a twenty over to him. "Keep the change."

The bartender cracked a slight smile as he scooped up the bill, mostly as acknowledgment of a good tip.

A plastered patron gripped a microphone, swaying from

side to side, staring up at a wall-mounted TV screen that was feeding him the lyrics to *Livin' On a Prayer* by Bon Jovi. He was totally off-key and screaming, but nobody paid him much mind. He was obviously a regular. When he finished his song, there was a smattering of applause, and the DJ operating the karaoke machine announced that Jewel was next. She downed the rest of her cocktail and slammed the empty glass down on the table to make some kind of point to Gunnar, then hauled herself up to her feet and marched unsteadily across the bar to the karaoke corner. She aggressively snatched the mic from the drunk guy, who she clearly was not fond of. He just stumbled off, his watery eyes looking lost, trying to find his table.

The music started and Jewel launched into *Hit Me with Your Best Shot* by Pat Benatar.

"She's not half bad," Liv noted as they huddled together near the bar.

Jewel's eyes were closed as she hit the higher notes, relishing her time in the spotlight, probably pretending she was actually performing at a decent venue in front of an adoring crowd instead of a dumpy bar where most of the patrons were ignoring her and talking among themselves.

When she hit the refrain again, she opened her eyes and they unexpectedly fell upon Liv, zeroing in on her. She was suddenly thrown and lost track of where she was in the song and fumbled the lyrics. She stopped singing, and the music continued on without her. She tried catching up, but it was hopeless at this point, and she angrily threw the mic down, frustrated, and made a beeline for the bar where Liv was standing with Jarrod and Brody.

The flustered DJ stopped the song and announced the next singer, who bounded over and began belting out *Sweet Child o' Mine* by Guns N' Roses.

Jewel marched over and got right up in Liv's face. "What the hell are you doing here?"

Both Brody and Jarrod stepped forward, forming a protective barrier in front of Liv.

Jewel did not seem to notice or care.

Liv kept her cool. "Jewel, this is my father Jarrod and my uncle Brody."

She was not impressed. "Why are you here? I told you to stay away from me and my family."

"We just want to talk to you," Liv said.

"About what?"

"Zel Cameron," Jarrod interjected.

Jewel was puzzled. "Who is that?"

"My boyfriend. He was directing the documentary about your mother Candy," Liv explained. "Someone murdered him."

This caught Jewel off guard, but she quickly recovered. "Boo-hoo. Sorry. I didn't know the guy. Why should I care?"

Liv pushed her way past Jarrod and Brody. It was her turn to get right up in Jewel's face. "The thing is, Jewel, you did know him. You and Gunnar showed up at his studio making all kinds of threats. Gunnar physically assaulted him. And then, the next thing you know, a day later, he winds up dead. Clocked in the back of the head. Bludgeoned to death. The police might think that sounds awfully suspicious."

Liv had finally gotten her attention.

When Jewel spoke this time, she was far less confrontational. "I'm sorry he's dead, but we had nothing to do with it. You wasted your time coming all the way out here."

By now, Gunnar had noticed Jewel had not returned to their table and had spotted them all clustered at the bar. Jarrod saw him slowly rising to his feet, eyes narrowing, as he pushed past the obliterated patron who sang Bon Jovi and stomped heatedly toward them. "Are they bothering you?"

Brody raised a hand to hold him back. "Dude, relax. We're just talking."

"Well, I wasn't talking to *you*," Gunnar growled, poking a

fat finger into Brody's wide chest. "So, get lost and leave my girl alone."

"Touch me again and we're going to have a serious problem," Brody warned.

"Is that supposed to scare me?" Gunnar scoffed.

Jarrod nodded and addressed Gunnar with a dead serious expression. "Yes. Trust me. It should. Really. Just a friendly warning. But yes. Be afraid. Be very afraid."

Jewel, sensing impending disaster, pulled on the sleeve of Gunnar's plaid shirt. "Come on, Gunnar, you're wasted, so why don't you back off? They just want to have a chat."

His pride now on the line, Gunnar bravely but foolishly poked Brody's chest one more time. Brody calmly reached up and grabbed his finger and twisted it back, almost breaking it. Gunnar howled in pain and then reared back to take a roundhouse swing at Brody. Anticipating the move, Brody casually sidestepped the blow and managed to get a hold of Gunnar's arm, twisting it behind his back and shoving him against the bar to immobilize him. Roaring with fury, Gunnar swung his free arm, knocking glasses off the bar, sending them smashing to the floor.

The bartender rolled his eyes in disgust at Gunnar. "Dude, come on. Don't make me call the cops again."

But there was no reasoning with him. Gunnar was embarrassed and humiliated at having been so easily dispatched. He managed to pick up a beer bottle and smash it against a bar stool, using the shards of glass as a weapon. Brody released him and stepped back to avoid getting stabbed. Then, like a martial arts expert, Brody pivoted his body, his leg arcing through the air at lightning speed, his foot striking Gunnar's gut, sending him staggering backward, gasping for air, the wind knocked out of him. He hit the floor with a thud. Brody then sauntered over and helped him to his feet, took him by the shirt collar, and dragged him out of the bar. Once he was at the door, Brody took a step back and gave Gunnar one more swift, hard kick in the backside, sending him sprawling to the gravel pavement outside.

The whole bar watched the scene in awe except for the oblivious karaoke singer, who was still performing the final notes from the Guns N' Roses song.

The bartender reached for his cell phone. "I'm sorry, Jewel, but I gotta call the cops."

"No, Tim, please, give him a break. He can't get arrested again. He's got so many priors, they might throw the book at him this time."

The bartender shrugged. "He might go to his truck and come back with a loaded gun. It's happened before. I can't take the chance someone in here might get hurt, or worse."

Jewel, distressed, sighed as she watched the bartender call 9-1-1 and report the incident. She turned to Liv. "Look, I know Gunnar's got a short fuse, but he didn't kill your boyfriend. When did you say it happened?"

"Last Thursday," Jarrod answered.

They could see the relief in Jewel's eyes. "See, it couldn't have been him. We were nowhere near Palm Springs that night. We were right here in Desert Hot Springs. All night."

Jarrod folded his arms. "Can you prove it?"

Jewel nodded. "Unfortunately. All you need to do is go outside and talk to the cops, who are probably pulling up to arrest Gunnar as we speak."

The bartender shook his head. "She's telling the truth. I had to call them that night because Gunnar started another nasty brawl with a tatted biker from Riverside. I would've eighty-sixed him from the bar a long time ago, but I have a soft spot for Jewel, who begged me to give him another chance."

"Thank you, Tim," Jewel said demurely.

"And what about you?" Brody asked Jewel.

"I went from here to my mother's house to ask her to help

me with the bail money, and then I drove straight to the police station, where I sat in the lobby until they let him out. Talk to the desk sergeant. He saw me sitting there on a bench all night."

Jewel did not wait to hear if they believed her story. She hurried out of the bar once she saw the flashing blue lights outside the smudged windows caked with desert sand.

Jarrod, Liv, and Brody followed her, and they watched as two officers handcuffed Gunnar. He was much more subdued now, knowing he was about to face more charges in front of a judge again.

"How're the kids, Dan?" Gunnar asked.

"Lori's a freshman now, Toby's in sixth grade," the patrolman calmly answered as he put a hand on top of Gunnar's head and helped him into the backseat of the squad car.

Obviously he had been arrested so many times before that he knew the arresting officers on a first-name basis.

CHAPTER 20

The Desert Havens Estates promised beautifully modeled homes and lush landscaping, an upscale enclave that served as a private hideaway to the rich and famous. However, when they arrived, the property proved to be something else entirely, the modest tapestry of a low-rent trailer park. As Brody drove them down the main street lined with homes, an eclectic mix of shapes and sizes, Jarrod studied the numbers painted on the mailboxes, looking for the one he had typed into his phone that Jewel had given him. Most of the mobile homes had patched roofs and peeling paint, and a few boasted extensions, decks, and small gardens to carve out a little comfort in the cramped spaces.

At the end of Mirage Street, Jarrod pointed out a trailer on a tiny corner lot. It was dilapidated, ignored in disrepair, desperate for a little TLC. The light was on inside, and Brody pulled his truck over to the curb out front. They got out and made their way across the overgrown patch of grass that had burnt from lack of water. Jarrod took the lead, with Liv hovering behind him and Brody waiting a few steps back almost out of sight, on duty in case they might need him to step in if Dale got out of hand.

Jarrod boldly rapped on the dirty fiberglass door. They could hear voices inside followed by an explosive laugh track, probably from a sitcom playing on TV. When no one came to the door after a minute, Jarrod knocked again, this time louder, and sighed in frustration.

"He's got the TV on so loud, there's no way he's ever going to hear you," Liv said.

Jarrod pounded on the door again.

This time they could hear the volume lower on the TV as the person inside finally was alerted to the knocking. They heard movement and then the door flew open, and a skulking Dale peered out at them standing on his tiny wedge of property.

"Whatever you're sellin' I ain't buyin'," he growled. "There's a sign posted at the front entrance that says, 'No soliciting'!"

"Dale, I'm sorry to show up here so late, but I'm Jarrod Jarvis." He stuck out a hand.

Dale's mouth dropped open in shock as he limply accepted his handshake, still reeling.

"I know you've met my daughter already. Liv."

Dale nodded slightly, confused, then collected himself. "You're not going to believe this. I'm in there watching you right now. I got old reruns of *Go To Your Room!* playing on Tubi!"

Jarrod could hear his twelve-year-old self impishly rattling off lame obvious jokes at a rapid-fire rate from the television set.

"It's the episode where your wacky new neighbor's experimental invention causes you to switch bodies with your dad, and everything goes haywire," Dale explained.

Jarrod had no recollection of this particular episode, just the old 1970s original *Freaky Friday* movie that it had been stolen from and repurposed as a 1980s sitcom plot.

"We did over a hundred episodes. It's kind of hard to keep track of all of them."

Dale studied Jarrod's face. "You look so old now."

Jarrod bit his bottom lip to stop himself from capping this guy's knees with a well-timed put down.

That was not why they were here.

Dale gave Liv a cursory glance. "Hey, sorry to hear about your boyfriend. That's rough."

Liv eyed him suspiciously. "Who told you?"

"Nobody. I heard it on the news." Dale quickly changed the subject, getting excited, eyes flicking back to Jarrod. "So did your daughter tell you about the business proposition I have that I'd like to discuss with you? That's why I'm bingeing your show. I figure if we're going to work together, I need to educate myself about you."

Jarrod smiled tightly. "Yes, but she didn't get into any specifics."

Dale glanced around nervously, as if afraid one of the other residents in the trailer park might be eavesdropping and could overhear his million-dollar idea. Then he lowered his voice to a whisper. "I'm thinking of opening a chain of diners, but they have a child star theme, you know, menu items named after the greats from *Leave It to Beaver* all the way up to the kids from *Stranger Things*. And we could get any of them who are still living, like the Brady kids, or any survivor from *The Partridge Family* or *Diff'rent Strokes*, you know, the old classics, to come around and take selfies with the customers! We might even be able to pay 'em!"

"That sounds like an interesting idea, Dale," Jarrod said evenly.

Dale grinned expectantly. "So do you want in?"

"I will be sure to speak to my business manager about it," Jarrod said.

There was no business manager.

Jarrod had given him up along with his agent when he left Hollywood for Palm Springs years ago. But he did not want to immediately trash Dale's horrific idea and get a door slammed in his face.

"I've been working on a prospectus I can give you," Dale cooed, dashing back inside the trailer. They could hear him rummaging around before he returned and handed Jarrod a bent file folder smudged with what looked like grease stains. "It's all in there. The initial investment numbers. The rollout plan. I've thought of everything. I just need a big name attached to get the ball rolling."

"I'm not sure I have the clout to get you a green light, Dale. I haven't done much acting in years."

"Out here, you're still somebody, and Palm Springs is a top tourist destination. We open our first location right in downtown and then just let the money pour in."

Jarrod frowned. "As exciting an opportunity as this sounds, Dale, we just have one problem. There can't be a whiff of scandal when we go to our first round of potential investors. We don't want to risk scaring them off, so you need to be absolutely honest and aboveboard."

"I can do that," Dale shrugged. "I got nothing to hide."

"The police suspect you might be involved in Zel's murder," Liv blurted out.

That was not technically true.

At least not yet.

But it did get a rise out of him.

"What? Why would they suspect *me*?"

"I told Zel how you were stalking me and he said he was going to come find you and warn you to stay away, and then he suddenly wound up dead."

Liv was treading water.

She was making things up as she went along just to gauge his reaction.

Dale proved rather convincing.

"You gotta believe me! I never had any contact with him!

Jewel mentioned something about some guy making a film about us, but that's it! I didn't even know his name until I heard it on the news. How would I have found him?" His eyes pleaded with Jarrod. "I swear I had nothing to do with anything she's saying!"

"I believe you, Dale," Jarrod assured him. "But be honest. Zel was making a documentary about your family that you had no say in. How did you feel about a complete stranger suddenly putting a spotlight on you? Did it bother you?"

"No! I thought it might help my business idea! You know, put us on the radar, get our names out there, and it got me to you! I was nothing but grateful for that guy."

"Maybe so, but it would help us enormously as I consider whether to go into business with you to know if you have an alibi for the night of the murder?"

Dale's face darkened, frustrated. "When was it, last Thursday night?" He thought about it. There was a slight cringe, which he quickly covered up. Then he nodded confidently. "I remember where I was. I was with Jewel and Gunnar. At the Dusty Mug. I wanted to show them my specs for the new business. They were impressed, thought I had it all worked out."

Jarrod raised an eyebrow. "The whole night?"

Dale thought about it some more. "Pretty much."

Liv stared at him. "Did you all leave together?"

"Yeah, I think so, around midnight. They dropped me off here on their way home."

Jarrod took a small step closer, stirring Dale's agitation into a lather. "That's funny, Dale, because according to Jewel, Gunnar got arrested after a bar fight that night and she spent the entire night trying to get him out on bail. Maybe you ought to get your facts straight."

He flinched, sweat beads forming on his brow.

Obviously caught.

Jarrod could almost see his mind racing in real time.

He looked at Jarrod with cool assessment. "I've spent a lot of time hanging out at that bar. Maybe I'm just getting my nights mixed up. That's right. I remember now. It was Wednesday night when they dropped me off here. Thursday, Gunnar got nailed for brawling again. Me and Jewel both went to the station in Gunnar's truck. I gave her all the money I had on me to help her out with the bail, and then I walked home because I needed to get up for an early shift. I work at a gas station convenience store a few blocks away."

His eyes bored into Jarrod, daring him to question his story again. He suddenly noticed Brody loitering on the street behind Jarrod and Liv. "Wait, who's that? Is he a cop?"

Brody stepped into the night light that was attached to the side of the trailer.

Dale's knees nearly buckled and he gasped in disbelief. "Is that Blackheart?"

Jarrod smirked. "You a wrestling fan?"

He pushed past Jarrod and Liv and ran out to the street to greet his hero. "You were the best, man. I always rooted for you, even though you were a bad guy. There was something about you. Like you didn't want to be evil but that was just your curse, your cross to bear. You had to play the part! Oh man. This is so awesome!" He pumped Brody's hand. "Would you mind me getting a selfie with you?"

Brody, uncomfortable by the attention, slung an arm around his shoulder as Dale held out his phone and snapped a series of photos. "You know, I was thinking of doing the same idea with diners but with pro wrestlers, you know with sandwiches like the Hulk Hoagie or a dessert named The Rock's Rocky Road Sundae. We should really talk, man."

Brody shoved his hands in his pockets and pivoted on his heel, heading to the car. "We gotta go."

"I'll get your deets from Jarrod!" He grabbed Jarrod's arm. "Are we good? No more worries? Full steam ahead?"

Jarrod hesitated, worrying Dale.

"Look, if you don't believe me, just call my sister. She'll back me up, I swear."

"Okay, I'll be in touch," Jarrod assured him.

As Liv passed, Dale spat out, "Night, sis."

Jarrod saw Liv shiver slightly.

She did not like the way he addressed her.

With an unwanted familiarity.

She gave him a quick nod and kept going.

As they walked toward Brody's truck, Dale called after them. "You should've worn that championship belt at least once, Blackheart! You was robbed!"

When they piled into the front of the truck, Liv in the middle, and Brody fired up the engine, he warned, "That guy was lying."

"There's one way to prove it," Jarrod replied, reaching for his phone and calling the number Jewel had given him. He turned to Liv and Brody. "Went straight to voicemail. I bet Dale has already got her on the phone begging her to back up his story."

They drove some more and then Jarrod tried calling again. This time she picked up.

"Yeah?"

"Hello, Jewel, it's Jarrod Jarvis."

"You're calling me already? I just saw you a couple hours ago," Jewel grunted.

"We were just with your brother, Dale. He claims he was with you on the night Gunnar got arrested, but you never mentioned him when we talked. Is he telling us the truth?"

She paused.

"Yeah, he was with us."

She was lying.

Dale had gotten to her too fast.

"Look, I gotta go. I can't leave Gunnar rotting in jail all night. I need to scrounge around for more bail money."

"How much you got?"

"Bail's ten thousand. I have to come up with a grand. So far, I've managed to drum up three hundred and thirty-five dollars. My mother refuses to help this time. She says this is going to keep happening, so she's not going to dole out any more money from her savings. She wants to start a college fund for her grandkids, if she ever gets any."

"I can Venmo you the rest of the amount you need right now."

Another pause.

"Why would you do that? You don't owe me anything."

"It's because I can. If you level with me."

"What do you want?"

"Just tell me the truth."

"About what?"

"Was Dale really with you on the night Zel was murdered?"

This time, the pause felt interminable.

As if Jewel was going through an internal struggle.

Making a choice between her brother or her boyfriend.

Finally, she made a decision.

"No. We never saw him that night."

CHAPTER 21

Dale stood slack-jawed behind the counter at the gas station and convenience store where he worked. He was barely able to choke out the words. "Jewel didn't back me up?"

Jarrod solemnly shook his head. "Nope. It looks like you're short one alibi."

"Why would she do that to me?"

Jarrod refrained from giving him the real answer that she was willing to sacrifice her brother in order to get her boyfriend out of jail.

That messy family dynamic was for Jewel to explain.

The bell on top of the door rang as an older customer in his seventies entered and took his place in line behind Jarrod and Liv to pay for his gas.

Dale's eyes nervously darted back and forth. "Look, I can't do this right now. I'm working." He talked past them to the customer. "What pump, sir?"

"Number seven."

Jarrod and Liv stepped aside but did not leave the store.

Dale quickly rang him up and ran his card through the machine. The man added a soda from the fountain behind them to his order, and once his card was approved, Dale printed him

a receipt, tearing it off the machine and handing it to him.
"You have a great day, sir."

The man gave him a half smile and wandered over to the
soda fountain to fill up his large paper cup.

Dale redirected his attention to Jarrod and Liv. "Hey, if
you're not going to buy anything—"

Liv plucked a plastic box of Tic Tacs from the candy rack
and dropped it down in front of Dale.

He bitterly punched some keys on his register and scowled.
"That'll be two sixty-seven."

Liv reached into her bag, withdrew a credit card, and went
to hand it to him, but Dale refused to take it and sneered. "We
have a ten-dollar minimum on all credit card purchases."

Without missing a beat, Liv dropped the card back in her
bag and took out three crisp one-dollar bills, spreading them
out on the counter evenly in front of Dale. Dale scooped them
up and shoved them into the register before counting some
change, nearly hurling the coins at Liv.

"Just an observation, Dale, but you look incredibly guilty
right now," Liv said.

"I didn't do it, okay?" he hissed under his breath.

"You're sure not acting like an innocent man. So what happened? Why did you show up at his studio and attack him?"
Jarrod theorized.

"I already told you, I was happy he got in touch with my
mom. Jewel was the one who had a problem with having a new
sister, not me!"

"But unlike you, Jewel has an alibi," Jarrod noted. "So does
Gunnar, for that matter."

Dale's bottom lip quivered. "Look, I could give a rat's ass
who ends up with Mom's house. I already got a place to live. I
was only interested in talking to you about my business proposition."

Jarrod's mind raced with more possibilities. "Okay, how about
this? You tried convincing Zel to hear your million-dollar idea

and he dismissed you, told you to get lost, and that made you angry, so angry that you—"

"Come on, man, I didn't kill anybody!" Dale slammed the register shut in frustration, startling the man with his cup of soda, causing some to spill on the floor before he could secure the plastic lid. He shot Dale an annoyed look and fled the store. Dale then leaned forward, seething. "When are you going to get that through your thick skulls?"

Liv watched as the older customer holding the soda got in his car and started his engine as another car pulled into the gas station behind him and a man got out. Liv tugged on her father's shirt sleeve. "Dad . . ."

Jarrod turned to her. "What is it?"

"Look who's here."

Jarrod glanced out the window of the convenience store, and his eyes widened in surprise as Detective Jordan filled his tank at one of the pumps and then walked directly into the convenience store with another younger plainclothes detective who followed behind him like a loyal puppy dog.

As Jordan entered, he stopped suddenly at the sight of Jarrod and Liv at the counter talking to Dale.

Jordan smirked knowingly. "I suppose you're going to tell me you were running low on gas and so you just happened to pull into this particular station to fill up your tank?"

"That sounds like a reasonable enough explanation," Jarrod chirped.

Liv raised her small box of breath mints. "Plus, I needed some Tic Tacs."

Jordan was not buying any of it. "Whatever. I need you two to step aside, please."

Jarrod and Liv, not wanting to rile up the detective any more than he already was, obeyed, stepping off to the right, allowing Jordan and his colleague enough space to move up to the counter and face Dale.

"Dale Lithwick?" Jordan asked in a heavy tone.

Dale nodded, confused, more than a bit scared.

"I'm placing you under arrest. Keep your hands where I can see them," Jordan ordered.

The junior detective produced a pair of handcuffs as Jordan ordered Dale to slowly and peacefully come out from behind the counter.

"I need to call my boss. Somebody's going to have to take over my shift," Dale said robotically, almost resigned now.

Jarrod's head was spinning.

Detective Jordan must have uncovered enough evidence to arrest Dale for Zel's murder before he and Liv had the chance. He had to admit that it was impressive he had been so focused and speedy about it. Jarrod was almost disappointed the case had been solved so quickly. He had been enjoying the time he was spending with Liv and now feared things would just go back to the way they were before.

Liv could not help herself. She had to know what they had missed. "Detective, can you tell us what specifically you found to tie him to Zel's murder?"

Jordan stared at her, probably debating about how much he needed to tell her, if anything. But ultimately, he could not resist. "I'm not arresting him for murder. I'm arresting him for burglary, criminal trespassing, and theft."

"What are you talking about?" Dale squeaked, but it was the worst acting Jarrod had seen since he hosted Bad Movie Nights at his Hollywood Hills home in the early aughts and subjected his guests to Elizabeth Berkley's train wreck of a performance in *Showgirls*.

Jordan looked toward Liv, deciding to indulge her. "Dale is a part of a crew behind a spate of break-ins all over the Coachella Valley. They stake out neighborhoods and hit the homes when they know the owners are out of town."

"I swear, you got the wrong guy! Where's your proof?" Dale

wailed, pulling his wrists apart, futilely trying to break free from the steel handcuffs.

"I got an eyewitness who saw you leaving one of the properties. A neighbor's security footage at another targeted location. The DA says it's going to be a cakewalk getting a conviction," Jordan said with a self-satisfied smile.

The younger detective led a shell-shocked Dale by the arm out of the store. Jordan started to head out too, but Jarrod called after him. "Detective, what about Zel Cameron's murder?"

Jordan shrugged dismissively. "I'm not going to discuss a case that's still an active investigation." Then he noticed the hurt in Liv's eyes and softened slightly. "We just don't have the evidence to connect Dale or any of his other cronies to the murder at Cameron's studio."

Liv's shoulders sagged, defeated.

"Look, we caught Lithwick red-handed, but we still don't have the identities of his accomplices in the burglaries. I bet the DA will be willing to cut him a deal if he coughs up their names and any other information he might have regarding Cameron's murder. You don't have to run around the valley playing some 'my dad and I solve crimes' game and getting in my way. Let me handle this. It's my job. I will keep you in the loop. I promise."

Jarrod suspected he was just paying them lip service.

Jordan knew he was coming off as dismissive and condescending so he decided to offer them a bit more. "Look, the reason I'd like you two to back down, at least for now, is because . . ." He stopped himself, not sure he was ready to divulge what almost came flying out of his mouth.

This only stirred up Jarrod's curiosity even more. "What is it, Detective? What were you about to say?"

Whatever he was going to tell them must be some kind of bombshell.

Jordan hemmed and hawed, fearing he would never get out of here if he did not confess to them what he knew. "We, uh, we do have a person of interest, not a suspect mind you, just a person of interest in the Cameron case, and it's not Dale Lithwick."

"Okay," Jarrod whispered, bracing himself.

"We canvassed the whole area near Cameron's studio, and there was no security camera anywhere that faced directly toward the crime scene, so we never saw anyone coming or going, but there was a surveillance camera set up down the street that picked up a person in the vicinity of the studio heading in that direction on the night of the murder."

"Who was it, Detective?" Jarrod pressed.

"Male. Mid to late thirties. Wearing a hoodie. We were able to blow up the image and identify him." His eyes fell to the floor, as if he was sad to have to be the one to tell them. "It was Brody Peters."

"Uncle Brody?" Liv gasped.

"One of the detectives recognized him instantly as Blackheart, one of his favorite pro wrestlers," Jordan explained.

Jarrod looked numbly at Liv, who was shaking.

"No, it couldn't be him. Why would he . . . ?" Liv's voice trailed off.

Jarrod loved his brother-in-law with all his heart.

But his troubled life was no family secret.

Brody had a lot of problems, not to mention a violent past both in and out of the ring.

But he was getting better.

Or so Jarrod thought.

There was just one big, looming question.

What on earth was Brody doing near the crime scene?

CHAPTER 22

They found him working out in the garage with some exercise equipment he had obviously found in the storage shed behind the casita. There was a power rack, adjustable dumbbells, and a pull-up bar integrated into the power rack where he was currently flexing his muscles with each heavy lift of his body, his count up to twenty-seven.

Jarrod and Liv stood at the entrance, waiting for him to reach thirty before Jarrod finally spoke. "I see you found Charlie's old gym equipment."

He nodded, and with a fresh burst of adrenaline, finished his thirtieth pull-up. Then he dropped down to his feet and wiped his face with a white towel. "I'm surprised you held on to it."

"I thought about getting rid of it, selling it online, before I moved to Palm Springs, but then I convinced myself I would actually use it to get back into shape with all the free time I was going to have on my hands. But of course, that never happened."

He failed to mention that he also hated tossing out anything that reminded him of his late husband. There were still a few clothing items—his old patrol uniform, the tux he wore at their wedding—that he just could not bear to part with.

As he watched Brody, who bore a striking resemblance to his older brother, exercising, he could picture Charlie working out on that same equipment, glistening with sweat, cheeks red. It felt as if he was still here, they were still together, and things were as they had been, both of them happy, content and very much in love. His heart still sometimes ached for that idyllic period in his life.

Liv snapped him out of his daydreaming. "Uncle Brody, we need to talk to you about something."

Brody dropped his towel and began to do some light stretching, taking his left arm across his chest and pulling the wrist with his other hand. "What's up?"

Liv nervously glanced at her father before taking a breath and plowing ahead, and her eyes fell to the brand-new pair of Nike Metcon 8 shoes Brody was wearing. Jarrod wondered how he could have afforded such pricey workout sneakers. He thought they went for close to a hundred bucks. But Brody always kept things like his personal finances close to the vest, and Jarrod did not feel it was his duty to pry.

"Pretty awesome, right? I've had my eyes on these for a while. A lot of my wrestling buddies swear by them as the best for training," Brody said.

"What size do you wear?" Liv asked as casually as possible.

"Twelve and a half," Brody replied without hesitation.

Roughly the same size as the dusty footprint found at the murder scene, according to Detective Jordan.

Brody was finally picking up on the tension. "Why? What's going on?"

Jarrod fretfully scratched the stubble on his chin. He had not shaved in a few days. "I spotted a shoe print at the crime scene with some unique dirt particles the police have yet to identify."

Brody shrugged. "What's that got to do with me?"

Liv could barely make eye contact with Brody. "Detective Jordan says the shoe size was twelve and a half, Uncle Brody."

He stared at both of them, stunned. "Are you suggesting . . . Oh, come on, guys! You're being ridiculous! Sure, I've been in a few scrapes with the law, but why would I have any reason to take out your boyfriend? Why would your minds even go there?"

"Because the police have security cam footage of you walking around in the vicinity of Zel's studio on the night of his murder," Jarrod said sharply.

Brody's mouth dropped open, horrified. *"What?"*

Jarrod pointed a finger at him. "Jordan says you're officially a person of interest. What were you doing there?"

Brody planted the palms of his giant hands over both of his eyes and wailed in frustration before trying to explain "No, it's not what you think—"

"Uncle Brody, you must understand why we had to ask. I mean it doesn't look good."

Brody cursed himself a bit, then dropped his hands and took a step closer toward them. "All right, I'll admit, I went over there after dinner that night."

"You said you were going to the casita," Jarrod sighed.

"I know, I know, I lied. I left your house and snuck out the side gate to my truck."

Liv's voice was shaky. "Why?"

"I was worried about you. I didn't like the sound of the guy. He struck me as opportunistic, maybe using you for his career or whatnot, so I decided to play protective uncle and go see for myself, talk to the guy, get my own impression."

"Oh, Uncle Brody . . ." Liv moaned.

"It was easy to find the studio address on his website. Frankly, I got a bad vibe from the guy the moment he opened the door. He asked who I was, I told him, we had a few words, and then I left. That was it."

Jarrod raised an eyebrow. "You had a few words?"

"Yeah, he knew I was checking him out to see if he was using Liv, and he didn't appreciate it. He said he resented some random dude showing up at his place, blasting him with questions. I admit, things got a little heated."

Jarrod felt a sense of dread. "Did anything physical happen between the two of you? Did you touch him in any way?"

Brody vigorously shook his head. "No. I mean, I may have poked him in the chest with my finger a few times, but that was it, I swear! I'm not an idiot! There's no way I'm ever going to do anything that sends me back to the slammer!"

Both Jarrod and Liv chose not to tug at the string of information Brody had just revealed, that he had recently been in jail. He probably had not meant to let that piece of info fly out of his mouth so freely.

It would have to be a discussion for another time.

"Jarrod, Liv, you gotta believe me. When I left that studio, he was still standing, very much alive!"

Jarrod put a firm hand on Brody's shoulder. "Of course we believe you, but we're not the ones you have to convince. Detective Jordan doesn't have enough evidence to arrest you yet, but he's working very hard on it."

"I'm sorry I didn't tell you before, but when I heard Zel had been murdered, I panicked. I was scared. I wanted to distance myself as much as possible. With my record, I knew the cops would automatically zero in on me if they knew I had been there that night. I've made a real mess of things by not coming clean, haven't I?"

"I'll be honest, it's not ideal," Jarrod admitted. "I'm surprised no one's shown up here looking for you yet, or at least tried calling you?"

"I've been here in the garage all morning, and I left my phone charging in the casita."

"I'm sure he's got eyes watching the house, waiting for you to come in or out. Just cooperate and be completely honest, and hopefully we'll find the person responsible so there won't be a dark cloud hovering over you anymore."

But Jarrod had a sinking feeling that even if they could prove Brody's innocence, there were a lot more dark clouds about to come rolling in.

CHAPTER 23

The yellow police tape had finally been removed from the front door of Zel's studio, and Liv was able to use the key her late boyfriend had given her to gain access with Jarrod.

Most of Zel's camera equipment and computers had been removed from the premises for the official police investigation, so it was immediately obvious there would be very few clues for them to uncover since the space was almost bare.

Jarrod noticed Liv grimacing. "What is it?"

"I was hoping his laptop would still be here. I know his password. It was my full name, Olivia. I was going to see if there was anything on there that might prove useful."

"Well, it's probably tagged and shoved in a police storage facility waiting to be analyzed by some digital forensic guy."

Liv tapped her toe on the floor, thinking. "I know he had an iPad. He was always losing it. I can't count the number of times he left it at my place."

"Do you think it still might be there?"

Liv shook her head. "No, I already looked."

"So the police must have it."

Liv's eyes darted around the studio. "Maybe."

She wandered over to a bookshelf filled with tomes dissecting the works of the world's greatest filmmakers, including Hitchcock, Scorsese, Tarantino, and famous documentarians including Michael Apted, Ken Burns, and Michael Moore. Wedged between the books on Apted and Moore was a leather-bound book with no title on the spine. Liv pulled it out and opened it, a smile creeping across her face.

She turned it around to show Jarrod.

It was Zel's iPad.

"I remember him telling me he kept it between his two biggest inspirations. He was obsessed with the *Up!* series Apted did and all of Michael Moore's movies. The cops must have missed it."

Jarrod rushed over to her side. "Do you think he used the same password as his laptop?"

"No, *Olivia* is too long. It has to be six numbers."

She thought about it and typed in her birthday.

No dice.

She tried his birthday.

Again no.

She was running out of tries before it would be permanently locked.

She steeled herself and tried one more time.

Eleven fifteen twenty-two.

It worked.

She had access.

Jarrod looked up at her. "What's so special about November 15, 2022?"

"It was the release date of his first documentary film project when he was still in college. He had a huge release party, and he got some really nice reviews. That day was really special to him. It was the first time he felt he wasn't a fraud, that he was a real filmmaker."

Liv started scrolling through his files in the cloud, hoping to find a clue that might lead them to his killer. Most of the files were video interviews for various projects he was currently working on or that were waiting on the back burner.

She was about to give up when she came upon a file labeled

"Candy Interview 10-3-25" that caught her eye. She wrinkled her nose as she opened the file and started to download the footage. "This is odd. The file label says this is the interview with Candy, but he's got the date wrong. I was there. We did the interview on October first. Normally I'm bad at remembering dates, but that day when he ambushed me with Candy I remember thinking to myself, 'What a way to start the month.'"

She began playing the video and immediately paused it when she saw Candy sitting nervously in a chair as Butch hovered around behind her adjusting some lights. "Wait, she's wearing a completely different outfit. He must have conducted a second interview without telling me."

She continued playing the video. Candy shifted in her seat, visibly uncomfortable, blowing on a strand of hair that kept falling in front of her face. Frustrated, she finally pulled it back with her hand.

They could hear Zel talking from behind the camera. "Thanks for coming back for another round, Candy. I sure do appreciate it. I wanted to hear your story without Liv here so you feel more free to talk openly about your experience."

Candy checked her appearance in a small hand mirror she had pulled from her purse. "Is this going to take long? I'm having my kids over for dinner tonight, and I need to get to the grocery store."

"We agreed on two hundred dollars for an hour of your time. I promise if I go over, I will make it up to you," Zel said.

Jarrod turned to see Liv's face fall.

"He *paid* her?" Liv gasped. "That's completely unethical. He knows better. Why would he risk doing something like that? If anyone found out, his career would be ruined!"

They kept watching.

Zel continued speaking off-camera. "Now regarding Jarrod and Charlie, the couple you helped, was there anything challenging about the process?"

She thought about it and shook her head. "No, not really. They were kind, supportive, generally good people."

There was a pause before Zel spoke again. "No hiccups? No conflicts? Surely there must be difficulties during such an emotional process."

"No, they were excited, nervous, like any normal expectant parents. At one point I think they may have been concerned that I would have an emotional attachment to the baby when she was born, which could make things complicated, but they were ready to work through it. And in the end, I knew I was being paid to carry their child, and so I was definitely not going to make any waves."

"So, you did have an emotional attachment when Liv was born?"

Liv flinched at the personal nature of Zel's line of questioning.

"He's digging for dirt," Jarrod growled.

But Candy held firm. "Of course. But I knew what I signed up for, and I was okay with that. As I said before, they assured me I could be a part of Olivia's life, but I eventually decided to step aside and let them raise their daughter on their own."

"So, they pushed you away?"

"No, that was *my* choice."

Another frustrated pause as Zel regrouped off-screen. "Candy, I need more than just a feel-good story. I want the raw, the real."

"And I would be happy to oblige if there was anything to tell. They trusted me, respected me . . . they treated me like family."

"But there must have been something. A disagreement? A moment of tension? I'm going to be candid with you. Our narrative needs more depth, more complexity . . ."

Candy shrugged. "I don't know what you want me to say."

"Okay, I guess that's it, then."

Candy started to get up. "Are we done?"

"Yes, we're done."

She stood in front of the camera, patiently waiting.

Finally, Zel spoke again. "Did you remember something you want to tell me?"

"No, I was just wondering if you were going to write me a check or Venmo me the fee for coming here today?"

Zel's voice was cold, detached. "You didn't give me anything."

Candy's whole body stiffened. "I gave you my time. That's what we agreed upon. It's up to you whether you use the full hour or not."

"I'm sorry, Candy, but this was a total waste of my time," Zel said flatly.

Candy's eyes blazed. "I'm not going to badmouth those nice men just because you want more depth and complexity."

"That's your choice. Doesn't mean I have to pay for you obviously holding back."

"I'm not holding back anything," Candy snapped.

"Look, Candy, I offered you good money for some information, and you gave me nothing."

Candy did not budge. Her whole demeanor started to change. The sweetness melted away, taken over by a hardened, disconcerting glare. "I told you, there's nothing to give. It was a clean deal and I've held up my end."

"You can see yourself out."

"You don't get it, do you? You think I'm bluffing? If you don't honor our deal, I could make your life very difficult."

"Ha! Yeah, right. I know your type."

Candy was shaking with anger now. "Oh? What type am I?"

They could hear Zel scoff behind the camera. "Don't make me say it."

"Trailer trash? Is that what you mean?"

"Your words, not mine."

Her voice darkened. "I don't take kindly to being played.

You have no idea who you're messing with. You owe me, and I don't take debts lightly."

"You don't scare me, Candy."

"You should be scared. This isn't the end of it. Not by a long shot."

Then she stormed off-screen, and Zel shut off the camera.

Jarrod and Liv exchanged surprised looks.

This was a side of Candy neither of them had ever seen.

And it was entirely possible that she had kept her promise that this ill-fated interview had not been the end of it.

Not by a long shot.

CHAPTER 24

When Kitty Reynolds decided to throw a cocktail party at her opulent Rancho Mirage estate, she never failed to go all out. Her home exuded an air of timeless elegance beneath the warm Californian night sky. Its sprawling grounds were adorned with sprinkling lights casting a soft glow over the lush gardens and vibrant flower beds. The murmur of conversation and clinking of glasses drifted through the evening air.

As Jarrod and Liv entered, they instantly spotted their hostess, a paragon of grace and sophistication, as she moved among her esteemed guests with effortless charm, her warm smile lighting up the room.

Kitty's parties were always packed with VIPs. Former senators engaged in animated discussions with Hollywood icons, while retired diplomats conversed with tech moguls. Jarrod always felt out of place at one of Kitty's parties, feeling he had never been important enough to deserve a spot on the esteemed guest list. He felt self-conscious as a former child star discussing peace in the Middle East with a former secretary of state.

Liv was another story.

She relished mixing it up with a bunch of retired Washington power players, making sure they heard the voice of the younger generation as they contemplated present and future policy matters while sipping on Kitty's signature handcrafted cocktails.

Jarrod and Liv weaved their way through the throng of guests to reach Kitty, who was in the middle of a legendary story about her wardrobe malfunction in front of the president of China while on a goodwill tour throughout Asia during her husband's first term in office. They patiently waited for her to finish her tale to raucous laughter until it died down and Kitty spotted them out of the corner of her eye.

"Jarrod, Liv, I'm so happy you're here!" Kitty exclaimed, turning to the small group huddling around her. "Excuse me, everyone." She hustled over and threw her arms around Jarrod's neck, pulling him close and whispering in his ear. "Thank God you came and rescued me. If I had to spend one more breathing moment with the former governor from Mississippi and his slavish wife right of *A Handmaid's Tale*, I would've died from boredom!"

Jarrod hugged her tightly but carefully so he did not accidentally wrinkle her immaculate designer dress. "Thanks for inviting us, Kitty. It looks like a great party."

"It's a complete disaster so far," Kitty moaned. "The caterer had a snit fit over not having enough oven space for the hot hors d'oeuvres and quit earlier this afternoon. I almost canceled the whole party, but then I called my old pal Laura Bush, who gave me the number of her favorite caterer in Houston, who had recently moved out here to Palm Desert. Luckily she was available to bail me out. I also suspect the bartender is downing more cocktails than he's serving to the guests."

"Well, everyone seems to be having a marvelous time," Jarrod assured her.

Kitty focused on Liv's wine-colored strapless wide-leg jumpsuit. "Darling, you look absolutely ravishing. Be sure to steer clear of those dirty old men hanging out near the fire pit. Former congressmen. You know how they can be. They're like the black flies back East. They'll eat you alive!"

"I'll be sure to watch my step, Kitty," Liv laughed, then pivoted. "Listen, I hope you don't mind, but I invited someone to your party."

"I told her she should have called and checked with you first," Jarrod scolded.

Kitty's eyes lit up. "I'm intrigued. Who is it?"

"My birth mother . . . I mean, the surrogate my dads hired . . ." Liv trailed off, unsure how she should describe her. "Anyway, she recently came into my life rather unexpectedly, and I'm still trying to figure out how this might work, if it's even going to work, and so I thought maybe getting to know her more in a social setting might be helpful."

"Her name is Candy," Jarrod added.

Kitty broke into a wide smile. "I think it's a lovely idea, and I'm very excited to meet her. What a way to add a little pep to my otherwise dull party!"

Jarrod scoffed. "*Dull?* I think I just spotted George and Amal Clooney walking through the front door."

"I know," Kitty sighed. "I try to keep the Hollywood types to a minimum, but he's directing a movie up in Idyllwild, so I felt obligated to invite them."

Behind the Clooneys, Candy slowly made her way inside the house, staring at the power couple in front of her as if she could not believe it was actually them. With her eyes fixed on George and Amal, she was not watching where she was going and bumped into a cater waiter passing by with a tray of canapes. Lucikly he managed to quickly balance his tray before anything slid off.

Candy apologized profusely.

Liv took a deep breath. "She's here."

Jarrod locked eyes with his daughter. "I know why you invited her, Liv. You thought by dropping her in the middle of a party, maybe loosening her up with a few cocktails, you might be able to get her to open up about her altercation with Zel to find out if she knows more than she's letting on about his murder."

Liv grabbed a canape off the tray as the waiter passed by them. "Am I that obvious?"

"No, you just take after me."

Liv waved at Candy, who appeared enormously relieved to see a familiar face. Straightening her simple knee-length black dress, slightly worn and outdated in style, Candy made her way over to Jarrod and Liv, stopping in front of them.

"Hello."

She was not sure whether she should hug them or just shake hands.

"Hi, Candy," Liv said, reaching out and giving her a quick innocuous squeeze. "I'm so glad you could make it."

Candy fixed her gaze on Jarrod. "Jarrod, you haven't changed a bit. Still as handsome as ever."

Jarrod turned to Liv. "Didn't I always tell you about how smart and observant she was?"

They all shared a laugh.

Candy's eyes began taking in her posh surroundings. "I don't think I've ever been in such a big, beautiful home before. I feel like I don't belong here, like I'm not cultured or classy enough."

Jarrod chuckled. "Believe me, Candy, you have nothing to worry about. This place is filled with Washington politicians. You're a hell of a lot more classy than any of them could ever hope to be."

"Let me get you a cocktail," Liv offered. "What are you drinking?"

"Uh, I don't know, I'm not much a drinker. Just one pretty much goes straight to my head."

Liv liked hearing that. "How about something airy and refreshing like a gin fizz?"

Candy hesitated but decided to go for it. "Okay, thank you."

Liv spirited herself away, leaving Jarrod alone with Candy. There was an awkward silence between them, neither one of them knowing what to say.

Finally, Jarrod decided to break the ice. "It's been a long time, Candy."

She nodded. "It has." She cleared her throat. "I was very sorry to hear about Charlie."

"Yes, it was rather sudden and unexpected. It's taken me a while to learn how to move on." He paused. "I'm still learning."

"He was a good man."

"That he was."

Another agonizingly long beat.

"Jarrod, I need to tell you something. I don't want Liv to know, but I have to get this off my chest."

"What is it, Candy?"

"I assume you know how me and Liv first got together, how her boyfriend called me out of the blue and asked me to take part in the movie he was making about the surrogacy process?"

"Yes, I'm aware. Liv told me."

"Well, I wasn't sure if I should get involved without speaking to you first, and I feel guilty I didn't call you before because maybe you would've tried talking me out of it, but it all happened so fast, and then I never—"

"Candy, you never needed my permission. That was always your decision and yours alone."

"It's just that it didn't go the way I expected. Don't get me wrong. Liv has been wonderful. I know she was surprised to see me, but she handled it well and has been very kind. You raised her right. But her boyfriend, Zel, the one who got killed, he wasn't who I thought he was. After that initial meeting, I believed we were done, but he kept calling me, badgering me, offering to pay me to talk smack about you and Charlie . . ."

Jarrod put a protective hand on Candy's shoulder. "I know, Candy. Liv and I saw the footage from the second interview."

Candy gasped. "You did? Even the part where I . . . ?"

"Threatened him for not paying you? Yes."

"I was never going to go through with it, I promise! I was just so angry in the moment. Honestly, Jarrod, after I left, I felt sorry for the guy. He struck me as this sad, damaged soul. I didn't think he was worthy of Liv. But who am I to pass judgment, given my own history with men? I guess I was just hoping that being with Liv might make him a better person."

"Given what we know now, I don't think even Liv is that kind of a miracle worker."

"Here we go!" Liv sang as she arrived and handed the gin fizz to Candy and a glass of red wine to her father. "What are we talking about?"

"Candy's argument with Zel."

Liv's eyes widened in surprise.

As Candy took a small sip of her cocktail, Jarrod leaned in and whispered in Liv's ear. "She brought it up before I even had the chance."

Jarrod could see the release of tension in Liv's whole body. Both of them knew in their hearts that Candy just did not have it in her to kill another human being. She was as sweet and kind as Jarrod remembered. He was not so sure about Candy's two adult children, however.

Alibis or not, they were still on his radar as possible suspects.

Liv threw a quick smile toward her father and then took Candy by the arm. "Come on, I'll show you around. I don't know a lot of the fancy bigwigs here, but I can introduce you to the few people I do know."

They shuffled off, leaving Jarrod to mingle on his own.

George and Leo, in matching plaid pink blazers, made a beeline for Jarrod, cocktails in hand.

"Was that her? The surrogate?" George demanded to know.

Jarrod nodded. "She's a lovely person."

"So is he!" Leo declared.

Jarrod sipped his wine. "Who?"

"Him!" Leo pointed over at Jim Stratton looking dapper in a blue sports coat, open-collar white shirt, and beige pants, standing near the kitchen, keeping a watchful eye over the party. "Sexy Secret Service Man at ten o'clock!"

George clasped his hands together excitedly. "We've been chatting him up all night! He's a dreamboat. Very impressive. He's smart, handsome, charming, witty. Totally not your type. I'm kidding. We decided you need to go out with him. Then you'll get married, and we can be a foursome."

"He means we can have a four-way," Leo giggled.

"Don't be crass," George sniffed before redirecting his attention back to Jarrod. "He's perfect. Come on, it's been almost ten years. It's time to get back in the dating pool and think of Leo and me as lifeguards here to make sure you don't drown."

Leo took Jarrod by the hand. "We honestly believe Charlie would approve."

"There is just one problem," Jarrod reminded them. "He hasn't asked me out."

George sighed. "Why can't *you* do the asking?"

The mere thought of that caused Jarrod to hyperventilate.

What if he said no?

Or worse, what if he said yes?

Then he would actually have to go through with a real date.

"You have thirty seconds," George warned.

"What happens after thirty seconds?"

Leo folded his arms. "George and I ask him out for you."

"You wouldn't dare."

George scoffed. "Have you met us?"

He had known them for years.

And he knew they were not bluffing.

Unlike Candy, they would have no problem following through on their threat.

Jarrod downed the rest of his Pinot Noir and shoved the empty wineglass at Leo. "Fine, I'll do it."

He could feel George and Leo watching him as he crossed the room over to Jim. Jarrod was instantly hit with the wafting intoxication of Jim's cologne. A warm and spicy smell that Jarrod suspected was a Tom Ford fragrance. It somehow caught him off guard, and he just stood dumbstruck in front of Jim, not knowing what the hell to do next.

Finally, Jim decided to offer a little help. "What can I do for you?"

Jarrod was not only stymied by his captivating aroma, he could not take his eyes off the light-brown chest hair peeking out of Jim's open-collar shirt or the broad shoulders filling out his perfectly fitted blazer. "I, uh, I came over here to ask you something."

Jim waited patiently as Jarrod retreated to an old version of himself, the awkward, pimply teenager who was no longer wanted on the cover of *TV Guide* or *People* magazine as America's favorite cherubic child star, totally unsure of himself.

Jim prompted him again. "What do you want to ask me?"

Jarrod opened his mouth but the words that came spilling out were not the ones he had silently rehearsed to himself on the way over here. "Where can I find the bathroom?"

"Down the hall to the right," Jim responded in a clipped measured tone.

"Thank you," Jarrod squeaked, his feet still not moving.

"Was there anything else?"

Jarrod shook his head. "No, that's it. Down the hall to the right. Got it. Thanks."

Finally managing to stumble away, he glanced back at George and Leo watching him expectantly and gave them a thumbs-up.

They both reacted with glee.

He figured he would admit the truth to them later, that he had chickened out, after the party so it would be too late for them to take matters into their own hands.

CHAPTER 25

"Jarrod, I just met a former secretary of state," a wide-eyed Candy gushed. "I've never been in a room with so many important people."

"Neither have I, to be honest."

Liv strolled up to them holding two cocktails and tried handing one to Candy, but she waved it off. "I better not. One was enough. That stuff goes right to my head, and I'm already nervous about saying the wrong thing as it is!"

Jarrod noticed a new arrival entering through the front door. His stomach suddenly twisted in knots. "Is that . . . ?"

Candy turned and her mouth dropped open in surprise. "Dale!"

Her loud-mouthed manipulative son.

Crashing the party.

Obviously out on bail after his arrest.

"What's he doing here?" Jarrod asked, his voice tense.

Candy turned to Jarrod and Liv, her voice shaky, her nerves starting to get the best of her. "He offered to drive me. He knew I was very worried about coming here tonight. He said he would drop me off, go hang out with some buddies of his here in town, and then pick me up whenever I texted him and told him I was ready to leave. But we agreed he would wait outside for me. I specifically told him *not* to come inside."

"Dale doesn't strike me as the kind of guy who does what he is told," Liv said curtly.

"I'm so sorry, I better go now. Thank you for a lovely evening, both of you."

By now Dale had spotted the three of them huddled together and had glided across the room to join them. He gave Liv a quick once-over. "Hiya, sis. Boy, you sure do clean up nice."

"Hello, Dale," Liv said flatly.

Candy slipped her arm through Dale's and gently tried to guide him back toward the door. "Let's go home, Dale."

Dale feigned disappointment. "What? I just got here, Mom. I thought I'd enjoy a little cocktail from the open bar. Besides, did you get a look at the bartender? She's *hot!*"

"No, Dale, I think we should just go," Candy pleaded.

Dale stuck a hand out to Jarrod. "Nice to see you again, Mr. Jarvis. You should have seen how excited Mom was when Liv invited her to this little shindig. I offered to be her plus one, but she refused. Can you believe that? What mother wouldn't want to spend quality time with her only son?"

Jarrod glanced over to see Secret Service agent Jim monitoring the situation, knowing full well that Dale was not on the guest list and so a potential threat.

Candy tugged on her son's arm. "Please, Dale, I'm tired and I want to go home."

Dale's face darkened. "What? You can't even let me enjoy myself for five minutes? When am I going to get the chance to mingle with VIPs like this ever again?" He gave Jarrod a snakish smile. "Since Mr. Jarvis here wasn't interested in my business proposition, I figure maybe I'd chat up the hostess with the mostest, big bucks over there, am I right?"

"I don't think that's a good idea, Dale," Jarrod warned. "At least not tonight. She's very busy with her guests. And you have enough on your plate with your trial coming up."

Dale grabbed a glass of champagne off a tray a passing waiter was carrying. "Those charges are bogus, you'll see." He chugged it down and glared at Jarrod. "Just because you're not willing to entertain such an amazing opportunity doesn't mean these other fat cats have to fall in line behind you."

Candy pressed her painted nails into the skin on his arm as she probably did when he was a little boy and acting out as a stern warning. "Dale, you heard Jarrod, this is *not* the time . . ."

Dale's voice grew louder as he confronted his mother. "You're always yelling at me to get my act together, but then you want me to shut up when I have a goal, when I'm trying to better myself! And yet here you are, hobnobbing with a bunch of rich folks while ordering me to stay outside in the car like I'm your personal chauffeur!"

Embarrassed, Candy kept her eyes fixed on the floor, knowing her son was causing a scene that was capturing the attention of everyone in the room. "You offered to drive me. I would've brought my own car . . ."

"I knew you'd be too embarrassed to bring your own clunker and have to hand the keys off to that sneering valet outside!"

Jarrod could tell the glass of champagne Dale had just downed had not been his first drink of the evening. "You're being a nuisance, Dale. Now I think it would be wise to listen to your mother and just go home. I will talk to Kitty, tell her your idea, and she can make her own decision about whether she wants to learn more, okay? How does that sound?"

Dale scoffed. "It sounds like a brush-off to me. Mom always said, 'Why put off for tomorrow what you can do today?' Didn't you say that, Mom?" Dale began swiveling his head around, trying to locate Kitty. "So where is she? Where's the former first lady of the grand ole US of A?"

"I'm right here," Kitty purred, magically appearing behind Dale as if on cue.

Dale spun around, slapping a bright, friendly smile on his face. "It's a pleasure to meet you, Mrs. Reynolds. I'm Dale Lithwick and this is my mother, Candy."

Candy could not bear to look at her. She just kept staring at the floor, as if she wanted it to open up and swallow her whole.

"I've met your charming mother. In fact, I've met everyone here who is on the guest list."

Dale decided to blow past the obvious dig. "Well, I sure do appreciate you inviting her. She doesn't get to go to many fancy parties like this with champagne and canapes. We're more of a beer and Chex Mix kind of family."

"My husband and I sustained ourselves through his first congressional campaign with beer and Chex Mix. I will be sure to have plenty of both on hand at my next party," she quipped before reaching out and taking Candy's free hand. "Where your mother will be most welcome."

"Thank you for a lovely evening, Mrs. Reynolds," Candy muttered, hand slightly shaking, still unable to make eye contact.

Kitty frowned. "Leaving so soon?"

"I have to work tomorrow."

Dale extricated himself from his mother's sharp nails and descended upon Kitty.

Jarrod took a protective step toward her.

Out of the corner of his eye, he could see Jim slowly heading in their direction.

"Before we go, Mrs. Reynolds, I'd like to talk to you about a very exciting business opportunity."

Jarrod protectively moved in front of Kitty. "Like I told you, Dale, I will discuss your proposition with Kitty, and someone will get back to you."

"I think Mrs. Reynolds, *Kitty*, might be interested in hearing it for herself," Dale spit out through gritted teeth.

"And you'd be wrong, my dear," Kitty sighed. "I'm sorry, Mr. Lithwick, but I need to tend to my other guests, my *invited* guests. Please, do yourself a favor and listen to Jarrod. I promise to give your idea the consideration it deserves."

Dale did not know how to react.

Was she serious or was she mocking him?

He decided to keep plowing ahead. "I swear this won't take long—" He tried pushing past Jarrod, but Jarrod blocked him like NFL defensive lineman Chris Jones.

Dale angrily stuck his chest out and tried butting Jarrod out of the way, but Jarrod held firm, although Dale was much bigger than him.

Suddenly Jim was behind Dale, grabbing him tightly by the wrist with his giant paw and twisting it up behind Dale's back as he yelped in pain.

The entire room watched in stunned silence as Jim forcefully escorted Dale to the front door and ejected him with a hard shove. All eyes in the room were now on studly Jim, who had so valiantly come to the rescue. It was a swoon-worthy heroic moment not lost on Jarrod or anyone else at the party, for that matter. They were either impressed or instantly smitten.

Unaware of all the attention he was suddenly receiving, Jim returned to his post, ignoring all the adoring eyes staring at him.

Humiliated, Candy, a hand over her mouth, shaking her head, said tearfully, "I'm sorry for causing such a scene. I'm so embarrassed . . ."

Kitty laughed. "This was nothing. I have a drunken son-in-law who is always causing scenes and mortifying us. We literally caught him swinging from a chandelier at one of my husband's inaugural balls. I didn't even think that was possible. I thought it was just a phrase people use. And don't get me started on my late husband's brother Samuel. He made Billy Carter look like a choir boy. Please don't worry. We all have family members who sometimes embarrass us, Candy."

"Thank you, Mrs. Reynolds. Despite all of this, I had a lovely time," Candy said.

"I look forward to seeing you again," Kitty said warmly.

Head down, Candy made a hasty exit.

Jim held the door open for her as she rushed out before quietly closing it behind her.

"She's a good woman," Kitty noted to Jarrod and Liv before spinning around and setting off to mingle some more.

Jarrod snatched a canape off another tray passing by and popped it in his mouth. "Kitty's right. She's a good woman who just happens to have a couple of lousy kids."

"They must take after their father."

"But Jewel has an alibi."

"And Dale doesn't. So, I guess he's our top suspect at this point," Liv concluded.

Although he detested Dale, Jarrod secretly hoped their instincts would be wrong this time, that Dale was not involved, because in his opinion, poor Candy had already been through enough and did not need her son, now facing a mountain of legal woes, to be exposed to the world as a merciless killer.

He feared Candy's heart might not be able to take it.

CHAPTER 26

Jarrod pulled his car to the curb in front of Liv's apartment building. It was going on midnight. Most cocktail parties in Palm Springs petered out before ten, but Kitty's soiree had a life of its own and did not break up until after eleven thirty. Per usual, Jarrod had been one of the last guests to leave. Throughout his entire life, he had had a habit of staying until the bitter end at social gatherings, fearing if he left early, he might miss something.

Liv had been quiet on the ride home, her mind far away. When she realized the car had stopped and they were in front of her apartment building, she forced a smile and reached over to hug her father good night.

Liv unbuckled her seat belt. "Good night, Dad. Thanks for driving."

"You want to talk about it?"

"About what?"

"What's bothering you?"

"Nothing's bothering me."

Jarrod shot her a skeptical look.

Liv straightened up in her seat, determined. "I think we should really focus on Dale. It's clear he's involved with Zel's murder somehow."

"Is it? Clear? I'm not so sure."

Liv scoffed. "Dad, he's a hothead who lied about where he was on the night of the murder, and he lacks a solid alibi. Plus, he just gives me the creeps."

"Doesn't make him a killer."

"I also noticed he has pretty big feet and might be the same shoe size as the imprint you found at the scene."

"A lot of men have big feet, Liv."

Liv sighed, frustrated. "Why are you suddenly defending him? I don't get it."

"I'm not. I'm just saying we need more hard evidence. We can't assume he's guilty simply because we don't like his personality and he has trouble with telling the truth. I know you're anxious to pin this on someone because you want to prove your Uncle Brody's innocent, but we need to be careful not to rush things and accuse the wrong person."

"Well, if it's not Dale, then who?"

Jarrod shrugged. "I don't know yet. We just need to stay focused, keep plugging away, look at the facts in front of us."

"Meanwhile, the cops are *this* close to arresting Uncle Brody and throwing him in jail! How can you just sit there and let that happen?"

"They're not going to arrest Brody just because he was in the vicinity of the murder and wears a twelve and a half size shoe. Detective Jordan is in the same boat as us. He needs more evidence. Uncle Brody is going to be just fine. We both know he didn't do it. There's no reason to worry."

Tears pricked Liv's eyes. "I've seen enough true crime shows to know the wrong guy can be convicted of a crime and sent to prison for decades before the courts realize he didn't do it."

Jarrod reached over and took hold of Liv's hand. "Honey, you're catastrophizing. There's something else going on here. What is it?"

Liv tried sniffing back her tears but one managed to roll down her right cheek. She wiped it away with her hand and took a deep breath. "I just can't shake the feeling that all of this is my fault."

Jarrod cocked an eyebrow. "How do you mean?"

"That I somehow triggered the events that led to Zel's murder, that my willingness to open this whole Pandora's box allowing all these people to come pouring into our lives, that I did this, that I'm somehow responsible."

"That's nonsense! You said yourself that Zel was the one who pushed the issue, it was his idea to get in touch with Candy for his film project, not yours, and that you were blindsided by the whole thing."

"I know, but I did go along with it when I could have immediately stopped him in his tracks. He kept telling me it was my decision, that he'd abide by my wishes, and I kept dithering. Maybe he'd still be alive if I'd been more forceful right out of the gate."

"I'm not going to let you blame yourself, Liv. You did nothing wrong. You were trying to be supportive. And we don't even know for certain that Zel's murder has any connection to the surrogacy project. There could be something else we're just not seeing yet, something totally unrelated."

Jarrod could tell his words were doing very little to assuage her guilt.

"Liv, do you know how many people in the world have a twelve and a half shoe size?"

She sniffed and nodded.

"We're going to find him. Or her. It could be a woman. Hell, Brittney Griner wears a men's size seventeen sneaker when she plays basketball."

"I don't think Brittney Griner had a grudge against Zel, Dad, I'm just saying."

She gave him a peck on the cheek and then hopped out of the car, slamming the door behind her. Jarrod watched her scurry through the gate and to her apartment, her shoulders sagging, still beating herself up, which just made him more determined than ever to find whoever killed his daughter's boyfriend.

CHAPTER 27

Jarrod detested the name of his group exercise class today. The powers that be at the gym where he worked out decided on "Young at Heart" instead of "Forever Fit." Jarrod was not quite sixty years old yet, and although he was one of the youngest members in the class, the oldest being the spitfire Joan at ninety-two, he believed the marketing geniuses responsible for naming the class should have gone with something a little less ageist and patronizing. Both he and George had fired off protest emails, but so far they had not heard back. Still, with its combination of cardio, choreography, and weight training, he made sure to sign up three times a week in addition to his usual outdoor hikes and yoga class. He was getting older and wanted to stay fit and healthy. He had seen too many sedentary friends suffer from aches and pains and a plethora of health problems from not living an active lifestyle. Plus, as an actor, he was still vain enough to want to look good.

Leo had a dentist appointment today, and George was holding court on his own as his usual group of admirers flocked to him like birds to a feeder, eager to hear his long-winded stories about his colorful past life as a Fosse dancer on Broadway, which he would illustrate during the choreography part of the workout using jazz hands, shoulder rolls, and lots of pivots and twists. Even the instructor, who was a bit envious of all the attention George was getting, would eat it up.

Jarrod tended to stay in the back because he knew he would inevitably screw up the routine and did not want to throw everyone else off who might be following him if he was in the front row. He kept his eye on the clock on the wall, counting down the minutes until the final stretches to Cher or Prince blasting from the speakers.

When class was over, Jarrod pushed his way through the throng of adoring women to get to George. They had carpooled together in George's silver Mercedes, and Jarrod told him he just needed to grab his bag and would meet him by the front entrance. George gave him a cursory nod as he prattled on to his audience about his verbal jousting with Stephen Sondheim after George had once told him point-blank that the book for *A Little Night Music* could have benefited from a punch-up. Sondheim also did not appreciate George taking credit for inspiring the title of another one of his hit shows, *Sunday in the Park with George.*

As Jarrod headed out of the exercise studio toward the locker room, his eye caught the back of a man with perfect calves, wearing a tank top and tight gray shorts and lifting a heavy barbell. There was a lot to admire about the man's perfectly muscled arms and broad shoulders that were on display. Jarrod could see a number of people nearby surreptitiously glancing over and taking in the man's incredible body.

As the man set down the weight and grabbed a white towel to wipe the sweat off himself, he turned around enough so Jarrod could see his face.

It was Jim Stratton.

Jarrod was caught off guard and was about to make a mad dash for the locker room before Jim spotted him, but he was too late.

Jim noticed Jarrod ogling him and gave him a polite wave.

Now Jarrod was stuck.

He could not just keep going.

That would be rude.

He had to go over and say hello.

But his feet refused to move.

Why was he so nervous?

Jim took the initiative and ambled over.

"Hey there," Jarrod mumbled lamely.

"Hi, I saw you earlier, dancing up a storm in there. What's the class?"

Humiliated, Jarrod dithered before finally admitting, "It's, um, it's called 'Young at Heart' . . ." Jarrod sighed. "Apparently they think we're all geriatrics."

Jim chuckled. "It looks like fun. Maybe I'll sign up for it next time."

"You'd be very popular with the ladies. You would certainly give my friend George a run for his money."

A stilted pause punctuated the conversation.

Finally, Jarrod broke the silence. "I didn't know you work out here."

"Normally I don't. But Kitty does. She's over there complaining to her personal trainer about how she hates doing squats with the medicine ball."

Jarrod glanced over to see a red-faced Kitty, clearly angry, trying her best, as her personal trainer calmly explained how this exercise would improve her strength, power, and coordination. It was obvious she did not want to hear it. Her mind was already on the glass of champagne she was going to have at lunch.

Jarrod turned and flashed Jim a smile. "I'll let you get back to your workout. It was nice seeing you again."

Jarrod started to shuffle off.

"Jarrod . . ."

He spun back around expectantly.

"I, uh, I was wondering if you might want to grab dinner sometime?"

"With you?"

Jim grinned. "Yes, with me."

"Did Kitty put you up to this?"

"No!" he barked too quickly. "I mean, let's just say she wouldn't be opposed to the two of us having dinner . . . without her."

Which was another way of saying Kitty definitely put him up to it.

There was nothing covert about her continuing matchmaking efforts.

And although Jim technically worked for the Secret Service, he was still beholden to Kitty and what she wanted.

Jarrod strongly suspected this had all been orchestrated by Kitty, and he did not feel right about her pressuring poor Jim into asking him out on a date.

"That's okay, Jim. I appreciate the gesture though. You can just tell Kitty that I said no, I'm very busy, and hopefully she'll finally let it go."

Jim did not know what to say to that.

He just nodded and went back to his weightlifting.

"You should be ashamed of yourself!" George huffed from behind him. Jarrod turned around to see George, all five foot three of him, arms folded, glaring at Jarrod, his gaggle of girl-friends having fluttered off to their cars.

"Why? What did I do?"

"That poor man just asked you out on a date, and you just heartlessly rejected him! Who in his right mind says no to a god like that? Trust me, that man has more sex appeal than Jason Momoa!"

"Exactly! Which is why I said no. He only asked me out because Kitty has been nagging him nonstop. The guy didn't have a choice if he wanted to keep his job, so I made it easy for him by saying no."

"Did you see his face when you turned him down? That wasn't relief on his face. That was wounded pride!"

Jarrod scoffed. "Come on, George . . ."

"Look at him!"

Jarrod cranked his head around to see Jim, a kettlebell between his legs, swinging forward and upward using his hips and glutes, but his focus seemed distant. There was a tension in his movements, his face bearing a veil of hurt, a mask concealing the sting of rejection.

Jarrod felt a twinge of guilt.

Had he completely misread the situation?

George was more confident in his assessment. "If this is how you choose to handle your personal life, perhaps it's time to rethink your strategy!"

As much as Jarrod hated to admit it, he gave George a slight nod. "You're right."

"I'm *always* right!"

CHAPTER 28

Back to square one, Jarrod and Liv returned to Zel's studio, hoping to find something that could lead them to a new clue, a lead that might jump start their investigation again. Neither of them were bullish on the prospect, having already thoroughly combed the entire place after the police and a forensics team had finished their own sweep. But with nothing new to go on, they were desperate enough to try anything.

When they entered the studio, Liv instantly noticed something amiss. Although Zel was the opposite of a neat freak, his creativity sparked by cluttered chaos, the studio was more of a mess than the last time they had been here. Papers were scattered all over the floor like fallen leaves, the shelf full of Zel's collection of books studying the careers of his favorite directors was knocked over. Desk drawers had been ripped open, files rifled through.

Liv's trembling hand found refuge in her father's firm grip. "Dad, I think someone's been here."

Jarrod nodded in agreement. "They were after something, but what?"

"Should we call the police?"

"Why? We have no idea if anything is actually missing. Maybe they didn't find what they were looking for. We might as well just take another look around, see if we find anything."

He moved to the shelf, picking up books and rifling through them. Liv headed over to the drawers and started thumbing through files, not at all confident she would magically come across something useful.

This was starting to feel like a pointless exercise.

Seated at Zel's desk, sifting through the same folders as before, Liv's jaw clenched in frustration as she brushed the papers aside. "This is a complete waste of time, Dad. We're not going to find anything new. I feel like we're just running in circles at this point. You know, they say the definition of insanity is doing the same thing over and over and expecting a different result."

"You sound like your papa Charlie. He always kept telling me to stop my meddling, but he knew I would never willingly let it go, and eventually through sheer determination, something would always eventually turn up, like it does in every Agatha Christie novel, every Sam Spade mystery, every episode of *Murder, She Wrote.*"

Liv smirked. "You're such a dork, Dad."

She stood up from the desk and made her way to the back of the studio. She stopped in her tracks. This room appeared to be even more ransacked than the other part of the studio with scattered film reels, shattered lenses, and a chaotic jumble of papers strewn across the editing table.

Liv took a steadying breath, steeling herself for the painful task ahead. As she approached the closet, swinging the door halfway open, Liv's eyes were drawn to a familiar sight. The iconic gorilla mask from Zel's favorite movie, *Planet of the Apes*, the original 1968 version, hung on a hook—a quirky and beloved memento that had often brought a smile to their faces. Zel had worn it to a Halloween party last year at the college, where they had first met.

With a heavy heart, she reached out to touch the mask, only for her fingers to brush against the coarse fur. Liv gasped, her eyes widening as the mask shivered. Panic clawed at her throat as she realized that it wasn't hanging empty.

Someone's head was inside it.

Before Liv could react, the closet door banged all the way open, revealing the masked intruder. Fear froze her in place as the man, hidden behind the grotesque guise, lunged at her with unexpected ferocity. Liv felt a powerful force collide with her, and the world spun as she crashed to the studio floor, gasping for breath.

The masked figure wasted no time. He darted past her into the next room, where he was surprised to find Jarrod. Liv could see the gorilla-masked man, fueled by desperation, deliver a forceful blow to Jarrod's ribcage, sending him sprawling to the side.

Driven by a surge of adrenaline and determination, Liv staggered to her feet. Ignoring the pain, she sprinted after the masked assailant, stopping first to check on her father.

"Dad!"

Jarrod clutched his side. "I'm okay!"

Before he could stop her, Liv sprang back up and out the door in hot pursuit of the gorilla.

Once outside, she scanned for any sign of him. Behind her, she heard the roar of a car engine. She spun around just in time to see a blue Toyota Camry barreling toward her, tires squealing. She leaped out of the way, high enough to land on top of her father's car that was parked at the curb. Rolling off, she focused on the license plate, managing to commit it to memory before the Camry screeched around a corner and disappeared.

"XYZ7890!"

She repeated it again.

"XYZ7890!"

She kept repeating it until she could hurry back inside the studio and write it down on a piece of paper on Zel's desk.

Jarrod was back on his feet, wincing a little but otherwise okay.

She handed the paper to her father.

"Is this the license plate number?"

"Maybe you could call one of Papa Charlie's police contacts and have them run a check?"

"Honey, I'm sorry, but I've lost touch with all of the people Charlie worked with at the LAPD. It's been over ten years. His old partner, Ned, and his wife send me a Christmas card every year, but they're both retired and living in Hawaii."

"There must be someone you know who can do it."

She could almost see his mind whirring.

And then he frowned.

She could tell that he had thought of someone, but he was reluctant.

"Who, Dad? I know you've come up with a name. It's written all over your face."

Jarrod reached for his phone. "I can try, but I have a feeling he's not going to be very enthusiastic about helping me." Jarrod checked his texts from Kitty. She had sent him his number just in case Jarrod wanted to get in contact with him. He tapped the number to make the call.

Jarrod heard his deep baritone voice after just two rings. "Hello?"

"Hey, Jim, it's Jarrod Jarvis."

Silence.

"I'm sorry to bother you, but I was calling to see—"

"Did you change your mind about dinner?"

"What? No, I mean, that's not why I'm calling—"

"So, you just want to rub salt in the wound by saying no to me again, in case it didn't land the first time?"

"No!"

Liv could plainly see this was not going well.

"I'm with my daughter, Liv, and we just came across someone breaking and entering in her boyfriend's studio, and well, I'm sure Kitty told you, the boyfriend was murdered, and Liv was smart enough to get the license number on the car he was driving, and, well, you're the only person I could think of who might be able to help us find out who the car is registered to . . ."

"I'm not a police officer. I work for the Secret Service, and we fall under the Department of Homeland Security."

"Yes, I know, but I'm sure you know lots of people in law enforcement and could—"

He spoke in a clipped tone. "You want me to call in a favor? For you?"

"I get the feeling I'm overstepping. I apologize, Jim. I realize now I never should've called you about this."

Another long silence.

"What's the number?" Jim muttered.

"I beg your pardon?"

"What's the license number?"

Jarrod referred to the piece of paper he was holding in his hand. Liv's face lit up in anticipation.

"XYZ7890."

"I'll see what I can do."

Then the call dropped.

Liv excitedly clasped her hands together. "So, he's going to help us?"

Jarrod shrugged. "I guess we'll just have to wait and see."

"If he comes through for us, you really need to go on a date with him, Dad."

Jarrod ignored her.

They did not have to wait long.

By the time Jarrod was pulling up to Liv's apartment building to drop her off, he received a text from Jim.

He had come through.

He had the name of the person who owned the gorilla-masked man's getaway car.

Jarrod's heart leapt in his throat as he read the name.

Illya Lipovsky.

Professor Illya Lipovsky of the College of the Desert.

Zel's teacher and mentor.

CHAPTER 29

Liv had never been a fashionista like Maude, who was always chasing after the latest trends, so she loathed dressing up in a flashy crop top and a pair of high-waisted jeans, accessorizing them with some chunky jewelry. But she considered her outfit a necessary part of her undercover assignment this evening. She and Maude were planning to attend an off-campus party where a lot of Professor Lipovsky's film students would be partying. When she had mentioned this mission to her father, he was not exactly happy with the idea of her crashing a college keg blowout, fearing what might happen at such an event. Mostly because he had probably attended his fair share back in the day and partook in all the debauchery that usually ensued.

But Liv was determined to suss out more information about the relationship between Zel and his professor, and who better to question than a bunch of eyewitnesses who knew them both well.

Liv studied herself in the full-length mirror in her bedroom as she applied the finishing touches, a little mascara and some eyeshadow, but not too much. She did not want to look like a raccoon.

Her phone on the nightstand lit up.

It was a text from Maude.

She was already waiting outside.

Ten minutes early.

Very unusual for Maude.

Liv figured she was just excited to be going to a party with lots of hot college guys. Liv had to remind her that this place was not going to be packed with big, muscly football players. This party was for students from the film program, so flirting with a Travis Kelce lookalike might prove to be wishful thinking.

Liv rushed out the door and out to the street where Maude was waiting in her cherry-red Honda Accord. As Liv opened the passenger door and slid inside, she could see the excitement and anticipation on Maude's face. She was decked out in a sleek fitted red bodysuit that matched the color of her car, a tight leather skirt, boots, and a denim jacket, which was her ready-to-party look.

Before Liv had the chance to shut the car door, Maude was speeding away from Liv's building toward Highway 111 and Palm Desert.

"I was desperate to do something fun tonight so thank you for inviting me!" Maude chirped.

"Why aren't you doing something with Butch?"

Maude scoffed. "The loser ghosted me!"

"What? You two seemed so good together!"

"That's what I thought. Things seemed to be going so well. I honestly believed he was genuinely interested in me, that maybe this time a guy I'm dating wouldn't turn out to be a grade-A creep. Wrong again!"

Maude swerved the car onto Highway 111.

"You forgot to turn on your blinker," Liv quietly reminded her.

"Liv, I'm having a moment of crisis. I can't be expected to follow *all* the traffic rules!"

"They're not rules, they're laws. Maybe I should have driven."

Maude eased up from the gas pedal with her foot so the car

at least slowed down to the speed limit. "I'll try to do better, Miss Goody Two-Shoes."

"So what do you think happened?"

"He did mention an ex-girlfriend of his had been texting him lately, trying to worm her way back into his life, but I didn't think he seemed to be into her anymore. But what do I know? They're probably planning a spring wedding as we speak! I also think her family has money and he's out of a job now that Zel's gone, so that might have played into it too."

Liv reached over and touched Maude's hand that gripped the gearshift. "I'm sorry, Maudie."

Maude scoffed. "Don't be. I probably dodged a bullet. I just want to go to this party, guzzle some beer, and forget all my troubles. I'm done with men. So, if some really hot guy sweeps me off my feet tonight, promise me you'll get me out of there before I make another horrendous mistake!"

"Somehow I don't think Prince Charming is going to be at this keg party, so there's probably nothing to worry about."

When Liv and Maude arrived at the modest house in a quiet residential section of Palm Desert, the party was already in full swing. The thirty to forty drunken college kids were all shouting to each other over Dua Lipa, whose siren voice wafted from the speakers. The sliding glass door leading to the backyard was wide open, allowing easy access to the three kegs set up near the kidney-shaped pool that was in need of a deep cleaning.

As Liv and Maude weaved their way through the throng of revelers to the backyard, they were intercepted by a lanky blond boy in a tank top and shorts. He stepped in front of Liv and went in for a hug. She recognized him from when she was in school but was blanking on his name.

"Liv, I'm so happy you made it!"

"Of course. I wouldn't miss it." Her mind raced to come up with his name. She was good with faces. Bad with names. She knew he had been a freshman when she was a senior. It was right on the tip of her tongue.

Joe.

No, Jeff.

What the hell was it?

Finally she took Maude gently by the arm and pulled her up next to her. "This is my friend Maude."

Maude's eyes twinkled. "Hello."

The kid was cute.

"Hi, I'm Jeb."

Jeb! Yes, of course!

"Let's get you two something to drink. We're doing tequila shots in the kitchen if that's your jam."

"We're fine with beer."

"Speak for yourself," Maude interjected. "Point me toward the kitchen, Jebbie."

Jeb smiled and steered her to the left, where Liv could see a group of kids slamming their empty shot glasses down on the kitchen counter before sucking on some sliced limes.

Maude flitted off to join them, and Liv made a mental note to insist that she be the one who drives home.

Jeb's eyes drifted toward the door. "I'll be right back. I gotta go say hello to some people who just arrived. But don't disappear. I want to hang with you. It's not every day the beautiful Olivia Jarvis-Peters graces us with her regal presence."

Liv chuckled as he squeezed her arm and headed in the direction of the front door. Liv wandered outside and grabbed a plastic cup. Another film student, this one portly and a bit disheveled, stood by one of the kegs. She recognized him as one of Zel's classmates, and she remembered Zel telling her once about this guy, how he was not a fan of Zel's work. The kid held the nozzle of the keg over her cup and pressed his thumb down, filling the cup to the rim with foamy beer.

She could not recall his name either.

"Kenny," he said as if reading her mind.

"Liv."

"Oh, I know who you are. You're Zel's girlfriend," he said before correcting himself. "I mean, you *were* Zel's girlfriend. Sorry, I didn't mean to—"

"No, it's okay."

"It was such a shock, to everyone, when we heard what happened to him."

She studied his face.

He was wearing a mask of indifference.

As if he felt the need to say the words, but in his heart he did not really mean it.

"Hey, did you ever finish that short subject project on the Coachella Music Festival I remember you were working on?"

He shook his head and said with a hint of bitterness, "No, I gave up on that long before I shot anything."

"It sounded like an excellent idea for a short film."

"Somebody else beat me to it with something similar, so I decided to drop it and work on something else."

Zel.

He had directed a short film about the festival.

He must have stolen the idea from Kenny.

But for whatever reason, perhaps out of respect to Liv and her relationship with Zel, he was not going to trash him tonight.

In fact, as Liv socialized with other students, most of whom she knew must despise Zel, they all dialed back on their anger toward him, possibly out of fear they might become suspects in his murder. No one was eager to talk about him and would quickly change the subject when his name came up.

After checking on Maude, who was still in the kitchen holding court with a swarm of new admirers, Liv continued casually questioning student after student, but none of them were willing to talk out of school about Zel and Professor Lipovsky.

She was about to give up when, as promised, Jeb intercepted her and steered her toward the couch where they could sit down and have a chat.

She noticed Jeb was more inebriated than earlier and was a bit handsy, touching her leg as they talked, which she gently swatted away a couple of times. She did not want to offend him because he was more loose-lipped than anyone else at the party she had encountered so far, but she certainly was not going to allow him to freely paw her either.

She rested her elbow on her leg closest to him and leaned in, smelling the liquor on his breath. "I get the feeling everyone at this party had a big problem with Zel."

"Yeah, pretty much. That guy was a real dickwad." His watery eyes tried focusing on Liv. "Oh, man, I shouldn't have said that. I forgot you and him were—"

"No, it's fine. It's terrible what happened but we were kind of on the outs when he died. I know Zel had a lot of enemies."

"A *lot*!" Jeb slurred as he threw back the rest of his cocktail.

"And not just his classmates. I heard a rumor one of his professors had a beef with him."

"Lipovsky! Yes! They were, like, at war with each other! It got really bad!" His eyes were now at half-mast.

Liv felt the need to keep him talking before he passed out or bolted for the bathroom to hurl.

"What do you suppose happened?"

"Zel handed in a film proposal that he completely ripped off from Jackson Taylor, a good buddy of mine. Most of the time Zel got away with it, but this time even Lipovsky couldn't ignore the facts, and so Zel flunked the assignment. Zel was out of his mind with rage. He pressured all of us to write really bad evaluations about Lipovsky in hopes of getting him fired."

Liv was taken aback.

She had never witnessed such a vindictive side of Zel.

He must have hidden it well when he was with her.

"We all held firm, we weren't going to trash a professor just because Zel was pissed, so when that didn't work, he went nuclear."

"How so?"

"He started making these TikTok videos painting Lipovsky as a fraud and questioning his talent as a filmmaker when he was back in Russia. He'd find these guys with Russian accents who claimed to be ghost directors who had done all the work while Lipovsky took all the credit, which was ironic given the fact that was Zel's exact MO. I mean it was ridiculous. But people were starting to buy it. I heard Lipovsky got called into the dean's office to explain himself. Zel did a real number on him."

"But none of it was true."

Jeb shrugged. "That's the thing about fake news. People sometimes believe it. It was driving Lipovsky insane. There was a rumor going around that it cost him a grant he had been awarded to direct his first feature in years."

Liv took a breath. "Do you think he might have been angry enough to—"

Jeb anticipated her question. "Definitely. All of us who were in Lipovsky's class with Zel, we all assumed the same thing when we heard he was murdered, that it was probably Lipovsky who killed him."

CHAPTER 30

Liv was ready to go. Maude, however, was now sitting on top of the counter in the kitchen, legs swinging, cup of beer in hand, leading enough male admirers to comprise the first string of a football team as they sang along to the classic Carly Rae Jepsen song *Call Me Maybe* while miming being on the phone with her free hand.

Liv gave a quick wave to get her attention and mouthed that she was ready to leave the party.

Maude nodded, then as the boys continued singing, she shouted over their wailing voices, "I'll be right there! Just let me say goodbye!"

"I'll be outside!" Liv tried screaming above the loud party conversation and blasting music.

Maude scrunched up her nose. "What?"

"I said I'll meet you outside!"

Maude seemed to nod in acknowledgment, but Liv could not be sure. She just wanted to get away from all the deafening noise. She had confirmation from enough students to know she should be focusing squarely on Professor Lipovsky as the number one suspect in Zel's murder and hoped Maude would find her way to her car at some point.

Outside the house, Liv stopped to check her phone to see

what time it was when she felt a hand clamp down on her shoulder.

"Hey, where are you going?"

She turned around to see Jeb, a lot drunker than he was before, his watery eyes now at half-mast, as he swayed from side to side.

"It's time for me to go home. It was nice seeing you, Jeb," Liv said tightly.

He did not let up on his grip. "No, don't go. Why don't you come back inside so we can talk some more? I really want to get to know you."

"Sorry, I can't." She shook her shoulder to free herself from his hand and tried to leave, her discomfort evident. "Good night."

He reached out and grabbed her wrist, stopping her once again. "Hey, why are you being such a vibe killer? Don't tell me you didn't feel the connection we were making earlier? Come on, let's go somewhere quiet so we can—"

"That's the beer talking." She yanked her hand hard to wrench it out of Jeb's grasp, but he held firm, not letting her go.

"Let go of me!" Liv demanded.

A darkness fell over Jeb's face.

He was drunk and angry and aggressive.

Liv steeled herself.

She had trained for this in a self-defense class her father had forced her to take when she was twelve.

She had nails long enough to do serious damage to his face.

She positioned her leg, ready to knee him in the groin.

He had no idea what a big mistake he had just made.

But then, before she even had the opportunity to defend herself, a massive hulk appeared out of nowhere in a flash, surprising both of them. A giant arm wrapped around Jeb's neck in a headlock and then flipped him over in a flawless take-down, slamming Jeb to the ground with a resounding thud, leaving him flat on his back, moaning.

Liv gaped at the towering figure of her Uncle Brody, who stood over Jeb's writhing body, a mountain of resolve. Out of the corner of her eye, she could see Maude hovering near the front door, having emerged just in time to witness the spectacle.

Jeb attempted to crawl back up to his feet, but Brody, with a subtle flex of his muscles, used the heel of his boot to push him back down, warning with a growl, "Stay." He then turned to his niece. "Are you okay?"

Liv's face flushed red with anger. "Uncle Brody, what the hell are you doing here?"

This furious reaction was not what he had expected, and he suddenly looked like a puppy dog who had just been swatted on the nose with a rolled-up newspaper. "Um, I was just watching out for you, kid. We, uh, I mean, I just wanted to make sure you didn't get into any trouble."

"*We?* Who's we?"

She caught Brody furtively glancing to his right. She followed his gaze to a car parked across the street, where she could plainly see her father Jarrod sitting behind the wheel and looking sheepish.

She spun back to Brody. "I don't believe this! Have you two been following me all night?"

"Your dad was worried, you coming to this party on your own, asking a lot of questions. I mean, we don't know who's involved and who's not, so he thought—*we* thought—it would be wise to, you know, keep an eye on you."

Liv's eyes flared, livid. "I'm not a child! I can take care of myself!"

Maude appeared at her side. "Point of order. He did actually just save you from that frat boy Harvey Weinstein wannabe."

"I was ready to handle him, Maude!" Liv snapped.

Jeb had rolled over on his side, clutching himself and wincing in pain. "Can I get up now?"

Liv and Brody both snarled in unison. "Stay down!"

Jarrod got out of the car and jogged across the street to join the group. "Liv, don't be so hard on your uncle. He was just doing what I—"

She furiously cut him off. "Oh, you don't have to explain. I know who the ringleader was in all this. When are you going to stop with this overprotective dad bit?"

Jarrod thought about it. "When you're forty-five?"

"That's not funny!"

Jarrod threw his hands up in the air. "You're right. I apologize. We shouldn't have tailed you. We'll leave. Come on, Brody." But before he turned to walk back to his car, he could not resist adding, "But aren't you glad I made you take that self-defense class when you were twelve? If we hadn't been here, I'm sure you could've—"

"Go! Now!"

"Right, right, sorry."

He was about to try and leave again, but then noticed Jeb on the ground, still moaning. He took a step forward. "If you ever come near my daughter again, I swear I'll—"

"Dad!"

"I'm gone! I'm gone!" Jarrod cried, racing off to his car with Brody marching like a foot soldier in lockstep behind him.

Maude stared lustfully at the backside of the former pro wrestler. "Your uncle is giving off major Marvel superhero vibes. I'm not even exaggerating. He's like seriously hot!"

"Not now, Maude!"

"I know you're upset, I'm just saying—"

Liv shook her head.

This was so typical Maude.

"I guess you're totally over Butch now."

"Who?" Maude joked.

Liv could not help but crack a smile.

"Butch? Who's Butch? Hmmm. Butch . . . Butch . . . Doesn't ring a bell. You know what does ring a bell? Brody. That rings a big bell."

"Take me home, please," Liv begged.

CHAPTER 31

"It is my honor today to stand before such a talented group of individuals who are on their way to making their mark in the world of film," Jarrod said, speaking into a microphone from behind a lectern in a large auditorium at the College of the Desert.

He was surprised by the turnout.

Most of the students in the audience had not even been born yet when he was a television star way back in the 1980s. The film department had been nagging him for months to join their guest speaker roster, but Jarrod had demurred, always coming up with excuses such as "I'm traveling that week," or "I have a scheduled engagement on that day," or most recently, "I'm deep into rehearsals for my new play. I couldn't possibly get away."

But when Professor Lipovsky emailed, hoping to slot him into the program, Jarrod finally relented, especially since Lipovsky himself would be the one to introduce him. It would be so much easier to confront him about why his car had been identified screeching away from the scene of a break-in at Zel's studio.

"Now, I know some of you might recognize me from my days as a child star back in the eighties on a little sitcom called *Go To Your Room!*"

Crickets.

Jarrod felt embarrassed. He had half expected at least a smattering of applause for his signature TV show. He cleared his throat before continuing. "You might remember the catch-phrase that became synonymous with my character: 'Baby, don't even go there!' It's funny how those things stick with you throughout your career."

Still nothing from the peanut gallery.

Just some uncomfortable shifting in their seats.

"But I'm not here to talk about that."

He could see the relief on a few faces down front.

"I want to tell you about what happened after that. I didn't fall into a hole of drugs and despair, like so many other former child stars before and after me tragically have. But my career did come to a screeching halt when, in my early teens, I found myself thrust unwillingly into the limelight, navigating the challenges of fame. At the age of fifteen, I made a decision that was both deeply personal and very public: I came out as gay. It happened at a gay rodeo, of all places, when the press got hold of photos capturing a moment between me and another child star. It wasn't easy, but at that point, as difficult and scary as it was, I felt it was essential to be true to myself."

A good number of the students suddenly sat up in their seats, a little more interested in hearing what Jarrod had to say. Gender, sexual identity, and orientation were big issues of interest for this new generation.

"I can go on about my journey. Transitioning to adulthood, the humbling experience of auditioning for under five guest roles in the 2000s after once appearing on the cover of *TV Guide*, trying to revive a moribund career, but the landscape had drastically changed and so had I."

Jarrod looked around the auditorium.

At least they were listening.

"My greatest achievement turned out to be my ten-year marriage to my adoring husband, Charlie. But you know the saying, if you want to make God laugh, tell him your plans. Life has a tendency to throw you curveballs, and I got hit in the face with a big one. My husband suddenly died. I couldn't stay in Hollywood anymore. Everything reminded me of him. So, I found solace here in the Coachella Valley. And in the midst of my grief, I discovered a new passion: writing and directing plays."

These were film students, so the mere mention of the theatre had the kids slowly losing interest again. Jarrod could literally see their eyes glazing over.

"So why am I sharing all of this with you today? Because it's not just about reminiscing about the past, it's about embracing who you are and finding your own path. Life may take unexpected turns, but each twist and turn contributes to the narrative of your own unique story. To the aspiring filmmakers and storytellers in this room, I encourage you to stay true to yourselves, face challenges with resilience, and never be afraid to go where others might tell you not to dare go. Embrace your journey, and who knows? You may just find yourself directing plays in the beautiful oasis of Palm Springs one day, or you may find yourself on stage accepting an Academy Award for your first feature film. It's up to you."

Much to Jarrod's surprise, the audience erupted in applause. He had gotten them in the end. He had purposefully kept his remarks short so he would have time for a thorough Q&A. He could see the students with their phones out, googling more about him, finally engaged, and he spent the next hour answering their thoughtful questions.

Professor Lipovsky served as moderator and when they finally wrapped up just before lunch and the students filed out of the auditorium after one more round of applause, Jarrod seized his opportunity to corner Lipovsky.

"Thank you, Jarrod, for making the time to come talk with us today," Lipovsky said, pumping his hand.

"I was happy to do it. I will admit, I was nervous at first looking out at all those folded arms and bored expressions."

"I'm sorry we couldn't pay you a speaking fee with our tight budget, but maybe I could buy you a cup of coffee in the cafeteria?"

"No, thank you, I'm good, but there is something I would like, if you don't mind."

"Name it."

"Two days ago, my daughter and I were at her boyfriend Zel's studio, and we ran into an intruder."

Worry lines spread across Lipovsky's forehead. "An intruder?"

"Hiding in the closet. Wearing a mask. I'd like to know if it was you."

Lipovsky's mouth dropped open in shock. "*Me?* What are you talking about? Of course it wasn't me!"

"Then why was he driving your car?"

"Jarrod, you must be mistaken!" Lipovsky snorted defiantly.

"My daughter memorized the license plate. We had it checked. The car is registered to you."

His mind was racing now.

Sweat began forming on his brow.

He grabbed his glasses off the bridge of his nose and wiped them with a handkerchief from his jacket's breast pocket.

"Is this why you decided to grace us with your presence today? Just so you could interrogate me?"

Jarrod did not bother to deny the allegation.

Mostly because it was true.

So why lie?

"Professor, I know about Zel's campaign to sabotage your position here. Some of his classmates said he was relentless with all those TikTok videos targeting you. That must have caused you a lot of undue stress."

"I didn't kill him!" Lipovsky roared, startling a janitor who had just arrived to mop the floor.

Lipovsky gave the janitor a weak wave and then spun back around to Jarrod and lowered his voice. "Two days ago, you say? What time did this supposed break-in occur?"

"Around two in the afternoon."

The tension drained from Lipovsky's face. "Well, there you have it. It couldn't have been me. I was right here. Teaching a class on film theory. In front of forty students."

That would be easy to prove.

Which meant the guy in the gorilla mask was not Professor Lipovsky.

Then who?

"Does anybody else around here have access to your car?"

"No, why would I . . ."

A thought suddenly dawned on him.

"What is it, Professor?"

"No, it couldn't be him."

"Who?" Jarrod pressed.

"Well, on occasion when I need something, I give the keys to my teaching assistant so he can run errands for me."

"What's his name?"

"Sammy Vine."

"Where can I find him?"

"He's in my office right now doing research for an article I'm writing for *Sight and Sound*, the British Film Institute magazine. Come on, I'll take you over there."

They scuttled out of the auditorium, leaving the janitor to do his work in peace, and crossed the campus to the faculty building. As they walked down the hall, they could hear the sounds of hip-hop artist Drake wafting out of Lipovsky's office. As they entered the office, Jarrod spotted Sammy Vine, feet up on the desk, chewing on red licorice, engrossed in reading some information on Lipovsky's computer. He did not even notice them at first.

"Sammy, this is Jarrod Jarvis, he'd like to talk to you about—"

Sammy's eyes slowly rose to meet Jarrod's. His face went pale, and then, without warning, he jumped to his feet, charged them, knocking both men aside, and hightailed it down the hall and out the door.

Lipovsky was on the floor, nursing a banged-up knee, while Jarrod, who luckily just slammed his shoulder against the door, quickly gave chase.

Outside, Sammy darted across the quad with Jarrod in hot pursuit just as an oblivious campus security guard in a golf cart crossed right in front of them. Sammy could not stop in time and ran right into it, lost his balance, then pitched forward, his face landing right in the guard's lap. The guard, finally alerted to the foot chase, grabbed Sammy by his T-shirt and casually glanced up at Jarrod. "What'd this one do?"

"We're about to find out," Jarrod said before bending down and talking in Sammy's ear. "That was you at Zel's studio, wearing a mask, wasn't it, Sammy? You ran because you recognized me from that day and knew you'd been caught."

The guard, a Latino man in his midthirties, big and strong, still held Sammy by his T-shirt as he climbed out of the golf cart. He hoisted Sammy up on his feet to face Jarrod. "Go on, answer the man's questions."

"There's no point in denying it, Sammy. We know there's going to be a traffic light camera down the street that recorded you speeding away from the scene in Professor Lipovsky's car."

"Doesn't sound too good for you, kid," the guard noted.

Sammy glared at the guard, then looked away, refusing to make eye contact with Jarrod. "I want to call my parents' lawyer."

"I'm not a cop," Jarrod said before addressing the guard. "Are you a cop?"

"Nope. I get paid more playing a cop on campus."

"We can't use what you say against you in a court of law. We just want to know the truth."

"I don't know what you're talking about," he spit out. "I wasn't at Zel's studio. I never wore any gorilla mask."

Jarrod nodded. "Okay, Sammy. The thing is, though, when I said you were in a mask, I never mentioned it was a gorilla mask. Now how would you know that if you weren't the one wearing it? Do you know what I'm saying, Sammy?"

The guard grinned. "I do. I know what you're saying. The kid's lying through his teeth."

Sammy's shoulders sagged as he mumbled under his breath. "Yeah, okay, it was me."

"Why were you there? What were you looking for?"

"I had been researching a project about the impact of the Salton Sea crisis that's been going on for a while now, water-quality issues, environmental degradation, and the impact on local communities. I had been talking to politicians, environmentalists. I got some real good interviews to start. I had been working on it for about six months when suddenly all my research and interviews just disappeared. As if someone transferred everything to a hard drive and then deleted it all from my computer and the cloud. I was sharing a house with five other guys. We were all coming and going all the time, so it wasn't hard for someone to gain access to my room. Then, about a month later, Zel announced *he* was going to do a film on the Salton Sea, and that's when I knew it had been him who stole everything right out from under my nose!"

This was becoming an obvious pattern.

First Kenny.

Now Sammy.

And undoubtedly there were more victims of Zel's ruthless ambition out there.

"I broke into the studio to retrieve what rightfully was mine. All that research, the video interviews, they belong to me! That's *my* hard work! I was just trying to get it back since Zel was dead and had no further use for it. I just wanted to salvage my project."

"Did you kill Zel, Sammy?"

The guard holding him gave a vigorous nod. "Oh, the dude killed him, no question in my mind!"

"No, I didn't!" Sammy protested.

"Then where were you on the night of his murder?"

"I was nowhere near Zel's studio. I was in my room getting high off a bong. I was there *all* night."

"Okay, then. You said you live with five guys in a house, so it shouldn't be difficult to prove you were there. One of your roommates must have seen you."

Sammy's face fell. "Uh, no, I mean all the guys went to a hockey game at the Acrisure Arena. Coachella Valley Firebirds versus the Tucson Roadrunners. I was the only one who stayed home. But you gotta believe me, I never left the house!"

Not exactly an airtight alibi.

Which meant Sammy Vine was far from being in the clear.

CHAPTER 32

Jarrod was halfway home from the College of the Desert, waiting at a stoplight, when he noticed the text from Liv: *Maude and I found something big at Zel's apartment. Need you here ASAP. Texting you the address.*

When the next text came through, Jarrod quickly typed the street address into the Waze app that was connected to his Apple CarPlay. The soothing woman's voice guided him to take the next left and drive north.

When he arrived at the single-level apartment complex on a quiet residential street on the north end, east of downtown, he spotted Maude in the doorway to unit seven, waving at him. He got out of his car and jogged over to where she was waiting for him.

"What's up? What did you find?"

"Come on in. Liv will tell you everything."

Upon entering, Jarrod immediately noticed the rancid smell of unwashed sheets and dirty laundry in the small studio. There were dirty dishes piled up in the sink and a film of dust on all the counters and tiny kitchen table. The place had not been cleaned in months, if not longer. Next to the mattress on the floor—there was not a boxspring in sight—were some opened cardboard boxes. Liv was kneeling down, poring through papers and hard drives. There was also an iPad lying on top of a rickety wooden nightstand.

Liv popped up to her feet, a look of concern on her face, as she scooped up the iPad and walked over to join Maude and her father.

"You're making me nervous," Jarrod said. "What's going on?"

Liv gripped the iPad in front of her. "Zel's landlord called me this morning. Apparently on his rental application, Zel listed me as an emergency contact. The landlord told me that I needed to clear out all of his belongings today. He needs to get the place painted and cleaned for the next tenant, who wants to move in on the first."

Maude scrunched up her nose as she glanced around at the mess. "That could take weeks."

"I argued that Zel was paid up until the end of the month, but the landlord said he owed back rent and was willing to forfeit it if I came over and moved everything out today."

Jarrod's eyes darted back and forth between Liv and Maude, a sense of dread settling in the pit of his stomach. "Okay."

"Zel and I always hung out at my place. I rarely came over here to see him."

"I can see why," Maude quipped.

"Anyway, Zel only used this as a crash pad. He was hardly ever here, which is why I never thought to come around and search for clues. Anything of value and importance would be at the studio. Or so I thought."

"We found a couple of boxes in the closet. One of them just had a lot of papers and mementos from when he was a kid, family photos, middle school report card, high school yearbook, that kind of thing," Maude explained. "But the other one . . ." She gestured toward the box she had been rifling through. "The other one was filled with a bunch of handwritten pages and printed-out articles for a super secret project he had apparently been working on."

"What kind of super secret project are we talking about?"

Liv tapped the passcode on the screen and handed Jarrod the iPad. "I've never seen this iPad before. It's an older version of the one he always carried around with him. There was nothing on it except one unlabeled video in a folder. I figured he must have downloaded it to this second iPad before wiping it from the cloud. He didn't want anyone to find it."

"What's on the video?" Jarrod asked, hesitant.

Liv pursed her lips. "Maybe you should just watch it."

Jarrod was not sure what to expect but went ahead and pressed Play. The video was grainy and dark at first, like the phone that was recording was inside someone's coat pocket. But then, as it emerged into the light, Jarrod could make out a familiar room. The image was shaky at first but soon settled right in front of the vibrant colors of the American flag and a large nineteenth-century partners' desk, one Jarrod had seen many times on the news.

It was the Resolute Desk, a gift from Queen Victoria of the United Kingdom to President Rutherford B. Hayes in 1880. The desk had been used by many US presidents since then and had become a symbol of the presidency.

Jarrod gasped. "This is . . ."

Liv nodded. "The Oval Office. At the White House."

"Who's recording this?"

"I have no idea, Dad. But keep watching."

A man in his thirties, in a Brooks Brothers suit and tie, was nervously pacing back and forth in front of the desk. Jarrod could hear a door opening off-screen. The suit stopped, halfway out of frame. "Mr. President, we need to talk."

A deep baritone voice answered. "Let's clear the room, please. I need to speak with Gerry alone. Except you, Chad. You stay."

Chad apparently was the one who was secretly recording the conversation.

Jarrod could hear some shuffling as people who had just entered promptly exited the Oval Office and a door closed behind them. A distinguished, handsome man in his midsixties with graying temples and a few lines across his face that bore the signs of stress from such a weighty job entered the frame, taking a seat behind the Resolute Desk.

Jarrod's heart sank.

This was President Frank Reynolds.

Kitty's late husband.

"What's got you in such a tizzy now, Gerry?"

"It's serious this time. Harcourt has been asking questions about the Jackson confirmation."

"Harcourt's always asking questions. That's all he knows how to do."

There was a pause.

"I'm not worried," Reynolds said quietly.

"You should be. Harcourt's the ranking member of the Senate Committee on Homeland Security and Governmental Affairs. What if he calls for an investigation?"

"He's free to do as he pleases. We can't stop him."

"You need to stop making light of this. If senate investigators start sniffing around, do you honestly think they won't find out?"

"Find out what, Gerry? Whatever transpired between you and Governor Jackson had nothing to do with me."

"Is that your strategy now? Just play dumb? Come on, Frank. We both know you were fully aware of what we were doing. Hell, you encouraged it. We laughed it off when Jackson claimed his first priority was to the good people of Wisconsin, when, meanwhile, behind the scenes, he's willing to do anything in order to get a Cabinet appointment."

"So what? Political favors are exchanged all the time. It's just part of the process. There's nothing new here for the press to chew on," Reynolds scoffed.

"You're deluding yourself. We're talking bribery, kickbacks, election interference. Without Jackson and his operation, we would've lost Wisconsin, and you would be a one-term president. This will be bigger than Watergate, Iran-Contra, and Monica put together!"

An ashen-faced President Reynolds gave a slight nod.

"We need to sweep this under the carpet. If Harcourt runs with this and the Dems find out, we're done, finished. There will be an unending news cycle with all of Washington calling for your resignation."

"I need to think about this," Reynolds insisted. "You and Chad are to stand down until you hear from me, got it?"

"Yes, Mr. President," Gerry said.

"Now, can we get on with the meeting? I have to get upstairs and change into my tux soon. I have that state dinner with the Australian prime minister tonight."

As they could hear the door opening and people filing back into the Oval Office, the video ended.

Jarrod stared at the blank screen. "Who's Chad?"

"I don't know," Liv said. "Gerry is obviously Gerry Conklin, the president's chief of staff."

"How did Zel get his hands on this?"

"Not a clue."

"They must have succeeded in burying this whole scandal because it certainly never came out when President Reynolds was still alive," Jarrod noted.

"But, Dad, if it came to light now, all these years later, it would permanently tarnish his legacy."

"Yes, but he died years ago. It can't hurt him now."

"Exactly. But there is someone it *could* hurt. The one person who has devoted her life to protect his reputation and legacy . . ."

"Oh, come on, Liv! Kitty? She's one of my closest friends!"

"I love her too, but if she somehow found out what Zel was doing, who knows what lengths she might go?"

"Liv, stop! Kitty would never. I mean, yes she's very protective of her husband's reputation, but it's ridiculous to think that she would ever . . ."

His voice trailed off.

Because that sense of dread that had settled in the pit of his stomach was starting to grow so fast now that he could hardly breathe.

CHAPTER 33

The sun had already retreated behind the majestic Mount San Jacinto as the former first lady of the United States sat in her dimly lit study, curtains drawn, her hands gripping both sides of the iPad that Jarrod had just handed to her.

Jarrod, hovering behind her, reached down and pressed Play. He had not given her much warning about what she was about to watch, just that it involved her late husband while he was still in office and how Liv had accidentally stumbled across it at Zel's apartment.

As the images unfolded, a mixture of nostalgia and apprehension played across Kitty's face. Jarrod observed her reactions like a director scrutinizing the emotional nuances of a pivotal scene.

Then came the moment where President Reynolds dismissed his staff so he could speak privately to his chief of staff. Jarrod held his breath as the scene unfolded, and the flickering images reflected on the first lady's face, a canvas of emotions. Her jaw tightened as her beloved husband, a specter of the past, seemed to engage in a conspiratorial cover-up.

The video finally ended.

The screen went black.

Kitty continued staring at it pensively.

Jarrod, sensing the gravity of the situation, and what he had just done, chose his words carefully. "I know this must come as a shock, but I'm fairly sure I was right to show you this."

Kitty did not respond.

"Am I wrong? Should I have kept this to myself?"

Finally, Kitty climbed to her feet and handed Jarrod back the iPad. "I need a drink."

Then she marched swiftly out of the room.

Jarrod jogged behind her, catching up to her in the much more brightly lit living room where she veered behind the wet bar, plucked a bottle of scotch off the shelf, and poured herself a glass.

She knocked it back.

"I thought you liked your scotch on the rocks."

"There was no time for rocks."

"Kitty, I have to ask, did you know about this?"

"Of course I didn't know about it! But after watching it, my own personal takeaway is that Frank thought about it and then decided to do the right thing and not participate in a cover-up. He probably washed his hands of the whole thing."

"If there was no cover-up, then why didn't the story ever come out in the press?"

"Maybe the journalists never got wind of it, or maybe they could never fully connect the dots. I don't know, but as far as I'm concerned, this video proves nothing. Even if it somehow found its way on the Internet, I don't think it would affect Frank's legacy in a negative way. If anyone comes off looking bad, it's Gerry Conklin. He's obviously pressuring Frank to do something illegal." She noticed the skeptical look on Jarrod's face. "You didn't know my husband, Jarrod, just what you saw on the news or the late-night comedy shows that caricatured him mercilessly. He was a good man with good morals."

"I know you loved him very much . . ."

"I didn't just love him, Jarrod. I knew his heart better than anyone. He was not a corrupt man. He always tried to do the right thing. Gerry is the real villain here. He's the one to blame. I never trusted him. I thought he was always out for himself and not concerned with remaining loyal to the president."

"Did you tell Frank how you felt about Conklin?"

"Yes, but I never pressed too hard. I remember the hell Nancy Reagan and Hillary Clinton went through when they tried offering their opinions on Cabinet choices and policy making. The press just wanted to talk about what dress I wore when I met the Queen of England, and how it was too showy."

"I remember that dress. You looked fabulous."

Kitty mustered a half smile. "I always thought Gerry would turn out to be his own worst enemy, show his true colors, get kicked to the curb, then in an act of pure desperation, write a tell-all book about his time in the White House to pay off all his debts, and then mercifully just vanish into history. But he lasted well into Frank's second term, much longer than I, or anyone else for that matter, ever expected."

"Where is Gerry now?"

"About a fifteen-minute drive away. He and his wife live in Palm Desert and spend most of their time on the golf course. Needless to say, we rarely socialize. I thought about taking up golf. Wouldn't Jim look so handsome in a classic Arnold Palmer golf shirt with khaki shorts to show off those muscular legs?"

As if on cue, Jim sauntered into the living room from the kitchen. He was in a casual print short-sleeved shirt, tight enough to accentuate his biceps and abs, and a pair of gray shorts. "Anything you need, Kitty?"

"No, Jim. We're fine. Thank you."

Jim did an about-face and walked back toward the kitchen. Jarrod and Kitty watched him go, their eyes involuntarily drawn to his perfectly round butt.

They exchanged a subtle glance.

Then Kitty broke into a sly smile. "Go on, Jarrod. Ask me."

"Ask you what?"

"Where I was on the night of that young man's murder?"

"Kitty!"

"No, I'm flattered that you would consider me a suspect. Why else would you show me that video? You wanted to gauge my reaction, see if I betrayed any hint that I knew about the cover-up or was somehow involved."

"I could plainly see that you were blindsided by the video, so no, Kitty, you're not a suspect in my mind."

"Still, I clearly had a motive. Can you imagine me, former first lady of the United States, Kitty Reynolds, a cold-blooded killer? But alas, darling, I have a solid alibi on the night in question. I was playing cards with four other ladies right here in this living room."

"So, you have five people, your friends and Jim, who can corroborate you being home all evening. That's not just solid, that's airtight."

"I love when you get all Jessica Fletcher on me. It's so endearing. Oh, but it was Carl, not Jim."

"Who's Carl?"

"Another Secret Service agent who rotates in when Jim is off duty."

"Jim was off duty that night?"

Kitty poured herself another drink. "I know what you're thinking, Jarrod. If I was aware of the video and I did want that filmmaker dead to protect my late husband's reputation, why not just have my loyal bodyguard carry out the nasty deed? If he's willing to take a bullet for me, why not go the extra step? It's a fanciful theory and utterly ridiculous, like the plot from a James Patterson novel," Kitty chuckled.

Jarrod found himself nodding in agreement. Although a part of him could not ignore the possibility that Kitty had just laid out the truth in brazen fashion.

What if he was wrong?

What if Kitty had performed her part superbly, feigning shock and indignation, pretending to be viewing the video for the first time when he showed it to her? After all, the woman had spent eight years in the White House wearing different masks since it was not politically expedient to show her honest emotions in front of the public all the time. All politicians and their spouses have to be professional actors in some respects.

If Jarrod did not know Kitty as well as he thought he did, then Jim was indeed a plausible suspect.

And he needed to be investigated.

CHAPTER 34

"Jim, I want to apologize for being so rude the other day at the gym," Jarrod said at the door as he was leaving Kitty's house.

Jim seemed surprised. But then he reverted to his familiar stony expression, pure professional all the way, and he simply shrugged. "No problem."

Jarrod looked around to make sure Kitty was not around. She had said she was going to her bedroom to change for dinner, and he knew if she overheard their conversation, she would immediately suspect Jarrod's motives.

And she would be right.

"I guess I kind of panicked in the moment. I haven't dated in a long while and, well, you're a lot younger than me, and I know Kitty has it in her head that we would make a good match. I didn't want you to feel obligated to ask me out—"

Jim shrugged again. "It's just dinner. I'm not looking to put a ring on your finger."

Jarrod chuckled. "You're right, you're right. Fun fact about me. I have been known to overthink things."

Jim smirked. "You don't say."

"So how about you let me make it up to you? Dinner, tomorrow night? I know it's your night off from Kitty duty."

Jim hesitated.

"My treat. You like wiener schnitzel? I know a great Viennese place in town, Johanne's."

"Okay. Tomorrow night."

"Great," Jarrod chirped, not knowing whether to shake hands or go in for a hug. He panicked at the last moment and just patted Jim's massive bicep with his hand.

It was very awkward.

"I'll text you with the details tomorrow."

Jim gave him a slight nod. "Good night."

And then Jarrod slipped out the door.

Mission accomplished.

He tried not to let the guilt consume him as he walked to his car. The whole idea of the date was to get Jim in a social setting, relaxed after a bottle of wine, maybe he could nudge him to talk, find out more about him, and if he actually was the kind of loyal bodyguard who would literally do anything to protect Kitty.

He hoped that Jim was as kind and morally upstanding as he appeared.

But he had to know for sure.

The following evening, Jim had already arrived and was sitting at a table for two by the window at Johanne's when Jarrod showed up. Of course the Secret Service agent was prompt while the flighty Hollywood actor rolled into the restaurant ten minutes late.

Jim stood up as Brigitte, the beloved white-haired German hostess in her late seventies who was wearing a sparkling black top and deep red lipstick escorted Jarrod to the table.

"Enjoy your dinner, Jarrod," Brigitte barked in a heavy German accent before rushing away to greet a couple who had just entered and were waiting by the hostess station.

"I see you've been here before," Jim noted.

"When you don't cook much, all the restaurants in town tend to know you."

Jim had cleaned up rather nicely.

Very Palm Springs smart.

A navy blazer, baby-blue shirt with the collar open to show off his bronzed hairy chest, white slacks. Jarrod clocked Kitty's favorite colors, and so he could only assume she had been consulted on his wardrobe choice. Which also meant Kitty knew what was going down. So far, she had not called Jarrod to protest. Maybe she assumed Jarrod's reasons for asking Jim out on a date were actually on the up-and-up.

And that just made Jarrod feel all the more guilty.

"You're looking very dashing tonight, Mr. Stratton."

"So are you," Jim replied, but his eyes were on the menu and not Jarrod.

After ordering a bottle of Pinot Grigio, the two of them decided to share a decadent cheese spätzeln loaded with lobster and bacon before ordering their main course. Jarrod noticed other tables, both women and men, stealing glances at them, but he knew their gazes were not fixed on him but rather the startlingly good-looking Jim.

They spent the better part of the evening discussing their backgrounds, their history, past relationships. Jarrod was very candid about Charlie being the love of his life who could never be replaced and how he was not even sure if his heart could be open to someone else, although it was worth a try.

Jim, much more reserved, kept things close to the vest other than what he already revealed about taking care of his ex after he suffered a debilitating stroke. In that respect, he was the opposite of Jarrod. Jarrod was an actor, after all, and actors love talking about their feelings, their desires, their hopes and dreams, and just about anything else that came to mind.

Basically actors love talking about themselves.

By the time their entrees arrived, both men had settled on the restaurant's signature dish, wiener schnitzel.

Jarrod knew the clock was ticking and that he had to somehow subtly steer the conversation in the direction of Zel's murder.

Subtle being the key word.

And Jarrod always struggled with being subtle, both as an actor and as a human being.

"I hope you can come see the play I wrote and directed. We open in a few days."

"I knew you were directing a play. I didn't know you wrote it."

"Yes. A murder mystery. Very Agatha Christie. I'm obsessed with murder and mayhem. I mean, not obsessed, that would be really creepy, but I have been known to dabble in a little crime solving every now and then."

"Kitty may have mentioned something about that."

"Anyway, I'm terrified of opening night. I hope we're ready. The rehearsals haven't exactly boosted my confidence. Plus I missed a couple recently because I've been so focused on a real-life crime, as I'm sure you know."

"Your daughter's boyfriend. Yes. I was very sorry to hear about that. How's she doing?"

"Better. It was such a shock. But the more I dig into this, the more I discover there was so much about him that Liv was in the dark about. I was floored when we discovered he was working on a secret project that was going to upset a lot of people. Important people."

Jim appeared curious but did not pry.

He just took another bite of his schnitzel.

"People you probably know."

Jim looked up from his plate. "Me?"

"I can't get into specifics at this time, but Zel was involved in an explosive project that could have hurt people close to you."

Jim set his fork down. "Are we talking about Kitty?"

"I can't say just yet."

Jim was becoming uneasy, sensing a shift in the atmosphere. "Then what are you trying to say?"

Jarrod, his palms sweaty, regretful over how he was handling the subject so far, chose to reverse course. "Nothing. It's not important."

But Jim was not ready to just let it go. "Are you suggesting that Kitty had a motive to kill that kid, and so by association, then I must be a suspect too?"

Boy, he was a master at putting the pieces together. He would no doubt make a better sleuth than Jarrod. And he would probably be a lot more subtle in his interrogation techniques to boot.

Jarrod was now feeling queasy.

This whole thing had been a mistake.

"Jim, I may have had an ulterior motive for asking you to dinner tonight, but let's just forget about all that and enjoy our dinner. I promise not to—"

It was too late.

Jim, insulted, pushed his chair back from the table and threw the napkin that had been resting on his lap down on top of his plate and stood up abruptly.

"Jim, wait! I didn't mean to upset you. I just—"

"I feel so stupid. I thought this date was legit. Not some ploy to pump me for information." He scooped his wallet out of his back pocket and pulled out a hundred-dollar bill, slamming it down in the middle of the table. "Good night, Jarrod."

He stormed out of the restaurant.

Jarrod, trying to salvage the situation, jumped up from his chair and chased him out, nearly colliding with a waiter carrying a tray with four entrees, and catching the ire of a bemused Brigitte, who did not appreciate him running around and screaming in her restaurant.

Outside on the street, Jarrod managed to catch up with Jim, who was halfway to his car. "Jim, I'm sorry. I never should have brought that up. Please, give me another chance."

Jim scoffed, frustrated. "Another chance? You used our

date to dig into my personal life as part of your own little murder investigation! I'm done, Jarrod."

Jarrod, desperate, tried to grab Jim's arm, but he yanked it away and stalked off into the night.

"Jim, please. I messed up. I didn't mean to ruin our evening!"

But Jim was already gone, and Jarrod was left standing alone on the sidewalk, regret written all over his face.

CHAPTER 35

Jarrod knew he was in deep trouble the moment Kitty called and said she wanted to see him immediately. It was in the aftermath of his disastrous date with Jim, and there was no doubt in his mind that Kitty had pressed him about the details when he had returned home.

And knowing Jim, he had probably been very forthright about Jarrod's abysmal behavior.

Jarrod had tried calling Liv to rush over to his house for moral support, but she had not answered. As for Brody, he was out for a hike and would not be home for hours, so Jarrod was all on his own to face the wrath of his dear friend, if he would still be allowed to call her that.

When Kitty arrived, she swept through the front door, a bundle of furious energy. Before Jarrod could even offer her something to drink, she was shouting at him. "Jarrod, how could you? I am beside myself! I am so disappointed in you!"

Jarrod, like a puppy with his tail between his legs, lowered his gaze. "I take it this is about my ill-fated date with Jim last night?"

"A *date*? Is that what you're calling it? It wasn't a date, Jarrod, it was more like a grilling, some intense police interrogation designed to illicit a confession!"

"Is that how he's categorizing it?"

"No, that's what I could only assume when I simply asked if he had a nice time with you. Believe me, Jim is a man of few words, so I had to drag the details out of him, but I managed to get the gist of how the evening went."

"Kitty, I'm sorry, but Liv and I are knee-deep in this investigation, and we can't ignore any possibility, even one as remote as—"

She raised her hand for him to stop talking. "Would you like to know where Jim was on the night Liv's boyfriend was murdered?"

"Uh, yes, if he has an alibi—"

"He was at Stonewall Gardens."

"The retirement home?"

"Yes, the assisted living facility for LGBTQ+ residents. Who knows, maybe you'll wind up there someday."

He let that one fly by.

Because he deserved it.

"Does Jim have a friend or relative who resides there?"

"No, Jarrod. He volunteers there on his nights off. He sits down with them, talks to them, plays cards with them, watches movies, and discusses books with them. He shares stories about his life in the Secret Service. I hear from the staff that the residents adore him and look forward to his visits every week."

"I'm sorry, Kitty. I didn't know."

"Of course you didn't. Because you never bothered asking me. I could have told you Jim had nothing to do with this sordid murder that you've become so obsessed with solving."

Jarrod looked out the window. "Where is he now?"

"Standing guard outside. I'm sure you understand why he prefers not to come in here. Jim is the most decent, honorable, morally upstanding man I have ever met. And I broke bread with Nelson Mandela and helped build homes with the Carters back in the day!"

"Of course. You're right. I should go apologize to him—"

"No, I think you've done enough."

"But I feel awful."

"I think the best thing would be for you to just let it go at this point. If you keep trying to contact him, you'll start looking like some sort of unhinged stalker."

Jarrod nodded, guilt-ridden. "I won't bother him again. I promise."

"Good," Kitty said with a crushing sense of finality.

As she turned to go, Jarrod reached out and touched her arm. "What about us? I hope this hasn't damaged our friendship beyond repair. I wouldn't know what to do without you in my life, Kitty."

Her mask of anger and indignation faltered slightly, but he could see that she was still furious and not about to cave just yet. "We'll talk when I've had the chance to cool down. Goodbye, Jarrod."

And then she stormed out.

At least there was a glimmer of hope.

He would take anything at this point.

CHAPTER 36

Jarrod could never bypass the giant Marilyn Monroe statue that had found its permanent home next to the Palm Springs Art Museum. The twenty-six foot statue, a tribute to Marilyn in all her glory, captures one of the most iconic moments in film history. Monroe stood atop a New York City subway grate, her white dress billowing up around her as a train passed below. The pose captured a perfect blend of innocence and sensuality, showcasing Monroe's beauty and charisma with a majestic backdrop of the towering San Jacinto Mountains behind her. No other art piece, now a must-see tourist attraction, could ever sum up the association between Palm Springs and the glitz and glamour of Hollywood by evoking a sense of nostalgia, contributing to the retro and vintage vibe that the city was known for with its rich mid-century modern architectural history.

After a brief stop to marvel at Marilyn's fabulousness, Jarrod checked his phone.

It was almost one o'clock.

Kitty had sent him a text earlier that morning informing him that she had a board meeting at the museum to review several upcoming exhibitions, but she expected it to be wrapped up by one. She wanted to meet with Jarrod and told him to wait for her in the hallway between the Meditations in Glass and Contemporary African Art exhibits.

Although Jarrod had a dentist appointment on the books for that morning, he rescheduled. There was no way he was going to miss the opportunity to apologize again to Kitty and hopefully patch things up between them.

The meeting ran late, and it was almost one thirty before Kitty finally appeared in a canary-yellow top and white skirt.

Jim, in a Lacoste navy-blue shirt and khaki shorts so tight Jarrod wondered where he could possibly conceal a weapon, shadowed her from behind.

At the sight of Jarrod, he stopped short and hung back as Kitty continued approaching.

"I was so happy to get your text," Jarrod blurted out. He reached out to hug her, ignoring Kitty's stiffened posture. It was an awkward hug, but Kitty did pat him a few times gently on the shoulder before taking a step back.

"I don't have a lot of time. I'm due at the McCallum Theatre to discuss adding a Renée Fleming concert to next season's schedule."

There was not a cultural event in the entire Coachella Valley for which Kitty Reynolds was not somehow involved in the planning.

"Kitty, I just want to say—"

She raised a hand to silence him. "I know you're sorry. I know you can't help yourself. George and Leo explained to me that it has always been in your nature to be nosy and rude . . ."

"I might have said curious and determined."

"I'm sure we'll be able to move past it, but right now this isn't about you. This is about Jim and his reputation and my intention to prove once and for all that he is a good and decent man incapable of any wrongdoing."

"I believe you," Jarrod said, glancing over at Jim, who was

pretending not to listen. "He was at Stonewall Gardens the night of the murder. There's no way—"

"I know. But I'm afraid if this video and the cockamamie theory about Jim committing murder on my behalf somehow becomes public, I don't want rumors running rampant on social media that perhaps he enlisted the help of one of his Secret Service buddies to do his dirty work for him or that there is some cabal of rogue agents running around assassinating anyone who might expose the misdeeds of the Washington elite."

"That's absurd. I promise it won't get out. We're the only ones who know so far, you, me and Liv . . . oh, and Liv's friend Maude."

She grimaced. "Yes, I've met chatterbox Maude. You can't make a promise like that. These stories always find a way to surface. That's just the world we live in now. Easily debunked conspiracy theories flooding social media and people actually believing them. Jim's reputation has been sullied, and I am here to make sure that if you and Liv insist on playing Holmes and Watson, then you should zero in on the person who is *actually* responsible for the murder."

"Do you have a name?"

"Yes, we already discussed him. Gerry Conklin."

"From the video?"

"Frank's chief of staff. As I mentioned, he's still alive and kicking, and he recently declared his candidacy for US Congress in his home district of Riverside County. The last thing he needs at the moment is for some political scandal from his past bubbling up to the surface and being revealed to the world in an incendiary documentary film. Something like that would blow up his entire campaign. Even in this day and age."

"Does Conklin really have the stomach for murder?"

"I've known Gerry Conklin for decades. I wouldn't put it past him," Kitty sniffed.

"That's a pretty heavy allegation."

"I don't point fingers lightly, Jarrod, because you never know when they'll be pointed back at you. But Gerry is, well, how did my daughter Patrice put it? Oh yes, Gerry's a real slimeball. Not one to be trusted. He's morally bankrupt, which is ironic because his whole campaign is about restoring honor and integrity to Washington politics. Can you believe that one?"

"So, you think he'd be willing to do anything to save his own hide," Jarrod noted.

Kitty nodded. "Even if he didn't do the deed himself, Gerry has built up his brand, this whole 'us against them' strategy, and he has enough blind followers devoted to his cause who might be willing to take care of a problem for him. You know, Jarrod, how you believed it was me who wanted that man dead and that I had Jim ready and willing to do my handiwork?"

The guilt returned to the pit of his stomach. "Kitty, I don't know how many ways I can apologize . . ."

"You can apologize by finding proof it was Gerry and his circle who are behind this."

"But he's never going to talk to me. I have no connection to him, no contacts who can even get me in the same room as him."

"I know," Kitty said with a sly smile. "But I do."

CHAPTER 37

The car ride in Kitty's Mercedes to Palm Desert was tense. Jim gripped the steering wheel so tight Jarrod could see the whites of his knuckles. Jim's eyes were fixed on the road, not even a crack of a smile, ignoring Jarrod who sat alone in the back as Kitty prattled on in the front passenger's seat about the reaction she was sure to elicit when she crashed Gerry Conklin's fundraiser party. She explained that technically she was not crashing because she had received an invitation via email, one of those generic political pleas for money trumpeting the possible end of democracy as we know it if Gerry was not elected to Congress where he can heroically fight for a better tomorrow. Kitty had just neglected to RSVP, and so no one would be expecting to see her, least of all Gerry. She thought the element of surprise could serve them well as they investigated whether or not Gerry was aware of Zel's top-secret film project.

As they arrived at the private gated driveway that led to the sprawling single-story family estate, Jarrod had to wonder where the Conklins got all their money. This property had to be worth between three to four million dollars and Conklin had spent his entire career in government service, with no rich book deals or pricey speaking engagements in his portfolio, at least from what Jarrod had been able to assess in his initial investigation into Conklin himself.

Perhaps his wife came from money.

A young valet dressed all in white jogged up to the car as they got out of the Mercedes and happily took the keys from Jim, who circled around to the passenger's side to help Kitty out, placing a protective hand on her lower back as he led her toward the house.

Jarrod lagged behind, still ignored.

The house was filled with casually dressed wealthy guests who looked as if they had just arrived straight from the golf course.

As Kitty swept through the front door to the expansive living room, heads immediately turned, their faces registering surprise, some even shock. Kitty reveled in the attention, grinning from ear to ear, waving at her many old friends and acquaintances in attendance.

It did not take long for word to reach the hostess that Kitty Reynolds was indeed on the premises, and a long lithe stick figure of a woman in a shimmering red cocktail dress glided across the room, like one of Capote's swans, emerging from the gaping crowd to greet them.

Jarrod hovered behind Kitty as Jim seemed to disappear into the background to keep silent watch.

The woman threw out her bony arms. "Kitty! How long has it been?"

"Too long!" Kitty lied.

The two women air-kissed.

Kitty snatched a glass of champagne from a passing waiter. "I heard you were holding a fundraiser this afternoon and I happened to be in the area, so I thought, why not drop in to show my support?"

The woman stared at Kitty incredulously.

This made no sense at all.

But she was too well schooled in social graces to call her out in the moment. She would suss out the real reason Kitty Reyolds was crashing her party at a later date.

"I can't imagine why you would just happen to pop over to little ol' Palm Desert, of all places. I thought you never leave the confines of the tonier Rancho Mirage."

"Darling, that's a matter of opinion. Over here, you have El Paseo, the Rodeo Drive of the desert," Kitty drawled.

She knew the only reason the Conklins moved to Palm Desert was to help themselves politically. There were many more like-minded voters here than in Palm Springs, or Rancho Mirage, for that matter. "You have a lovely home, Debbie."

Debbie Conklin glanced around. "Yes. It's getting there. We bought it from a gay couple, so I thought when we moved in, there would be very little for me to do design-wise. I mean, I expected perfection, but it turned out they were just two mailmen who won the lottery. So needless to say, *new money*, which of course means limited taste. I had to start over from scratch! God, I went into the walk-in freezer and found a pornographic ice sculpture left over from one of their birthday parties they forgot to get rid of." Debbie guffawed. "Nice guys, though."

"Debbie, this is my dear friend, Jarrod," Kitty cooed, gesturing toward him.

Speaking of gays.

Debbie extended her long bony arm. Jarrod noticed her skeletal hands were rather big for her stick figure. "How do you do?"

Jarrod shook her hand lightly, fearing he might break her brittle fingers if he squeezed too hard.

Debbie's eyes drifted toward the door. "And who is the hot stud too shy to come all the way inside?"

"My Secret Service protection, Jim. He'd prefer that you just pretend he's not even here."

"I'm afraid that's going to be utterly impossible, my dear,"

Debbie whispered, a lustful look in her eye. She glanced around at a few of her guests whose eyes were drawn to the sexy muscular man guarding the door. "He's already garnering more than a few fans just standing stoically by himself in the corner."

"Do you think Gerry will mind that I'm here?" Kitty asked quietly.

Debbie scoffed. "Are you kidding? Gerry would roll out the welcome mat for Charles Manson as long as he's willing to make a donation to his campaign."

"I had to ask, given our history."

Books had been written about the contentious relationship between President Reynold's wife and his chief of staff. Nancy Reagan had gone through a similar situation during her husband's presidency, with a full-blown public feud between her and Reagan's chief aide, Donald Regan. Nancy had worked hard to get him fired after he hung up on her during a phone call. Then Regan, out for revenge, later exposed an embarrassing scandal in a tell-all book about how Nancy consulted an astrologer, Joan Quigley, on her husband's schedule and policies. It was all-out war.

Kitty, when going through the same conflict with Conklin, even consulted Mrs. Reagan for advice on how to handle the toxic relationship. Kitty had always kept Nancy's advice to herself, but as many in the press suspected, Kitty ultimately prevailed in the court of public opinion and Gerry's influence over her husband waned during the final days of his presidency.

So, for the two of them to be in the same room after all these years would have been a political reporter's dream, if anyone had been given a heads-up that it would be happening.

Gerry, for his part, was keeping his distance at the moment, although Jarrod could see him occasionally tossing a quick glance their way as he chatted up his fat-cat donors.

Jarrod knew that Kitty was not exactly fond of Debbie either, having described her as a "serpent" on the car ride to

Palm Desert, but they had remained cordial over the years. Kitty also noted that she would never turn her back on Debbie for any reason, lest she wind up with a sharp knife in it.

Jarrod slipped his hand out of Debbie's, but then she grabbed it back and pulled him closer toward her. "Wait, it just dawned on me. I know you!"

Here it comes, Jarrod thought to himself.

She was just the right age to remember it.

Debbie's face lit up and her wide grin revealed some pretty big blinding white teeth. "Please! Say it! You have to say it!"

"It's been years," Jarrod murmured with a shy smile.

Debbie clapped her hands for encouragement, making him feel like a show pony. He knew he was never going to get out of this, so he struck the familiar pose, one hand on his hip while wagging the other, and shouted, "Baby, don't even go there!"

Debbie erupted in pure delight, laughing and clapping. "Oh my god, when I was in high school, I had a T-shirt with that phrase on it. I thought I was *so* cool!"

Debbie was obviously a couple decades younger than her husband.

"I loved that show, *Go To Your Room!* You were hilarious! When I saw you come in, it took me a moment to recognize you, but now I totally see it. You still have that same twinkle in your eye that you had as a little kid. You're still adorable, by the way!"

"Thank you," Jarrod whispered demurely.

Debbie gripped Jarrod's wrist, dragging him away from Kitty over to a gaggle of similarly skinny women. "Babs, look who it is! Do you remember him from when you were a kid?"

The startled woman stared at Jarrod as if he was a monkey who had just escaped from his cage at the zoo before registering a hint of recognition. "I think so. Was he the boy who starred on *Silver Spoons?*"

"No! That was Justin Bateman!"

Jarrod tried to be helpful.

They were getting it all wrong.

"Actually she's thinking of Ricky Schroeder. Justin Bateman played a supporting character." He turned to the still stumped Babs. "I was on *Go To Your Room!*"

Babs brightened. "I loved that show! Of course! Oh my god, please do the thing. The thing. What was it? What did you always say?"

Definitely a show pony.

Jarrod sighed, struck the pose, and did it one more time. "Baby, don't even go there!"

The gaggle of swans all brayed in unison, then surrounded him and pummeled him with questions about his former glamorous Hollywood life. Jarrod hated to disappoint them. He talked mostly about the many years post-child stardom, slogging to one audition after another, getting resoundingly rejected for almost every role he read for, the curse former child actors endure except for a few lucky ones like Bateman, Jodie Foster, and more recently Selena Gomez.

After a few more agonizing minutes reliving his patchy acting career, Debbie mercifully latched onto Jarrod as if he personally belonged to her, like a Boston terrier, and dragged him around the room to meet everyone. Jarrod lost sight of Kitty, but he could only assume that she was circling Gerry and entertaining herself by making him exceedingly nervous.

Debbie swept Jarrod off on a grand tour of her home after he offhandedly agreed with Kitty about what a lovely house the Conklins had recently bought. After a long dissertation about all the renovations that were necessary to turn the house into Debbie's personal showcase befitting for a political power couple, Debbie led Jarrod to her lush garden outside, a tapestry of colors, with an array of vibrant blooms that painted the landscape in hues of red, orange, purple, and yellow.

Clutching Jarrod by the hand, Debbie guided him down the

stone pathway away from the din of the party, past towering palm trees and graceful eucalyptus shading them from the warm California sunshine.

Jarrod marveled at the abundance of flourishing plants and trees and flowers. "I wish I had your green thumb. It's amazing how lush your garden is given the harsh, unforgiving heat."

"It's all in how you tend to it," Debbie explained. "My secret is I use a super soil. My own special mixture. Organic worm casings, steamed bone meal, Bloom bat guano . . ."

It was as if she was speaking in a foreign tongue.

Her lips curled up into a seductive leer. "But I didn't bring you out here to drone on and on about my garden."

Jarrod's voice cracked. "You didn't?"

"You certainly have grown up since the days when I watched you on TV in *Go To Your Room!*"

"I would say so. I'll be sixty next year."

Was this really happening?

Was Gerry Conklin's serpent wife about to actually make a pass at him?

Had the impromptu tour of the house been orchestrated to lure him out into the garden, away from the other guests, for a secret romantic rendezvous?

Debbie must have missed the scandal back in the 1980s when the paparazzi took photos of Jarrod kissing another post-adolescent child star at the gay rodeo in LA. He had thought the whole world knew he was gay at that point.

He had never tried to hide it ever since.

But alas, Debbie Conklin was clueless because she wrapped her bony arms around Jarrod's waist, pulling him close enough that she could purse her augmented lips and plant a wet kiss directly on his mouth.

Jarrod tried to gently wriggle free but did not want to insult her. But at the same time, she was acting wildly inappropriate, given that her husband was just a few hundred feet away, trumpeting family values in order to replenish his coffers.

This was insane.

For such a stick-thin woman, Debbie Conklin possessed a surprisingly robust physical strength.

Only the sound of a woman's cackle broke Debbie from her spell. She opened one eye to see who was so rudely interrupting her rom-com moment in the garden with Jarrod before quickly shoving him away from her.

It was Kitty, fresh glass of champagne in hand, enjoying every minute as she watched Debbie debase herself. "I lost track of Jarrod, and one of your kind guests pointed me in the direction of your lovely garden. I guess it's true what they say. A leopard can't change its spots."

Debbie wiped her mouth with the back of her hand, humiliated. "We, uh, we just got caught up in a moment."

"*We?* Oh, Debbie, I highly doubt that. I know you're not Jarrod's type. You lack one important and necessary ingredient."

"What's that?"

"A penis."

Debbie's eyes nervously flicked to Jarrod, not sure she believed what Kitty was saying.

Jarrod just stood frozen, not knowing what to say.

"Yes, Debbie. Jarrod is gay. Gayer than a picnic basket."

"Excuse me," Debbie muttered, bolting past Kitty back toward the house.

Kitty, amused, folded her arms and opened her mouth to speak, but Jarrod stopped her by throwing a hand on his hip and wagging his finger in her face. "Baby, don't even go there!"

CHAPTER 38

Jarrod and Kitty made their way back inside, where the party was still in full swing, the atmosphere a little loud and loose after the free-flowing cocktails.

An ashen-faced Debbie had quickly rejoined a few of her fellow swans but kept stealing glances over at Jarrod and Kitty, mortified they might be gossiping about her behind her back.

Nothing could have been further from the truth.

Jarrod's only focus at this point was poking around the house for clues that might implicate Gerry in Zel's murder.

"Okay, Kitty, I trust you can regale everyone with your colorful backlog of stories from the White House in order to distract the guests while I go snooping."

"So, you're utilizing me as a diversion like Barbara Bain in *Mission: Impossible*? I loved her character Cinnamon Carter, who was both alluringly sexy *and* cold as ice."

"Nobody under sixty would even know what you're talking about, Kitty. They only remember Tom Cruise."

"Then they're clearly missing out. The original was by far the superior version. Go, Jarrod, do your thing. I will entertain the masses as best I can. But don't take too long. Most people here have already read my autobiography and could get bored very quickly."

Jarrod squeezed her hand and shuffled off toward the back of the house. Before rounding the corner in the direction of the bedrooms, he swiveled his head around to make sure no one was watching, only to spy Debbie, half listening to one of her stick-figure BFFs, glaring at him.

Jarrod froze in place before collecting himself and mouthing to Debbie, "Bathroom?" He pointed his finger down the hall.

Debbie nodded, eyes still warily fixed on him.

Jarrod gave her a thumbs-up and then scurried down the hall. He started with the main suite where Gerry and Debbie obviously slept. It was furnished with a king-sized, custom-designed bed featuring a stylish tufted headboard and high-thread-count linens in soothing desert-inspired colors. There was a spacious sitting area within the suite, including a designer plush sofa, positioned to take advantage of the breathtaking views and opposite a fireplace for cozy evenings.

Jarrod scoured the room, opening dresser drawers and rummaging through the massive walk-in closet with a wardrobe rivaling Carrie Bradshaw's from *Sex in the City*, but found nothing of significance.

He checked the bathroom, marveling at the sleek, floor-to-ceiling glass walls that offered breathtaking views of the surrounding desert landscape and towering palm trees. A free-standing sculptural bathtub took center stage, positioned strategically to maximize the panoramic views. Jarrod resisted the urge to stop his searching and fill the tub for a long, luxurious bubble bath.

Oh, how he sometimes envied the rich.

The medicine cabinet was stocked with blood pressure and cholesterol meds, Viagra, and lots of over-the-counter headache products like Tylenol, Ibuprofen, and Excedrin for migraines.

The search was a bust.

But Jarrod was not about to give up yet.

There were five bedrooms in this house.

He slipped out of the main suite and across the hall to another guest suite where Gerry kept a lot of his mementos from his time in Washington. Photos of him with various world leaders, an engraved version of the official White House seal, framed presidential speech scripts. But none of them raised any kind of red flag.

The third bedroom struck Jarrod because it was the first that actually appeared to be lived in. The bed was hastily made, the attached bathroom had a used toothbrush and rolled-up toothpaste tube lying next to the sink. There was a half-empty can of spray deodorant and the shower had soap stains.

Someone had definitely been staying here.

Jarrod made a beeline for the closet and found dirty socks discarded on the carpeted floor, one nice suit on a hanger, and lots of wrinkled and balled-up shorts and T-shirts piled high on the top shelf.

Then his eye spotted something in the corner, and he let out a gasp. Kneeling down to do a closer inspection, Jarrod reached in and grabbed a large pair of boots. He stuffed his hand inside one of the boots to check the label.

Size twelve and a half.

The same size as the footprint found at the murder scene. Jarrod turned the boot upside down to examine the heel.

A chill ran down his spine.

The soil caked onto the boot matched the distinctive composition he had found at the murder scene.

It also appeared to be the same kind of super soil that Debbie had just bragged about using in her garden that made it so lush and enchanting. If tests proved that the soil was the same unique mixture Debbie described, then these boots would be conclusively tied to the dirt found at Zel's studio after the murder. This would be the link the police would need to prove it was Gerry Conklin who killed Zel to stop him from exposing his long buried White House scandal.

Without warning, the door to the bedroom flung open and a voice bellowed, "What are you doing in here?"

Jarrod's heart stopped.

He jumped to his feet and spun around, only to be surprised by Jim looming in the doorway.

Jarrod's heart slowly started beating again. "I could ask you the same thing. Aren't you supposed to be watching Kitty?"

"She had to use the powder room across the hall. I can't go everywhere she goes. There are limits."

Jarrod dashed across the bedroom and grabbed Jim by the shirtsleeve, yanking him inside and closing the door behind him and locking it.

"What the hell is this? I can't leave Kitty!" Jim protested.

"I'm sure she's in there with the door locked. I think we both can assume she's safe for a few minutes from a terrorist group that might want to kidnap her!"

He dragged Jim over toward the closet. "You need to see what I found."

Jarrod pointed to the boots. "I believe these are the same boots the killer wore when he murdered my daughter's boy-friend."

Jim looked at him skeptically. "Are you sure?"

"Yes, I'm sure! What, you don't trust me?"

"No, I don't trust you! Yesterday you thought *I* was the killer!"

"It was nothing personal. It's my job to look into anyone who might have had a motive."

"But you're not a detective. You're an actor. And from what Kitty tells me, you don't even do that anymore."

Jarrod's nostrils flared. "That was low, even for you."

Jim sighed. "I'm not trying to insult you. Why are you so sensitive? Is that an actor thing?"

"Don't reduce me to your idea of what an actor is. I'm not a stereotype. Although if we're talking stereotypes, take a look in the mirror. It must be exhausting playing the hard-nosed, humorless Secret Service guy who never cracks a smile. You're more of an actor than I am. I've been watching you."

"I know. You can't take your eyes off me."

Jarrod's mouth dropped open.

He tried mustering a modicum of indignation, but he had been called out accurately and that just made him even more furious.

And neither of them could deny the palpable tension in the air that could possibly lead to one of those classic movie moments when the two leads give in to their attraction in the heat of the moment and passionately kiss.

But it was not meant to be.

Because suddenly someone was rattling the doorknob and knocking.

Jarrod frantically whispered, "Quick, we can't both be found in here. It would lead to too many questions! Get in the closet!"

"No, I have to get back to Kitty."

Jarrod handed the boots to Jim and gave him a forceful shove. "She'll understand. She's supposed to be the diversion for this whole plan, which is why I'm stymied by her sudden decision to go to the powder room during such a crucial moment!"

The knocking at the door persisted.

"Just stay in the closet until the coast is clear."

"The irony of this won't be lost on anyone."

Jarrod slammed the closet shut and made his way over to the bedroom door to unlock it and hopefully con his way out of a heap of trouble.

He took a deep breath before opening the door to find Debbie Conklin with a confused look on her face.

Think fast.

What was he doing in one of the spare bedrooms with the door locked?

This did not look good.

And Debbie, arms folded, was impatiently waiting for an explanation.

CHAPTER 39

Before Jarrod could open his mouth to speak, Debbie planted a hand on his chest and pushed him back in the room, slamming the door shut behind her. Then she grabbed both of Jarrod's cheeks, pulling him closer and kissing him hard on the mouth.

Jarrod struggled to free himself, but Debbie was more determined than she had been in the garden.

Finally, Jarrod managed to wrench his lips free and come up for air.

Debbie took a step back, folding her arms triumphantly, a self-satisfied smile on her face.

"Debbie! Like Kitty said, I'm gay."

"So were most of my college boyfriends, but with a little encouragement and a couple of shots of tequila, they always managed to rise to the occasion. Come on, Jarrod. I just assumed you were being discreet. When you made eye contact with me and gestured toward the bedrooms and then you didn't come back, it didn't take a world-class detective to deduce you were waiting for me in one of these rooms that just happen to have a bed."

"Couldn't you read my lips? I was just looking for the bathroom!"

Debbie looked around, amused. "And yet here you are. You're

right to avoid the main suite. There's a higher chance Gerry might walk in on us. Plus, that man has the nose of a blood-hound. He picks up on scents and would probably know you were tumbling around in his sheets."

Jarrod gripped Debbie by both arms. "Mrs. Conklin . . ."

"Debbie, please. We're too familiar with each other now. I think it's time we dispense with formalities."

"Debbie, this can't happen."

"Yes, it can." She began unbuttoning his shirt as he tried to slap her hand away, but she was undeterred. "Gerry is so wrapped up groveling for money with those stuffed shirts out there, he won't suspect a thing."

"I'm not talking about your husband. This has nothing to do with him . . ."

"Well, I am married to him, so at least tangentially what we're about to do *might* concern him . . ." Frustrated with his shirt buttons, she finally gave up and just ripped the whole thing open.

"Debbie, please, I beg of you, stop talking and listen to me. I'm gay. A homosexual. Maybe not on the scale of the Judy and Barbra and RuPaul-worshipping homosexual, but a homosex-ual nonetheless! This, right here, you and me, this is not going to happen. It's *never* going to happen."

"Then what are you doing in here?"

Before Jarrod could muster up some plausible reason for sneaking around the bedrooms, Gerry Conklin appeared in the doorway, a scotch on the rocks in his hand. "Darling, is everything all right? You suddenly pulled a vanishing act, and I need you out there buttering up the donors . . ." His voice trailed off at the sight of Jarrod with his shirt open. "What's going on?"

"Nothing!" Jarrod blurted out.

Gerry's eyes narrowed and his mood darkened. "Then why do you have my wife's lipstick smeared all over your face?"

"This is not what it looks like!" Jarrod tried assuring him as he began wiping off the lipstick with the back of his hand. But he knew the moment those words escaped from his lips that whenever anyone said, "This is not what it looks like," it usually meant this was exactly what it looked like.

Gerry was not buying it for a second. His eyes flicked to his smug wife, who was enjoying his slow meltdown.

It was obvious she craved any kind of attention from her husband.

Jarrod began to suspect that he was just a pawn in Debbie's game to make her husband jealous.

"I will bury you," Gerry growled at Jarrod.

"Debbie, tell him. Tell him nothing happened here," Jarrod begged.

"I can deny we had sex until I'm blue in the face, but Gerry is immensely jealous. He'll never believe me. So, there's no point in trying to convince him," she said, her lip curling up in a self-satisfied sneer.

Jarrod could see Gerry balling his hands up into tight fists, preparing to strike.

Jarrod's first thought as a longtime actor was, *Oh God, not the face!*

At that moment, Kitty breezed into the room, past Gerry, who reared back, startled by her sudden appearance. She landed right in the middle between Gerry on one side and Jarrod and Debbie on the other.

She glanced around, slightly bewildered. "Where did Jim go?"

"He's not here," Debbie sighed, frustrated at Kitty's interruption, as her desired showdown between her husband and imaginary lover was just getting underway.

"He texted me and told me to meet him here when I was done in the powder room. Where did he go?"

"Well, as you can plainly see, Kitty, he must have left," Debbie said.

There was a thump.

The noise had come from the closet.

They all froze.

Jarrod guessed Jim had probably dropped one of the boots he was holding. He marched over and flung the door open, revealing Jim standing there, holding one boot while the other laid at his feet. In his free hand was his phone.

Jarrod marched over and grabbed Jim around the neck and planted a deep, long kiss on his lips.

Debbie gasped.

Kitty had to suppress a giggle.

Gerry just looked flabbergasted that there was a strange man in the closet.

Jarrod spun around. "This is what I was doing in here, what I was trying to tell you. I came in here to hook up with Kitty's bodyguard, Jim. Look how hot he is!"

Debbie gave him the once-over.

It was obvious she wholeheartedly agreed.

Jarrod stared pointedly at Debbie. "Do you believe me now?"

She just shrugged, still not entirely convinced or perhaps not ready to accept the honest truth.

Gerry scrunched up his nose and turned to Jarrod, confused. "So you didn't sleep with my wife?"

Jarrod threw his hands up in the air. "No!"

Gerry studied Jarrod closely, trying to gauge whether or not he should trust him. "And you snuck in here with him, not Debbie?"

"Yes!" Jarrod cried.

"This is like a French farce, very Molière," Kitty purred.

Jim crossed to Kitty, still holding the boot. "Kitty, I am so sorry. This was completely unprofessional behavior. I would understand if you decide to contact my superior and file a complaint."

"Why would I do that? On what grounds?"

"Dereliction of duty," he said, glaring at Jarrod. "I never should have left your side," he said, anguished, before pointing at Jarrod. "I never should have let *him*—"

Kitty cut him off. "Don't be silly, Jim. No one's filing any complaint. I've been trying to get the two of you together for weeks now, and it looks like I've finally made some progress. I couldn't be more thrilled."

"No, you don't understand. We're not, we didn't . . ." Jim did not know what to say. He obviously wanted to explain to Kitty that there was nothing romantic going on between him and Jarrod while not exposing the fact that he had caught Jarrod casing all the bedrooms for clues that might implicate Gerry Conklin.

But one undisputable fact he did not count on was finally brought up by Conklin himself.

Gerry took a step forward, eyes fixed on the boot Jim was absentmindedly still holding in his hand. "Do you mind telling me what you are doing with that?"

Jim meekly held up the boot. "This?"

"Yes. Were you going to steal it? Do you have some sort of boot fetish? Please, tell us. We're all on pins and needles," Gerry seethed.

Jarrod knew there was no wriggling out of this one.

It was time to come clean.

"We were going to turn the boots over to the police," Jarrod calmly explained. "They're evidence."

"Evidence of what?"

Jarrod walked over and scooped up the other boot off the floor of the closet and then spun around and held it out toward Gerry Conklin. "They tie you to the murder of Zel Cameron."

CHAPTER 40

"Who the hell is Zel Cameron?" Gerry bellowed. "I've never even heard of the guy!"

Jarrod shot him a skeptical look.

Gerry grimaced. "Okay, this is obviously your big Hercule Poirot moment. We're all gathered here, not exactly a stately drawing room but it will have to do. So go on, tell us. How does this murder mystery end?"

"Very well," Jarrod muttered, accepting the challenge. "You're in the middle of a very heated congressional race. The polls are tight. The election could go either way. Any stumble, any unexpected revelation, could sink your campaign before you reach the finish line, so you have to be steady and beyond reproach. You thought you had it in the bag. But then came some very troubling news. A particularly odious scandal from your Washington days working for the Reynolds administration suddenly surfaced. Now I'm not sure whether Zel contacted you for an interview and that's how you found out or you discovered the film project he was working on independently, but let's just say, for the sake of argument, it came to your attention."

"You're way off base, Poirot," Gerry snarled before sneering, "or should I say Miss Marple?"

"Oh yes, let's add homophobia to your bag of tricks. I'm sure your more moderate voters will really love hearing that."

Gerry opened his mouth to respond, but Debbie squeezed his arm, silently begging him to stop talking.

"There was a video of you during your days in the White House orchestrating a cover-up that was floating around. There was no getting around it, no spinning it. You had to stop that footage from ever getting out for public consumption, at least not before the election anyway. So you took matters into your own hands. You went to Zel's studio to somehow convince him to abandon the project, either by bribes or threats, but he was intractable. This was his ticket to the big time. Thoughts of CNN, Fox, all the news networks covering this outweighed whatever you could possibly promise him. He'd be a household name. You persisted, things got out of hand, maybe there was a scuffle, you grabbed whatever heavy object you could get your hands on and bashed the poor kid in the head before slipping out, hoping the police would assume it was just a robbery of some kind."

Gerry stood motionless for a few seconds and then began clapping his hands together. "Bravo. Well done. You've certainly watched your share of *Murder, She Wrote* episodes. I'm impressed. I'm not going to deny what was on that video. I could claim it was some AI-generated deep fake. But it's not. Yep. That was me. I was responsible for the scandal, the cover-up—I cop to everything. I knew there was a chance that whole incident might one day surface during my campaign, but I had already factored in the fallout. It was already baked in. Most of my voters would see that video and think, man, he was willing to do anything to protect his boss, the president of the United States. Those who would be appalled were never going to vote for me anyway. So, when I got word there was a video out there and a documentary underway about the whole affair, I did have my people contact the filmmaker—I never knew his name, by the way—and try to see if they could make it all go away."

Gerry shrugged. "But he was not interested. Our entreaties were dead on arrival." He stared at Jarrod impassively. "You were right about that. He had stars in his eyes. He was picturing himself on stage at the Academy Awards. The next Michael Moore. There was no reasoning with him."

"So you killed him," Jarrod whispered.

Gerry groaned. "No. I didn't. I would never take another human life for *any* reason."

"Then how do you explain the boots I found with the same soil from your garden embedded in the heel, the same super soil, your wife's own personal mixture, that was found at the crime scene?"

Gerry stole a glance at Debbie, who looked utterly perplexed.

"They can't belong to your wife," Jarrod continued. "She has small feet. These boots are size twelve and a half."

Gerry stepped forward and grabbed the boots and sat down on the bed. He kicked off his loafers and shoved his feet into them. He stood back up and tried to walk, almost tripping, then with a self-satisfied grin, announced to those in the room, "I'm size nine and a half. I'm swimming in these. If I tried to wear these boots to go murder someone, I'd fall flat on my face. In the immortal words of the great Johnnie Cochran during the OJ trial, 'If it doesn't fit, you must acquit.' So there. Try convincing a jury it was me!"

He was right.

His feet were way too small.

Then who did the boots belong to?

Jarrod looked around at the messy, lived-in room. "I found the boots in that closet. Who is staying in this room?"

Gerry and Debbie exchanged tense glances.

"It's a spare guest room," Debbie answered weakly.

Kitty piped up. "Debbie, didn't you mention to me earlier that one of your sons has recently moved back home?"

Debbie frowned at Kitty.

She did not dare speak.

Both Gerry and Debbie remained mum.

"Who are you trying to protect?" Jarrod pressed.

Kitty tapped her chin, trying to remember. Then, it came to her. "It's your youngest, Zachary, isn't it?"

"Does Zachary wear a size twelve and a half shoe by any chance?" Jarrod asked pointedly.

Gerry reached for his phone in his pants pocket. "I'm calling our lawyer."

Jarrod marched over to them. "Where is your son now?"

"He's not here," Debbie wailed.

"When is he coming back?"

"I don't know!"

Gerry spoke frantically into the phone. "Hi, Kayla, it's Gerry Conklin. I need to speak with Ray . . . I don't care if he's in a partners' meeting, get him out. It's an emergency!"

Jarrod's mind raced now. "Wait, I remember seeing a family portrait hanging over the fireplace." He dashed out of the bedroom and down the hall, back through the throng of donors and over to the wall with a large portrait of the Conklins and their three grown sons. Jarrod zeroed in on the obvious youngest, and his heart nearly stopped.

He instantly recognized him.

He had met him before.

At the crime scene just hours after the murder.

It was Butch.

Zel's assistant.

Butch was probably Zachary's nickname.

Something his family and close friends called him.

Debbie had mentioned how her sons often helped her out in the garden. Butch must have made the fatal error of not changing out of his boots before heading over to Zel's studio to murder the man he had been working for, all in a misguided effort to protect his father's reputation and legacy and current political campaign.

Jim suddenly appeared at Jarrod's side. "We just caught Debbie sending a text to her son, telling him not to come home. We need to call the police and have them go pick him up before he vanishes into the ether."

Jarrod grabbed his phone to call Detective Jordan.

If Butch was on the run and desperate, there was no telling what he might do.

Chapter 41

Maude, slack-jawed, gaped at Jarrod and Liv, who stood inside her shabby, messy apartment. After bringing Liv up to speed on what they had discovered at the Conklin home, Jarrod and Liv raced over to Maude's to question her more thoroughly about the night of Zel's murder.

Upon mentioning that Butch may have been involved, Maude, stunned, teetered on her feet, causing Liv to worry she might pass out and hit the floor. Liv gently reached out and took her by the arm, trying to steady her.

Once she managed to compose herself, Maude vigorously began shaking her hand. "No, it's impossible. It couldn't have been Butch. He was here with me the whole night. We were together until the following morning when we left for the studio and ran into you and your dad at Zel's studio, where you found the body."

Liv now gripped her by both arms. "Are you absolutely sure? There was no time you two were not together, that you both weren't here in the same room?"

"No, I'm one hundred percent sure. Believe me, I would love to finger that jerk for the murder. How dare he break it off with me by ghosting me! What kind of an a-hole does that?"

Liv put an arm around Maude and guided her to the couch, where they both sat down.

Jarrod stood off to the side, trying not to judge the dirty dishes piled high in the sink and the massive amount of dust-balls on the floor that threatened to take over the apartment like the Tribbles in that classic original *Star Trek* episode.

It was almost worse than Zel's pigpen of a crash pad.

"Walk me through that night, Maude. Where did you go? What did you do? We need to establish a timeline that comports with the time of the murder," Liv pressed, her arm still around Maude's shoulders, comforting her.

"Okay," Maude nodded. She thought for a few moments, collecting her thoughts before speaking. "He picked me up here around seven-thirty and then we went to dinner."

"Where?"

"Lulu's. It was pretty crowded and we didn't have a reservation, so we had to wait for a table. I think it was around nine before we were even seated."

"And you were there how long?"

Maude shrugged. "Ten thirty, maybe eleven. I remember the service was super slow, but I chalked that up to them being so busy."

"What happened after that?"

"We went for a drink at the Village Pub, which was packed. The music was so loud, we decided to head to my place where we could talk some more."

"Do you remember what time you arrived here?"

"Not exactly, but it was before midnight."

"Are you sure?"

"Yes. Positive. I have my lights programmed to turn off at midnight, and I remember they were still on when we got here."

"And then?"

"We had some wine and stayed up talking for a while."

"How long?"

"Maybe twelve thirty, one, I don't remember exactly. We were both a little tipsy when we . . ." She stopped herself.

"When you what?"

246 / LEE HOLLIS

Maude eyed Jarrod guiltily.

Liv immediately picked up on Maude's hesitation. "Liv, you know my dad's not a prude. He lived in Hollywood for years. He's seen it all. When you two went to your bedroom and had sex?"

"Don't say it like that! I'm not a slut. We made love, or at least that's how I thought of it. It seemed pretty romantic to me, but who knows what was going on in that lying prick's— excuse me. I meant to say that lying creep's mind?"

Jarrod suppressed a smile.

"After that, we were both really tired and just passed out. It was probably around one thirty."

Jarrod rounded the couch to face Maude. "Is it possible he waited for you to fall asleep before he snuck out to Zel's studio?"

Maude thought about this scenario and then shook her head. "No."

"Why not?"

"Because I woke up about forty-five minutes later, and Butch was right there, sleeping next to me in bed. I remember seeing the time on the wall clock. It was two fifteen."

Liv sat up, frustrated, looking at her father. "It would have been impossible for Butch to drive to the studio, kill Zel, and then make it back to Maude's place in less than forty-five minutes."

Jarrod rubbed his face with his hands. "Even with the boots as evidence, we can't definitively place him at the crime scene, given what Maude just told us. Like it or not, *she's* his alibi."

"No! I was so hoping to take the stand in his murder trial and see him squirm in his seat as I testified against him. I have the perfect outfit to wear with matching shoes and everything!"

"Sorry to ruin your big Alexis Carrington moment," Jarrod cracked.

"Who?" Liv and Maude asked in unison.

Jarrod rolled his eyes.

He was always forgetting just how young everyone was.

Or maybe how old *he* actually was.

"So, we're back to square one," Jarrod lamented.

Liv stood up and circled the apartment, ignoring the dust-balls and dirty dishes, trying to think. Was it possible they had once again fingered the wrong person for Zel's murder?

But what about the boots?

She and her father had been so certain they belonged to Butch.

Had he lent them to someone?

Was there another suspect who was not on their radar?

As flighty as Maude could be sometimes, she was certain about her reconstruction of the timeline. And like she said, she had no motive to protect Butch after the way he treated her.

Liv's eyes swept across the apartment in a last-ditch effort to see something they were missing.

That's when she noticed the microwave above the stove.

She walked over to it, checking the time on her phone. "Maude, did you know the clock on your microwave is off by an hour?"

"What?"

"It says it's five twenty-three, but it's actually only four twenty-three."

"Did you forget to change it for daylight savings?" Jarrod asked.

"No, it's supposed to automatically adjust for that," Maude said, sitting up, suddenly curious.

Liv tapped a few buttons on the microwave to bring up the settings and check to make sure Maude was correct.

She was.

"The daylight savings feature is on. You don't have to man-ually change the time."

Jarrod crossed over to join Liv. "So why is it off by an hour?"

Maude sighed, stumped. "I-I can't explain it."

Liv gasped, having a eureka moment. "Hold on. You said you woke up at two fifteen and Butch was right there beside you, right?"

"Yes."

"What if it was actually three fifteen?"

Jarrod broke out into a wide smile. "He changed the clocks."

"The wall clock over the television, the one in the bedroom, the stove, the microwave. He changed them all back one hour in order to make Maude believe she was awake at two fifteen when in reality it was three fifteen. And if it was three fifteen, that's plenty of time for him to slip out, kill Zel, and make it back here in time."

"But wait, what about her phone?" Jarrod challenged. "He couldn't have changed the time on her phone."

Maude shot to her feet. "Wait, I remember when I woke up, I couldn't find my phone to see what time it was. I asked Butch if he had seen it, but he was more interested in getting busy again, if you know what I mean, but I was too exhausted. That's when I noticed the time on the bedroom wall clock so I wasn't going to worry about finding my phone until morning. I just figured I left it on the kitchen table."

"And then you passed out again?" Liv asked.

"Pretty much."

"Why were you so tired?"

"It was two in the morning, or so I thought, I was full from dinner, I had downed three glasses of wine, we had just, you know, screwed for like half an hour. Who wouldn't be tired?"

Jarrod approached Liv, curious to hear what was going through her mind. "Do you think he spiked her wine?"

Liv nodded fervently. "Yes. I think Butch slipped something into Liv's wineglass when she wasn't looking that would make her sleepy and waited for her to pass out. He could have then changed all the clocks back an hour, stashed Liv's phone somewhere she couldn't find it, and then snuck out to murder Zel. When he returned to the apartment, he could have climbed back into bed with Maude before gently nudging her awake. Her first instinct would be to check the time. When her phone wasn't handy, she relied on the clock hanging on the wall, confirming it was only two fifteen. But it was three fifteen. When Butch became amorous with her, he knew she was still feeling the effects of the drug and would probably put him off, wanting to go back to sleep. Once she passed out again, he got out of bed and reset all the clocks to the correct time, and then moved Maude's phone to the kitchen table where they had been drinking wine earlier, so she would just assume she had left it there when they had gone to bed. He knew when they awoke in the morning, Maude would have no clue he had manipulated the time in order to give himself an airtight alibi. But he made one unforced error. In his haste, he reset the clock on the oven timer but completely forgot about the one on the microwave. Which is why it is still an hour behind."

Maude applauded Liv's ingenuity and sharp analysis.

But Jarrod was less forthcoming.

He was clearly bothered by something.

"What is it, Dad?"

"If your theory holds up, our only evidence is the time on the microwave clock. That's not nearly enough to build a case."

"And the boots! You have the boots!" Maude exclaimed.

"We spoke to Detective Jordan. He doesn't think the boots are enough to get an arrest warrant, not until they get the test results back on the soil," Liv reminded her. "He's just going to bring him in for questioning at this point."

"If they can find him. But Jordan's right. So far, the boots may not be enough to convict him," Jarrod sighed. "In order to really build a case, the prosecutor is going to need more, and we don't have any physical proof that Butch spiked Maude's wine that night."

"Yes, we do!" Maude declared, scampering over to her kitchen sink. She began grabbing the dishes piled in the sink and setting them aside on the counter until she was able to find a discarded wineglass. Using a dish towel to avoid contaminating any possible evidence, Maude carefully held up the wineglass. "This is the wineglass I drank from that night. If Liv's theory of the case is correct, then there should be remnants of some kind of sleep drug still on it!"

Jarrod rushed over and hugged Maude. "Maude, I love you! Thank God your spirit animal is Pig Pen!"

"Who?" Maude asked.

"Oh, come on. Work with me. What is it with you Gen Z-ers? Pig Pen! From *Peanuts*?"

Maude turned to Liv, confused. "What's he trying to say?"

Liv chuckled. "I think he's just really happy you don't believe in basic housekeeping and that your apartment is a filthy mess."

"That sounds like a backhanded compliment to me," Maude huffed.

CHAPTER 42

Detective Jordan listened politely as Jarrod, Liv, and Maude explained their theory of the case and who they believed killed Zel Cameron, sometimes talking all at once.

Jordan had to raise his hand twice to ask that they speak one at a time because he could not make out what any of them were saying.

Liv allowed her father to take the lead, but Maude just could not keep her mouth shut. She was furious about falling under the spell of a cold-blooded killer and kept inserting her own color commentary.

"He should be arrested immediately!" Maude interjected as Jarrod tried to explain how the microwave clock played a critical role in solving the case. "He drugged me! What if he had put too much in my wine? I could have overdosed! I'd be dead right now, another one of his victims!"

Liv touched her knee. "Maude, please, let Dad finish."

Jarrod shot Maude an admonishing look, then redirected his attention to Detective Jordan. "It all adds up. The time frame of the murder. Turning back the clocks in Maude's apartment one hour to give himself time. The sleeping drug that knocked Maude out so he could slip out unnoticed."

Jordan clasped his hands together and rested his fingers on his chin. "What kind of sleeping drug did you say he used?"

"We don't know," Jarrod answered.

"So, you didn't find a vial or bottle?"

Jarrod shook his head. "No."

"Then how do you know she was drugged? Maybe she just passed out from too much wine."

"Are you suggesting I was lit after three measly glasses of wine?" Maude snorted. "For your information, I have a very high tolerance for alcohol! My mother was Irish!"

Anticipating Jordan's question, Liv reached into her tote bag and extracted the wineglass in question that was wrapped in one of Maude's dish towels. She set it down on the edge of Jordan's desk. "I'm sure if you test it, you'll find traces of whatever drug Butch Conklin used."

Jordan cocked an eyebrow. "This is the wineglass she drank from?"

"Yes," Liv said.

"And it hasn't been washed? It's been like weeks."

Maude folded her arms and let out a heavy sigh. "Okay, I confess! I'm not a neat freak! I'm a slob! Is that a crime? Are you going to arrest me right here?"

Liv squeezed Maude's knee harder. "Maude, stop."

Jordan leaned back in his chair and considered everything they had just told him. Then, he reached across the desk and carefully picked up the wrapped wineglass. "All right, let's see if you're right. I'll give this to the lab guys so they can test it."

Jarrod felt relief washing over him. "Thank you, Detective."

Jordan waited for them to get up and leave but none of them budged. "Is there anything else?"

Maude raised her hand like she was asking a question about microorganisms in her high school biology class. "When are you going to arrest him?"

Jordan held up the wineglass. "Well, we need to get the test results back, and then, if they corroborate your story, we'll get a warrant."

Maude tapped her foot impatiently. "And how long will that take?"

"A day or two. Maybe less."

Maude stomped her foot. "No! It'll be too late! You have to arrest him now."

"I'm afraid it doesn't work that way."

"He'll be long gone by then!"

Jordan looked to Jarrod for an explanation.

"We are fairly certain his parents have tipped him off that the walls are closing in, and so we're very concerned he might do something drastic like try to leave—"

"Don't you see? He's going to flee the country!" Maude cried. "He'll escape to Mexico and hide out in some remote village and change his identity, and his parents will secretly wire him money through back channels so he's able to survive, and then he can live a whole new life and prey on some other unsuspecting girl, and you'll never catch him, and justice will never be served! Do you want that on your conscience?" She had to stop to catch her breath.

Jordan was unmoved by Maude's plea of urgency. "Look, we already brought him in for questioning but didn't have enough to hold him. Tell you what, I'll ask the lab guys to put a rush on it. That's about all I can do. Now, if you'll excuse me, I have other cases I need to work on."

Jarrod and Liv stood up, but Maude remained firmly planted in her seat. Liv tugged on her sleeve, signaling her that it was time to go. Maude finally relented, hauling herself up to her feet and giving Jordan some side-eye before being led out of the office flanked by Jarrod and Liv.

Outside in the hallway, Maude leaned against the scuffed marked wall and banged her head against it. "Why can't he see how dangerous Butch is? How can he just let him wander around freely? He should be behind bars where he can't hurt anybody else!"

"He's got rules he has to follow, Maude," Jarrod said quietly. "If he doesn't go by the book, it will only damage the prosecutor's case against Butch later. One wrong move could get the whole case dismissed."

"It doesn't seem right," Maude muttered.

She banged her head against the wall again in frustration.

Liv forcibly pulled her away from the wall. "My God, Maude, you're going to give yourself a concussion."

"I'm just so angry with myself!"

"What? Why? How are you in anyway responsible for this?"

Tears pooled in Maude's eyes. "I gave you so much grief about your relationship with Zel. How you weren't seeing his true self, how I didn't trust his intentions. I thought you were being so naive and gullible. I seriously questioned your judgment, Liv. And now look. I'm the one who is a damn fool. I completely missed Butch's dark side, and Zel is dead because of it."

"You can't take on that burden, Maude," Jarrod said. "Come on, there's nothing more we can do here. Let us take you home."

Jarrod and Liv guided a distraught Maude down the hall and out of the Palm Springs Police Department. After dropping Maude and Liv off at their respective apartments, Jarrod drove straight home.

He was exhausted.

Playing detective was not as easy as it had been when he was a young man in his thirties, living in the Hollywood Hills, married to a hot homicide detective. Now his bones seemed to creak despite his regular yoga sessions and Young at Heart classes. He would sometimes walk into a room and forget what he came in for. Life was marching on, and he feared he might not be up to the task anymore.

Sixty was the new forty, but sometimes he felt like sixty was more like seventy-five.

But he knew he had to see this through.

He knew how much it meant to Liv.

By the time Jarrod warmed up some leftover casserole for dinner, loaded the dishwasher, and poured himself a nightcap before settling in to watch some Netflix, he received a call from Detective Jordan.

Jordan had not been humoring them.

He had put a rush on it.

The lab tests were back, and it had only been a few hours.

The results were irrefutable.

Although the tests were negative for the usual array of drugs, so-called "party" drugs like ketamine, a sedative, and GHB, a depressant, that predators tended to use in nightclubs, there was a positive result for Ambien, which made sense with their theory. Maude would be of no use to Butch if she was rendered completely incapacitated, but a sleep aid like Ambien would make her drowsy without the effects of the harder stuff, which could cause memory loss, immobility, impaired speech, and loss of coordination. Spiking her wine with Ambien would serve his purpose much more effectively, manipulating her sleep patterns and memories of her time awake.

Jordan informed Jarrod they were in the process of getting an arrest warrant for Zachary "Butch" Conklin.

If they were not already too late.

CHAPTER 43

The heavily painted woman in her late sixties with teased-out blond hair was wearing a rainbow-colored caftan. She stood stoically in front of a defeated, hunched over man in a butler uniform in his late forties, his eyes downcast as she pointed an accusing finger at him.

"It was *you* all along, Reginald! How could I not see it before?"

"Because you don't see me at all! You're only concerned with your snooty, rich, well-connected social circle!" the man moaned. "But me? A lowly servant? I was nothing to you, so why would I ever come across your radar? But you're just playing guessing games. How could you possibly know that I was the one who killed Anthony Towers?"

"Frankly, I don't need to guess. It's the irrefutable proof I have uncovered that has done you in. That fingerprint we found on the night table lamp. We compared it to the one you left on the silver serving tray at my cocktail party yesterday. It was a perfect match."

"I'm a butler. It's literally my job to turn off the lights in Mr. Towers's bedroom!"

"The small cut on your left arm you explained away as a cat scratch from Mrs. Towers's Afghan Millie. We found traces of your skin underneath the victim's fingernails from when he desperately tried fighting for his life as you strangled him in his own bed!"

"But what motive would I possibly have to do away with my employer, the man who signs my paychecks, who ensures my livelihood?"

The woman in the loud caftan locked eyes with the seemingly harmless butler. "You're right. Reginald Blackdown has no motive to kill Anthony Towers. But Scottie Campbell does."

The butler shivered.

"That's your real name, isn't it?" the woman continued. "From Modesto. Whose nine-year-old daughter was killed seven years ago in a hit-and-run accident. When Anthony Towers was there to meet one of his mistresses and was driving drunk."

Off in the wings, Jarrod watched the scene, mouthing the words as they rolled off the actors' tongues.

The butterflies in his stomach had mostly subsided during the first act, but now, as the debut of his new play barreled toward its exciting conclusion and the final curtain, those pesky butterflies had returned again.

They were so close to bringing his baby home.

The actors, whom he feared would crumble on opening night, had actually made him proud.

After a disastrous dress rehearsal, they had rallied with a pep talk from their director, who was like a Super Bowl coach whose team was down by ten at halftime, determined to draw, or rather drag out, their best possible performance.

And in the end, they had not let him down.

By some miracle, everyone had hit the stage running, and they were now effortlessly sailing through the last climactic scene, the classic Agatha Christie drawing room moment when the truth was finally revealed.

Jarrod could see Liv and Brody seated in the front row, eyes glued to the lead actress, Talia, who was channeling her best Margaret Rutherford at the moment.

Suddenly Jarrod felt a sharp pain in the small of his back,

258 / LEE HOLLIS

like the tip of a knife. He tried to turn around, but someone behind him grabbed his face with his hand, smothering his nose and mouth tightly, so it was impossible for him to cry out. Then he felt hot breath against his ear as someone leaned forward and whispered, "Not a sound."

He was roughly yanked away, out of the wings, the knife jabbing him so hard, he could feel a stream of blood trickling down the small of his back toward his buttocks.

Jarrod's eyes frantically searched around for anyone to help, but there was no one else in the wings. All the actors were onstage for the final scene, and the stage manager, Ava, was on the opposite side at a podium with a small penlight following along with a script just in case anyone fumbled their lines, completely oblivious of the assault occurring on the other side, stage right.

Jarrod could sense that the man dragging him away through the wings was big and strong and broad-shouldered. He felt like he was a rag doll in the guy's grip. He glanced down to see the man's large foot, size twelve and a half or thirteen.

There was no doubt in his mind that this was Zachary "Butch" Conklin.

Jarrod reached up to try and pry Butch's thick fingers away from his mouth, but Butch anticipated the move and pressed them down harder, and then angrily shook Jarrod so hard his head started spinning.

He also felt the knife go deeper into his back.

After a few moments, Butch kicked the door to a dressing room open and hurled Jarrod inside. Jarrod tripped over some high heels left lying on the floor and stumbled forward, face-planting right next to the makeup table.

He knew they were in Talia's dressing room.

He heard Butch slam the door shut and lock it from the inside.

Jarrod slowly rolled over and looked up in horror to see

Butch, a wild glint in his eye, unhinged, towering over him, tapping the gleaming tip of the knife against his thigh.

"You're crazy to come here, Butch! There's a warrant out for your arrest. The cops are looking for you everywhere."

"Somehow I don't think the police are here to watch the opening night of your crappy play!" Butch roared.

"Everyone knows what you've done and why. The cops are keeping a close watch over your parents so they don't try to help you flee the country. You're on your own. You might as well end this now and turn yourself in. There's no point in running."

Butch sneered and shook his head. "If I wanted to run, I would be long gone by now. But here I am. Exactly where I'm supposed to be." He knelt down and thrust the knife at Jarrod, who flinched. "Right here with you."

"I know you were just trying to protect your dad by getting Zel out of the picture, but the truth has a funny way of coming out eventually. Your father would never have been able to suppress that video for long, especially if he was elected to Congress. He would be under the spotlight more than ever."

Butch menacingly kept flicking the knife at Jarrod's face, his eye, his nose, his mouth, ready to slash at the slightest provocation. "See, I have another take. Zel was a selfish prick, everybody hated him. There were people who, dare I say, were happy to see him wind up dead. In fact, that frat party you and Liv showed up at, that was kind of a celebration to commemorate a truly joyous moment. Zel Cameron was finally out of our lives!"

"You were there?"

"Oh, I've been busy watching you for a while now, both you and Liv, and I have to say, for an old guy, you've still got smarts. I wasn't worried at first about you running around like some fool wearing a deerstalker and carrying a magnifying glass like some pathetic Sherlock Holmes fanboy. But then you started getting too close, and that made me nervous. By the time my parents texted me, I knew I had made a mistake not taking you seriously. Or Liv. Liv. Wow. What a hottie. Truth be told, I was actually just using poor Maude to stay close to Liv, hoping I might be able to swoop in and comfort her in her time of need. You know, play out that classic storyline, where I'm there for her to wipe away the tears and support her during this difficult time—poor Zel—only for our shared grief to unexpectedly evolve into something more, something romantic and long-lasting. We could have had such a beautiful relationship. I deserve that."

"You don't deserve her!" Jarrod spat out.

Butch gripped the handle of the knife tighter, raising it up, his face reddening with anger. "Well, one thing I know for sure is that Liv has major daddy issues, so I came here, as a friend, to do her a favor and make them all go away."

The knife was high above his head now, his face a mask of rage, as Butch straddled Jarrod, about to plunge the knife deep into his chest like a vampire hunter's stake.

Jarrod, consumed with panic, suddenly jolted his right knee upward, smashing it into Butch's groin. The breath in Butch's body whooshed out of him, and he was speechless, stunned, and knelt frozen in place, the pain ripping through him.

Jarrod had learned that move from a stunt coordinator when he was thirteen and guest starring on *Magnum P.I.* playing the son of a wealthy industrialist kidnapped for ransom by a surfer gang while his family vacationed in Hawaii. Jarrod remembered two things from that week shooting in Waikiki: how sexy Tom Selleck was shirtless and the knee-to-the-groin move he was taught by the stunt coordinator to help Magnum bring down the bad guys in the big climactic rescue scene in act four.

Seizing the opportunity, Jarrod skittered out from under Butch and then did a swift kick to his chest with his right foot, knocking him to the ground. He clambered up to his feet and raced for the door to the dressing room, trying to yank it open but quickly realizing Butch had locked it.

As he fumbled to flip the lock open, he heard Butch behind him, springing to his feet.

Jarrod spun around in time to see Butch, still clutching the knife, lunging at him.

Jarrod ducked in time, and Butch slammed the knife into the door, embedding it in the wood and slicing his hand. He howled in pain.

Jarrod crawled over to grab one of Talia's high heels. He remembered a ridiculous scene from an old movie where somebody got impaled in the forehead with the sharp heel of a shoe, so he hurled it at Butch. It didn't drive through his forehead, but he got a good poke in the eye and grabbed at his face, moaning, giving Jarrod enough time to push past him, unlock the door, and rush out of the dressing room.

He could hear the cast were in the final moments of the play, the last few lines of dialogue.

With an enraged Butch now chasing him down, Jarrod burst out onto the stage in full view of the audience, the klieg lights blinding him as he stumbled around, his actors staring at one another in bewilderment.

Butch stopped short of following him out on stage and stood back in the wings, waiting for his chance to finish him off.

The audience, most of whom were aware that Jarrod was the playwright, just assumed the show was over and the writer was ready to receive his accolades. The theatre erupted in applause, and the curtain started to fall but not before Jarrod caught a glimpse of Liv and Brody in the front row, confused, wondering what was going on.

Two of his actors, Talia and Ira, rushed to Jarrod's side to find out what was happening as Kent pointed off into the wings stage right. "Who's that?"

Jarrod made eye contact with Butch, who never took his furious eyes off him. He kept pounding the handle of the knife against his thigh, anxious to finish what he had started.

Suddenly the ornate red-and-gold drape rose again for the final curtain call.

They all joined hands and smiled and took a deep collective bow. Jarrod was stuck in the middle.

When he glanced over in the wings, Butch was gone. The curtain fell again, and Jarrod bolted off stage right.

He frantically looked around.

Butch had vanished.

As he poked around for any sign of him, he could hear the rustling of the audience filing out of the theatre in an orderly fashion, unaware that a knife-wielding maniac was loose somewhere backstage.

Jarrod reached for his phone to call 9-1-1 when he was joined by Liv and Brody.

"Dad, what's wrong?"

"It's Butch. He's here."

"In the theatre?" Liv gasped.

Jarrod nodded. "He's got a knife."

Brody shook his head. "Man, that guy's got balls showing up here tonight."

"He's not thinking straight. He knows he's boxed in. He's desperate, which makes him even more dangerous," Jarrod warned. "He's got nothing to lose at this point."

Brody, his face etched with grim determination, charged forward. "Come on, let's fan out and find this wingnut."

Brody disappeared into the shadowy recesses of the theatre, searching, before climbing a steel ladder up into the rafters with all the hanging lights where he could get a bird's-eye view of backstage.

The stage manager Ava had called a security guard, who was

now checking all the dressing rooms, and the actors and stage crew were ordered out of the theatre for their own safety.

The security guard, gripping a rubber baton, his only weapon, approached Jarrod and Liv as they helped with the search.

"I think it might be better if you two waited outside," the security guard said.

Liv opened her mouth to protest, but Jarrod spoke before she had the chance. "He's right, Liv. Let's go join the others. The police will catch him."

The security guard headed off in another direction as Liv walked ahead of her father toward the exit when they were surprised by a guttural war cry as Butch suddenly leapt from the shadows, arm raised in the air, ready to slash Jarrod's face with the knife.

The stunned security guard reached for a gun holster that was not there, realizing he only had the rubber baton, which he flung at Butch, but it was a wide miss.

There was no time left to do anything else but watch in horror. Liv screamed at the top of her lungs as Jarrod cowered, expecting the blade of the knife to rip off his flesh.

And then, a body hurtled down from the rafters, smashing into Butch's back, driving him into the floor and onto his stomach, his hands splaying open, the knife clattering across the hardwood floor backstage.

Without wasting a beat, Brody positioned himself on top of Butch, using his knees to pin down Butch's legs, then grabbing his wrists using them as a crossface to control his head and neck, expertly securing a dominant position and limiting his options for escape.

"Blackheart is back, baby!" Brody crowed.

The security guard whooped and clapped, obviously a fan.

Jarrod turned to Liv, who hugged herself, shaking.

He enveloped her in a hug. "It's okay, honey, we got him."

"I-I saw him come at you, and I thought you were going to die, and, and . . . I was so scared, Dad. I didn't want to lose you too."

She broke down sobbing, and Jarrod held her for a long time, even as the faint cry of sirens grew louder and Detective Jordan and the Palm Springs police department soon swept into the theatre, taking custody of Butch from superhero Brody and snapping handcuffs on his wrists before forcefully leading him away.

As all that happened around them, Liv kept holding on to her father as if she was never ever going to let him go.

CHAPTER 44

It only took one phone call from Kitty Reynolds to the owners of Oscar's to secure the location for the opening night after-party. Oscar's, a prominent downtown Palm Springs hotspot that features a diverse lineup of talented singers, dancers, and drag performers and boasting an indoor cabaret space that spills out into a large, beautiful courtyard, was the perfect place to celebrate the play's successful opening, despite the confusing appearance of the playwright on stage during the final moments of the performance.

With most of the audience and a few online theatre critics assuming Jarrod's surprise appearance was actually written into the show, Kitty chose not to shine a light on the awkward moment and just pretended it never happened.

With Jim shadowing her, Kitty weaved through the crowd, greeting her guests, encouraging them to check out the open bar and to taste the handpicked hors d'oeuvres she had personally selected from Oscar's ecletic menu.

Jarrod had urged her not to go overboard, knowing with Kitty in charge, the budget for the after-party would be costlier than the entire production of his play. But Kitty rarely listened to anyone when she was on a mission, and she was determined to mark the event with a fabulous party that would be remembered long after the play closed.

Jarrod, Liv, and Brody arrived late, having stayed behind at the theatre to give statements to the police.

The courtyard was at capacity, and Jarrod thought they might be turned away by security, but as Jarrod was the guest of honor, the guard at the wrought iron gate that led into the courtyard happily welcomed them all inside.

They scanned the crowd for any sign of Kitty.

Brody spotted her by the stage, holding court with a few adoring local gay men Jarrod recognized and a couple of fawning drag queens. Although Kitty's husband had been very careful not to alienate his more conservative constituents during his administration, Kitty was far more accepting, making her views known publicly about her support for gay marriage and basic human rights, much to the consternation of a few of her husband's more hard-line cabinet members. She even hosted a drag brunch at the White House, which Frank had gone along with by stating, "Everyone is welcome at the White House. This is the people's house."

Still, he would have probably lost some key Southern states if he had been able to run for a third term.

Liv whipped around to her father and uncle. "I'm going to get drinks. Red wine, Dad?"

"Yes, thank you."

"Brody?"

"Uh, just a water, thanks."

Liv breezed away, stopping to greet some familiar faces.

"How long have you been on the wagon?" Jarrod asked Brody.

He shrugged. "Not long. Trying to make some positive changes in my life. We'll see how it goes."

Jarrod could see in Brody's hangdog expression that he was not convinced he could do it. He placed a hand on Brody's shoulder. "I want to thank you."

"For what?"

Jarrod chuckled. "Uh, saving my life?"

"Oh, that. It was fun. Made me feel like I was back in the ring again."

"Well, as much as I know you'll try to brush it off, you must know that if you hadn't been there, I probably wouldn't be here now."

"It was nothing. Easy peasy."

"See? Brushing it off. Brody, having you here these last few weeks, it's been comforting. Being around somebody who knows me better than most people here. We have a long history. I haven't felt this way since Charlie was still around . . ." His voice trailed off.

Flushed with embarrassment, Brody avoided eye contact, staring at the ground just as the retro disco music swelled from the DJ booth that had been set up on the outdoor stage and people started dancing. "I, uh, I . . . I just want to say, it's been nice being with family again . . . I'm going to miss it when I head out soon."

"There's no rush. The casita is yours for as long as you want it."

Jarrod could see tears start to pool in Brody's eyes, but he quickly looked away. "I don't want to overstay my welcome."

"You said it yourself, Brody. You're family." Fearing if he got too mushy, Brody might bolt, Jarrod added, "Besides I've got plenty of ideas on how you can earn your keep."

Brody suddenly lit up. "You mean, like, being your muscle in your next murder investigation? I can totally do that. Knock a few heads if they get out of line! I was born for that kind of gig!"

"I was thinking more along the lines of home improvement projects. Painting, caulking, roof repair, things like that. Trust me, the whole amateur detective thing was a one-off. It won't happen again."

"Yeah, right," Brody scoffed. "Charlie and I had more than

a few conservations about your addiction to crime scenes. Say what you want, but I know the real deal."

Jarrod had to suppress a smile.

Brody was right.

Still, he could at least try to stay out of police business in the future.

For a little while anyway.

Kitty and Maude accompanied Liv, helping her carry the drinks back to Jarrod and Brody.

"Well, it's about time," Kitty said. "I thought the guest of honor was going to be a no-show!"

"Sorry, Kitty, there was the little matter of someone trying to murder me on opening night, so that might have put us slightly behind schedule!"

"I just heard through the grapevine that Gerry Conklin released a statement an hour ago suspending his campaign. Now that his son has been arrested for murder—"

"*And* attempted murder!" Maude interjected.

Kitty guzzled her Manhattan. "Yes, and that. My God, there was more drama backstage than in the play."

"I really didn't need to hear that," Jarrod joked.

"Anyway, the Conklins have decided to put Gerry's political career on hold while they support their son during his legal troubles and are asking for privacy during this very difficult time," Kitty gushed breathlessly.

"They're making it sound like he just got a DUI or something," Liv marveled.

"He murdered your boyfriend!" Maude exclaimed. "*My* boyfriend murdered *your* boyfriend! How crazy is that? It's so hard to comprehend. I stream this stuff all the time. I go to sleep listening to *Forensics Files* or some true crime podcast about somebody's homicidal dentist, and you never think your life will turn out to be an episode someday, but here we are! They just better get someone pretty to play me. I'm not expecting a supermodel, but I hope she's at least got some style. I'm guessing they'll cast the glamour girl to play Liv, and I'll get a reliable character actress to portray the gullible slightly annoying best friend who is too blind and stupid to see that her new boyfriend is a deranged killer!"

"I'm just nauseous thinking there might be a movie about this someday," Liv moaned.

"Well, there is one positive outcome from this whole awful experience. I now know, with full certainty, that I am done with men. Completely, uncategorically done, finished!" Maude declared.

"I'll drink to that," Liv said, clinking glasses with Maude and taking a sip of her cosmo.

Jarrod swished the red wine around in his glass and then reached over to join the toast. "My daughter and I don't always see eye to eye, but in this case, I agree wholeheartedly."

Liv raised an eyebrow. "You agree with what, Dad? That I should swear off men, or that you should too?"

Jarrod took a sip of his wine and thought about it. "Both," he said with a sly smile.

Kitty laughed. "Well, I think it's ridiculous. You've been basically a hermit for ten years, went out on one date with an incredibly handsome and charming and available man, and now you're ready to run and hide again? You have one life, Jarrod. Liv is young. She can take her time. But you, ticktock, not getting any younger." She noticed Jim hovering nearby, listening. "Let's consult the incredibly handsome and charming man in question. Am I right, Jim?"

Jim shifted to one side, not eager to jump into this particular conversation. "I'm paid to watch, not talk."

"Indulge me," Kitty urged. "Should Jarrod step away from the dating scene for the foreseeable future?"

Jim paused, thinking, then glanced over at Jarrod, and replied with a smirk. "Yeah, I think that's probably a good idea."

Jarrod busted out laughing.

At least the guy had a decent sense of humor.

Jim winked at him before slapping on his Secret Service stone face again and returning to professional mode.

Jarrod could not help but think what might have been if he had not screwed it all up so badly.

But as he had just declared, he was done with men.

CHAPTER 45

Jarrod smiled awkwardly as he poured Candy a glass of wine and handed it to her. This dinner had been his idea, but now that Candy was in his house, he did not know what to say.

Luckily Liv was there to help break the ice.

"Thank you for coming tonight, Candy. I know this probably isn't how you expected to spend your Sunday evening."

"No, I was happy you called," Candy said, self-consciously sipping her wine. "What smells so good in the kitchen?"

"My famous chicken parmesan casserole," Jarrod said, pouring another glass of wine and handing it off to Liv. "It's pretty much the only thing I know how to make. I got the recipe online during the pandemic when I was going through an experimental phase like taking up cooking because there was nothing else to do. Liv likes it, so I figured why not give it another try, even though I tend to add too much garlic, but garlic is good for you, right? And I really want to know why I can't stop rambling right now, I mean I know why, it's because I'm so nervous . . ."

Liv reached out and touched his arm. "Dad, relax. There's nothing to be nervous about. Right, Candy?"

"Speak for yourself. My heart is pounding so hard right now, I'm afraid it's going to burst out of my chest."

She gulped down her wine.

"That's a lovely outfit you're wearing, Candy. Teal can sometimes be a tricky color, but you wear it so well. I feel I should completely reevaluate my opinion of that color. Look, I'm doing it again. I'm rambling. I can't seem to stop."

"Thank you, Jarrod," Candy said, grinning.

Liv sat down on the couch next to Candy. "With everything that's happened since we first met, I can only imagine how you must feel about us. I want to apologize for everything, how we contacted you out of the blue, putting you in such an awkward position with that interview and then dragging you and your kids into a messy murder investigation. Honestly, I'm surprised you even returned my call."

"You've been very kind and sensitive from the start, Liv. I was very happy you reached out."

Liv took a deep breath and glanced over at her father, who stood frozen in the middle of the living room, holding the half-full wine bottle. She turned back to Candy. "The thing is, I've done a lot of thinking, and I don't want us going our separate ways again. I guess what I'm trying to say is, I want you in my life, Candy. If you're open to it, of course."

After a long pause, Candy nodded, slightly at first, and then more vigorously. "Yes. Yes, I'd like that." She squeezed Liv's hand, eyes sparkling, but then her gaze drifted apprehensively over to Jarrod. "As long as Jarrod is okay with that. I would hate stepping on any toes."

"I'll be honest. When I first learned Liv was in contact with you, I wasn't sure how to feel. We hadn't spoken in so many years. I had no idea you even lived nearby. I didn't know what to expect . . ."

Candy waved her hand. "I completely understand."

"But being with you here, now, I can't tell you how happy I am. I'm awash in so many wonderful memories of that time in my life when Charlie and I were making that monumental decision to become parents, how you were such an integral part of the process. You were like a part of our family. I know you have your own family now, but I'm hoping, *we're* hoping, we can start a new chapter together."

Candy stood up and set her empty wineglass down on the table and crossed to Jarrod.

He reflexively tensed up, not sure what she was about to do but relaxed when she put her arms around him and gave him a warm hug.

They both stood there embracing for a long moment before Candy whispered in his ear, "Speaking of my family, I promise you from this day forward, I will keep those two kids of mine in line."

And then they all busted up laughing.

CHAPTER 46

After Candy had said good night and drove away to her home in Desert Hot Springs, Jarrod and Liv sat down together out on the patio for one last nightcap, staring up at the dark sky dotted with twinkling stars and a couple of faraway planets.

The bright moon was nearly full, its reflection shimmering across the surface of the kidney-shaped swimming pool as father and daughter sipped their Cabernet in silence before Jarrod finally spoke, looking at Liv with a mixture of pride and gratitude. "You know, Liv, I honestly never thought we'd find ourselves here, working side by side, but I have to tell you, it feels good. And for the record, you turned out to be a pretty damn good sleuth."

Liv bumped shoulders with her father. "That's because I learned from the best."

There was so much Jarrod wanted to say, especially how right George and Leo had been.

Teaming up to solve Zel's murder had brought them closer together.

Somehow through this whole ordeal they had rediscovered their relationship.

"When your Papa Charlie was still around, you two had such a strong bond, you worshipped him, and I sometimes felt like the odd man out, the bad cop parent, laying down the rules, in charge of all the discipline. I couldn't compete with the great Detective Charlie Peters. Super Dad. I mean, he wasn't just a hero to you, *everyone* looked up to him. He was such a force of nature. And there I was, the perpetually unemployed actor scooting to one failed audition after the other, desperately trying to reclaim some semblance of fame, who felt lucky just to be with him, basically holding on for dear life the whole time."

Liv laughed. "Papa Charlie was just as lucky as you were. I mean, come on, he snared the *Young Sheldon* of his day. The People's Choice nominated Favorite Child Star of 1985! You were on the cover of *TV Guide*. Twice. That's huge!" She glanced over at Jarrod, who was misty-eyed and trying to keep it together.

She reached over and took his hand, almost reading his mind. "I miss him too, Dad. I can't help but think he's been watching us stumble around together in search of clues like Veronica Mars and her dad and having a good laugh over it."

Jarrod nodded, sniffing, determined not to cry.

Liv's gaze softened. "I do know one thing after going through all this. I'm going to focus on grad school. I'm not yet sure what I'm going to do with my degree—law school maybe, forensics, who knows—but I may have finally found my calling."

"Yeah, I'm probably too old at this point to enroll in the police academy. I should probably stick to directing cheesy murder mystery plays. Much more in my wheelhouse."

"I hear *Eye of the Desert* is going to give it a rave. Next weekend should be a sellout."

"From your lips . . ." Jarrod chuckled.

"Oh, and there is one more thing I learned from all this."

"What's that?"

"I really think you're ready to date again."

Jarrod nearly spit out his wine. "Ha! No, I think that ship has sailed. No, wait. Let me rephrase that. I think that ship has sunk."

"I'm serious, Dad. I can totally see it."

"We're in the sweltering desert. It's probably a mirage."

"Stop joking. It's time. And deep down, you know Papa Charlie would want that for you. I'm guessing your psychic Isis would also agree."

"You have to admit, Isis turned out to be right."

"Dad, let's not, shall we?"

Jarrod chuckled. Then shook his head. "Liv, please, I don't want to play the Mystery Date game. If that's even still around. I'm not going to open the door and just find the man of my dreams in a tux or leather chaps or in scuba gear. I've lived in this town for ten years, and I learned very quickly that most gay men in Palm Springs are already paired up or just in from out of town for the weekend in search of a little fun."

"What about Jim?"

Jarrod scoffed. "Jim? I think I can safely say I blew it with him. There's no coming back from that one."

"Not necessarily. I see the way you two look at each other. There's definite chemistry, whether you're willing to see it yet or not."

"Not Jim. Not in a million years. Next topic."

"Call him."

"I'm not calling him."

"Are you scared?"

"You're not going to goad me into calling him."

"I'll bet you a hundred dollars if you call him and ask him out to dinner, he'll say yes."

"Forget it. I'm not calling."

"Two hundred."

"When did you start gambling? Please tell me you haven't been hanging out all night at the casinos."

"I will Venmo you if I lose." She picked up Jarrod's phone that he had set down on the wicker coffee table on the patio. "Call him."

Jarrod sighed and reluctantly snatched the phone out of her hand. He punched in his passcode and tapped the phone app.

Liv leaned over to get a glimpse of his screen.

"Oh, look, he's right on the top of the list of recent contacts."

Jarrod gave her some side-eye before tapping the call button. After a few rings, Jim picked up, catching Jarrod off guard.

"Oh, hi, Jim. This is Jarrod . . . Jarrod Jarvis, remember me? Yeah, that's right. Anyway, I know the last time I saw you, I proclaimed I was finished dating for the foreseeable future, but now that a few days have passed . . ." Jarrod paused, listening, then cracked a smile. "Hours, okay. A few hours. I know we both swore not to ever go out together again after the last time went slightly awry . . . Okay, yes, it was a fiasco, I will give you that one. I-I am so, so sorry about that. And believe me, if my ex-husband was still alive, he would tell you just how rare it is for me to apologize for anything. I'm also very risk-averse, so the fact that I'm even calling right now to ask you this is truly astounding—"

"Dad, you're rambling again," Liv whispered.

"Would you . . . would you . . ." Jarrod stammered, having trouble getting the words out. His eyes widened in surprise. "Friday? Sure, that works. Friday it is. You can choose the restaurant. Or I can make dinner here. No, it's probably best if we go out, my cooking can be tough sledding—"

"Dad, hang up."

"Anyway, I did make my chicken parmesan casserole tonight, and it tasted pretty good, so maybe I'll try making it."

Liv tried grabbing the phone. "Hang up, Dad."

"We can decide later. Okay, gotta go. See you Friday."

He mercifully ended the call.

Liv snatched the phone from him and began tapping the screen.

Jarrod watched her, confused. "What are you doing?"

"Downloading the Venmo app so you can send me the two hundred dollars you owe me."

"Baby, don't even go there!"